16

The NEVER-OPEN DESERT DINER

The NEVER-OPEN DESERT DINER

A NOVEL

JAMES ANDERSON

CROWN PUBLISHERS
NEW YORK

Copyright © 2015 by James Anderson

All rights reserved.
Published in the United States by Crown Publishers, an imprint of the Crown Publishing Group, a division of Penguin Random House LLC, New York.
www.crownpublishing.com

CROWN is a registered trademark and the Crown colophon is a trademark of Penguin Random House LLC.

Originally published by Caravel Books, New York, in 2015.

Grateful acknowledgment is made to W. W. Norton and Company, Inc. for permission to reprint "Degrees of Gray in Philipsburg." Copyright © 1973 by Richard Hugo, from *Making Certain It Goes On: Collected Poems of Richard Hugo* by Richard Hugo. Used by permission of W. W. Norton & Company, Inc. All rights reserved.

Library of Congress Cataloging-in-Publication data is available upon request.

ISBN 978-1-101-90652-1
eBook ISBN 978-1-101-90653-8

Printed in the United States of America

Jacket design by Will Staehle
Jacket photograph: inigocia/Shutterstock

10 9 8 7 6 5 4 3 2 1

First Edition

For BRUCE BERGER, *for his love of deserts, and* JAMES A. LAWSON, *for his love of the cello*

Dedicated in memoriam to the following authors for creating characters who became some of the best friends I've ever had, real or imaginary:

ROSS MACDONALD *(1915–1983)*
for Lew Archer (California)

JOHN D. MACDONALD *(1916–1986)*
for Travis McGee (Florida)

JAMES CRUMLEY *(1939–2008)*
for Milo Milodragovitch (Montana)

ROBERT B. PARKER *(1932–2010)*
for Spenser (Boston)

STEPHEN J. CANNELL *(1941–2010)*
for James Rockford (California)

& very special thanks to STERLING WATSON,
who kept those friendships from being forgotten

Isn't this your life? That ancient kiss

still burning out your eyes? Isn't this defeat

so accurate, the church bell simply seems

a pure announcement: ring and no one comes?

Don't empty houses ring?

—RICHARD HUGO, "Degrees of Gray in Philipsburg"

A red sun was balanced on the horizon when I arrived at The Well-Known Desert Diner. Sunrise shadows were draped around its corners. A full white moon was still visible in the dawn sky. I parked my tractor-trailer rig along the outer perimeter of the gravel parking lot. The "Closed" sign hung on the front door. To the left of the door, as if in mourning for Superman, stood a black metal and glass phone booth. Inside was a real phone with a rotary dial that clicked out the ten white numbers. Unlike the phones in the movies, this one worked—if you had enough nickels.

Curiosity usually wasn't a problem for me. I treated it like a sleeping junkyard dog. As a general rule I didn't hop the fence. Jagged scars on my backside reminded me of the few times I had violated that rule. Just because you can't see the dog doesn't mean it isn't out there. Sure, I look through the fence once in a while. What I see and think I keep to myself.

On that Monday morning in late May I was dangerously close to the fence. Walt Butterfield, the diner's owner, was a junkyard Unitarian: he was a congregation of one and his own guard dog. His junkyard was The Well-Known Desert Diner, and he didn't bark or growl before he tore your throat out. I liked him, and his junkyard. The place was a kind of odd shrine. Over the years the diner had become a regular rest stop for me as well as a source of fascination and idle speculation. It was always my first stop, even when I had nothing to deliver to Walt. Sometimes it was my last stop, too.

Out of habit, I tried the front door. It was locked, as usual. This was Walt's face to the world. Walt slept in what had been a small storage room attached to the kitchen. Behind the diner, across a wide alleyway of sand and flagstone, was a 50-by-100-foot galvanized steel World War II Quonset hut. This was where Walt really lived, alone with his motorcycles, and tools and grease and canyons of crated parts that reached to the ceiling.

Walt's motorcycle collection totaled nine of the finest and rarest beasts ever to have graced the roadways of America and Europe. Among them was his first, a 1948 Vincent Black Shadow. It was the same motorcycle he was riding, his new Korean War bride hugging his thin waist, the day he first rode onto the gravel of what was then called The Oasis Café. He was twenty years old. She was sixteen and spoke no English. They bought the place a year later, in 1953.

Walt kept the diner, like everything else in his life, in pristine shape. I peered through the glass door at the lime-green vinyl seats of the six booths and twelve stools. The platoon of glass salt and pepper shakers stood at attention. The trim along the edge of the counter shined its perpetual chrome smile back at me. The brown and ivory linoleum tiles reflected their usual wax and polish. A 1948 Wurlitzer jukebox hunkered against the far wall. Behind the counter, the same order ticket as always hung lifeless from a wire above the stainless steel kitchen pass-through. As far as I knew it was the final ticket from the last meal prepared for a paying guest, probably sometime in the autumn of 1987.

I returned to my truck and off-loaded a heavy carton filled with the usual motorcycle parts and wheeled it to the door of the Quonset hut. On Wednesday of the previous week Walt had received some unusual freight from New York—six boxes, all different sizes. They didn't have the sloppy heft of motorcycle parts, though that alone wasn't what got my attention. Each carton had a different return address in New York City, but all of them were from the same sender, someone named Chun-Ja. No last name. They had arrived in pairs, all originating on the same day, each set of two sent through one of the big three corporate carriers— FedEx, UPS, and DHL. By special contract I delivered for FedEx and UPS, but not DHL.

I had set my four next to the two left by the DHL driver. They weren't gone until Friday morning. That meant they had been left out for two days and two nights, which wasn't just odd—it had never happened before in all my years of making deliveries to Walt.

There was really only one possible explanation for why Walt failed to bring his freight inside—he had been out of town, except to my knowledge he had no family or friends, and absolutely nowhere else to go. Given his advanced age, the logical assumption would have been that he had died of natural causes and was stretched out stiff as a board somewhere in the recesses of his diner or workshop, or lay broken in the desert after an accident on one of his motorcycles. You had to know Walt to appreciate just how far-fetched such death scenarios were.

I pounded on the door of the Quonset hut. Just once. Walt's hearing was perfect. At seventy-nine, all of him was damn near perfect, except his attitude toward people. No matter where he was on the property, or what he was doing, he had a sixth sense that told him if someone was around. If he didn't show himself, he was ignoring you. The smartest and safest action you could take was to leave—the sooner the better. The only thing pounding and yelling did was piss him off. If there was one seventy-nine-year-old man on the planet you didn't want to piss off, it was Walt Butterfield.

I was probably the only person to have seen the inside of Walt's Quonset workshop in at least twenty years. These occasional excursions into Walt's world, always by gruff invitation, never lasted longer than the time it took for me to slip freight off a hand truck.

I left the new box of parts next to the door and did the smart thing. It was a piece of good luck that Walt hadn't answered my knock. I might have done something stupid, like ask him where he'd been or what was in the six cartons.

I always hoped to catch Walt, or rather have him willing to be caught. On a handful of occasions we sat in the closed diner. Sometimes he talked, though usually not. I always listened when he wanted to talk. A few times he actually fixed and served me breakfast in the diner. He had been around the area longer than anyone, or at least longer than anyone who had a brain that worked and a reliable memory.

I returned to my truck determined not to dwell on the strange freight or Walt's absence. The really big mysteries in life never troubled me much. How the pyramids were built or whether Cortés was a homosexual didn't bounce my curiosity needle. On the other hand, Walt's absence and his odd freight were hard to resist. The diner and I contemplated each other. Like Walt himself, it had a long and colorful past.

U.S. 191 is the main highway north and south out of Price, Utah. North led to Salt Lake City. Due south took you to Green River, and eventually Moab. The turnoff for State Road 117 is about twenty miles from the city limits of Price. Ten miles east, down 117, on the left, surrounded by miles of flat, rugged nothing, you came upon The Well-Known Desert Diner.

From 1955 to 1987 the diner appeared in dozens of B movies. There were the desert horror-thriller movies, the desert biker mayhem movies, and the movies where someone, usually an attractive young woman, drove across the desert alone and some bad shit happened.

Once in a while it's possible to catch one of these low-budget gems on cable. I always cheered when the diner filled the screen. My personal favorites involved atomic monsters or aliens terrorizing small-town desert locals. The locals eventually triumphed and saved the planet. Their victory was usually accomplished with little more than a car battery, a couple of Winchester rifles, and a visiting college professor who had a crazy theory—and a wild, beautiful daughter.

The diner was originally built in 1929. Its pale gravel driveway, antique glass-bubble gas pumps, white adobe walls, and green trim made it seem familiar, almost like a home you had known all your life but never visited. Even the most hardened, sun-struck driver slowed down and smiled.

Two billboards, one facing 191 South and another facing 191 North, advertised the diner to traffic. "Homemade pie ... Cool drinks ... Just ahead." The billboards were aged and faded. Through the years so many people had stopped to find the diner closed that one irate motorist spray-painted the northbound billboard to read: "The Never-Open Desert Diner." Though this was not entirely true, it was true enough. On that rare occasion when it had not been true, the experience had turned out to be an unfortunate event for those who found the front door unlocked and Walt behind the counter. Though I didn't know for certain, I'd always suspected that infrequently Walt took down the "Closed" sign and unlocked the door just to lure people in so he could run them off.

I emptied the last drops of coffee from the thermos into my ceramic mug and considered myself lucky, even though business was getting so bad I had been floating my diesel on a Visa card and trying not to wonder if I could survive another month. Still, every morning I got up feeling like I was headed home. To be sure, my luck was often *hard* luck, but good luck all the same, though lately I had felt more and more like a grown man still living at home with his poverty-stricken, ailing, and peculiar parents—which might have actually been the case if I'd had any.

Under my skin I wasn't feeling nearly as lucky as I had in times past. Below that was a rising shiver of cold desperation. Things had to change. I wanted them to change. Like most people who said they wanted change, all I wanted was enough change to keep everything the same, only better.

The highway ahead lolled in sunlight. It was mine and it made me happy. It didn't bother me that it was mine because no one else wanted it. The brakes hissed, and I glanced over at the diner one more time before I pulled out onto 117 to begin the rest of my day.

2

All the coffee caught up with me a few miles down the road from the diner. I searched for any spot large enough to allow me to safely pull over my twenty-eight-foot tractor-trailer rig. A narrow turnout appeared ahead. It was almost hidden at the bottom of a slight hill that came at the end of a long gentle curve. It wasn't a turnout at all—it was a road, though I didn't realize that until I had stopped and climbed down out of the cab. Dirt and sand have a special feel under your boots. This ground had a contoured hardness to it.

I scuffed at the sandy surface with a boot tip and stood there amazed at what I had uncovered—a slab of white concrete. I followed the concrete about fifty yards up a gentle slope. At the crest of the hill were two brick pillars connected by an iron arch. Inside the arch, in cursive metal script, were the words "Desert Home."

It seemed strange to me that I had never noticed the entrance before. I'd driven by it twice a day, five days a week, for twenty years. A car sped by on the highway below. The pillars were just high enough and far enough from the road they couldn't be easily seen, even if you were looking for them. Given the height of my cab and the level of the sloping highway, the entrance was nearly impossible to spot from 117.

For a moment I reflected on what had once been a grand entrance. It was somebody's dream gone sour and lost—probably a ranch. When I lowered my gaze a bit, the distance came into focus and I could make out a series of shallow, dry creek beds carved into the sands, all intertwined and attached.

It took a minute for the truth of the scene to register. They were not creek beds at all, but lanes and cul-de-sacs that had never made good on their promise of homes, except one, probably a model, that stuck out like a sturdy tooth on an empty gum. It was down the hill a couple blocks on my right.

A gust of wind kicked up a miniature twister of dust at my feet. My discomfort returned. Relieving yourself in a wind can be tricky business. The abiding loneliness of what lay ahead seemed to beckon, and the one-story model house offered a chance to get out of the wind. I had no idea I might be hopping any sort of fence.

Walking down the hill toward the house, I could almost hear the sounds of children playing and the happy drone of families enjoying weekend barbecues. It was a ghost town without the town and without the ghosts, since no one had actually ever lived there. I imagined ghosts of ghosts, less than ghosts, and I felt oddly welcomed into their company.

The model house had held up exceptionally well through the however many years it had been sitting there abandoned to the elements.

Maybe, like most orphans, I thought too much about houses. I'd never owned or lived in one as an adult. I had strong opinions and a tendency to evaluate houses in a particular way—windows first, placement mostly. Then the porch, whether it had one and what direction it faced. I liked porches and I've always been partial to those that were eastward facing. Finally, the roof. I've never liked a roof that's too pitched. If I wanted a hat I'd buy a hat. A sharp-pitched roof always seemed to put me off for some reason.

The house was alone in a bed of sand and the windows were unbroken and clean, and placed slightly lower for the cooler morning air. The porch faced east toward the sparkling mica-flaked mesa about fifty miles away. Any desert dweller will tell you the true beauty of a desert sunset can be best appreciated by looking in that unlikely direction, the east, away from the sun. A single faded green metal lawn chair relaxed on the porch. Someone would have been happy sitting there on a fine cool evening. The roof had a graceful, easy pitch that welcomed instead of threatened the sky.

I walked around the house. There was no sign anyone lived there, or had ever lived there. In the backyard I paused and took in the unhindered view all the way west to the Wasatch Mountains. The south side had the least wind. I stepped up close and rested my forehead on the shady wall just beneath a clean window. In the freedom of the moment and the beauty of the setting, I unbuckled my belt so I could fully abandon myself to the long-anticipated event.

It was almost quiet in the shade. Wind made a high whistling complaint as it slipped in and out of the eaves above me. When I looked up at the whistling, my sight traveled past the window—a kitchen window, I guessed. In that fraction of an instant my eyes glided over the disapproving face of a woman.

A good many bad behaviors have been honestly attributed to me over the years. Most of them I have just as honestly and sometimes even cheerfully acknowledged. Pissing on the side of someone's house, however modest or isolated, had never been among them. Such a breach surpassed bad manners and marched straight into the territory of criminally stupid. In the Utah desert it is likely to get you shot.

In my haste to retreat, my jeans slipped to my knees. I stumbled backward and over. Despite my best efforts, the flow continued undeterred while I thrashed around on my backside. It occurred to me at that moment I might have borne a striking similarity to a cheap Walmart lawn sprinkler. All that was miss-ing were a couple of brats in swimsuits jumping over me—and, of course, the lawn.

By the time I got control of the floodgates and up on my feet again, the face in the window was gone. But I had seen her. I was certain of it. I walked around to the front of the house to check again for signs of a resident. There were no tracks, human or machine. There was no evidence of any kind that would have warned me I was trespassing. I expressed my apology to the porch. I waited. I announced myself again, this time a little louder. Only the wind answered me. A block away, as I headed up the slope to the arch, I heard a woman's voice tell me to go away. She didn't need to tell me twice—or even once.

Under the arch I turned and squinted back down at the model home with all the glass in the windows and the chair on the eastern-facing porch. At my truck I looked up toward the archway and realized it was just high enough on the hill and far enough away that it couldn't be seen from the highway. I wondered if it had been designed that way.

My next stop was the Lacey brothers' place. I spent the thirty miles convincing myself to forget what had just happened. I could not be an unrepentant house-pisser. There was also her face, which I easily remembered and then struggled to forget. Maybe it wasn't exactly a beautiful face in the popular way of advertise-ments and magazine covers. The face was oddly striking, with a high forehead and a wide nose and no-nonsense lips, all framed in thick black hair that lightly settled upon her shoulders. It was a face with staying power.

3

My company, Ben's Desert Moon Delivery Service, consisted of one truck, one trailer, and one driver: me, Ben Jones. Several years earlier, as the result of a serendipitous tragedy, I was given exclusive contracts to deliver for FedEx and UPS. My route on 117 took me back and forth across a particularly remote hundred-mile stretch of Utah's high desert. The highway dead-ended up against the granite face of a towering mesa just outside the small former coal-mining town of Rockmuse, population 1,344. I also trucked whatever else was freight-forwarded through various shippers. My bread and butter, which had become mostly bread and damn little of that, came from the scattered locals who lived out in the desert and placed orders directly with me for whatever they needed.

I delivered to lonely cattle ranches along the way and sometimes to the odd desert rats holed up in their aluminum trailers that rose shimmering out of the brown distance like so much tinfoil pinned against the horizon. Rancher or crazy old sun rat, all had chosen to tuck themselves away in the rolling dirt, sand, and tumbleweed miles down rutted side roads that had no names.

Such folks were a special breed. I knew every one of them, though the sum total of every word ever exchanged between us might not equal what could be squeezed onto the back of a drug-store postcard. Entire life histories were swapped in three or four words with a narrow squint or a wave thrown in for punctuation.

Between hello and good-bye was a thick slice of silence that told a story you couldn't forget even if you wanted to. Conversation in the high desert was parceled out like water and often with less enthusiasm, each drop cherished for the life it represented.

The Lacey brothers, Fergus and Duncan, lived a mile off 117 in two sand-scoured red boxcars that had been welded together and placed on top of a foundation of gray cinder blocks. I didn't know how long the brothers had lived there or where they had come from, or their ages, or what they did, if anything, outside of running a scrawny bunch of cattle and horses. They never offered and I never inquired. How boxcars got out in the middle of the desert when there were no train tracks within seventy-five miles was a bit of a mystery. I mused upon it when it occurred to me, which was probably too often.

Fergus had seen me for several minutes as I made my way over dips and bends accompanied by squeaks and rattles across the ruts and holes of their nameless road. When I pulled into their dusty turnaround, he was half sitting, half leaning on a large wooden spool that had once held heavy-gauge cable. Nearby were two gray plastic milk crates that served as chairs, which I had never seen the brothers use. This was their yard furniture, reserved for entertaining guests that might have included the lost coyote or buzzard and not much else.

The Lacey brothers were small and scrappy, raw-boned men who wore their years in the desert like leather armor. What had once been red steel-wool hair had become a calico with short tufts of orange popping out between patches of white from the backs and sides of the dirty Stetson hats they rarely removed. Lopsided boot heels made them look as if they were always fighting a strong crosswind, and the wind was losing. Even in winter they wore T-shirts with jeans held up by red suspenders. Their clear, ice-blue eyes further identified them as brothers. Never blinking, those eyes did all the work for their beard-stubbled faces.

Fergus lowered the brim of his sweat-stained hat an inch or two by way of a hello. Together we unloaded three rolls of barbed wire and ten cases of Hormel chili. As usual, we stacked everything against the side of the boxcars. He signed for his goods and paid me in cash. My delivery completed, I turned to leave.

Fergus hoisted a work glove. "Hold up, Ben."

Duncan stepped out of the boxcars holding a shallow pie tin. "Birthday cake," he shouted.

"Which one of you old farts is having a birthday?" I asked.

Duncan set the cake, which was not actually a cake, down on the wooden spool table. The two brothers looked at each other and then at me.

Duncan said, "It's your birthday, asshole."

They both laughed.

I lifted my cap and dragged the back of my wrist over my wet brow. "I guess it is," I said. It wasn't.

Something passed between the two brothers, an unspoken thought, which I supposed was not uncommon between brothers. Duncan muttered a curse under his breath and disappeared inside.

Fergus shook his head. "Appreciate it, Ben. Duncan is having strange spells these days. For some damn reason he's convinced it's your birthday. It isn't, is it?"

"Nope," I said.

Fergus sniffed the air. "It don't matter to me, Ben," he said, "but I think you might have pissed yourself."

I didn't feel like explaining. I ignored his observation.

Sounds of rooting and banging came from inside the boxcars. Fergus released a slow, good-natured sigh. "I'll go help him."

A short while later they reappeared. After all my years of driving a truck I knew a road flare when I saw one. Duncan held one in his hand. Fergus carried three cans of beer. We met at the table.

Duncan admired the cake for a moment. "It's jalapeño corn bread," he said. "Made the frosting out of Velveeta cheese." Judging from the pride in his voice, he considered the Velveeta frosting an inspired invention on the order of penicillin and toilet paper.

The charred letter *B* floated upon the cheese lake of orange frosting. Fergus added, "It was my idea to make your initial out of bacon."

I nodded and tried to exhibit the appropriate amount of insincere admiration.

Duncan pulled the strike cap off the flare and struck the ignition end with the cap still in his teeth. The flare burst to life and spewed a bright flame into the already warm air. "Let's see you blow this out."

With a flourish worthy of a pile driver, Duncan jammed the lit flare into the center of the corn bread. The two of them sang "Happy Birthday" to me. They let the flare burn a few seconds. Suddenly Duncan threw his hands into the air and danced an animated but nonetheless pitiful jig around the table.

It didn't taste half bad. It was all bad. Whatever the recommended daily allowance of phosphorus was, after a few bites there was enough of it in our systems to meet that requirement for a lifetime and well into whatever came next. The beer was surprisingly cold, and not just welcome but medicinally necessary.

A very short time later I pulled through the turnaround. The remains of the cake sat next to me on the seat. Burn holes still smoldered in the Velveeta icing. My side mirrors caught the flare blazing behind me in the dirt where Fergus had thrown it. Fergus and Duncan were acting like two little boys, scuffing up a fine dusty haze into the air as they kicked the dying flare like a soccer ball back and forth between them.

It wasn't my birthday, but it was a birthday I'd remember until the day I died, which at the moment had never seemed closer.

A courteous distance down the road, well out of sight of the boxcars, I pulled over and buried the cake in a shallow grave. There was a big chunk of sandstone nearby. I used it to seal the tomb. Some poor scavenging desert creature might thank me.

If it was true that it's the thought that counts, I didn't want to know what Duncan Lacey was thinking when he made that cake. On the other hand, the ten cases of canned Hormel chili and other foodstuffs I regularly brought them needed no explanation. I took some solace in the fact that, though it wasn't my birthday, God willing, it wouldn't be my birthday again for another year.

4

I drove west, homeward, into a fiery late-afternoon sun. I cranked down my window and gulped at the clean desert air that had already begun to cool in anticipation of a spring evening.

No other vehicles appeared in either direction for almost an hour. I searched the road ahead for the turnout to Desert Home, unable to decide if I was going to stop. It wasn't until I'd parked and set the brake and listened to the engine relax that I began to wonder why I had stopped where I was so clearly unwelcome— the famous "scene of the crime." My wondering was short lived. I knew from experience that if you're about to do something you probably shouldn't do, the best advice you can give yourself is not to think about it too long. It ruins the surprise when the worst happens.

The wind picked up in ferocious gusts that roared in my ears and partially obscured my view of the model home. I hiked down the slope. Blowing sand burrowed inside my clothes and forced me to squint. Well away from the porch, I threw my "hello" toward the house. The chair was gone. I shouted several more times, gradually moving closer each time. With each step the wind scooped up my voice with the sand and sent them both to parts unknown. I knocked on the door. The wind took that, too.

The front windows were now covered with blankets from the inside. Newspaper had been taped across the picture window on the north side. Two of the sheets didn't completely overlap and allowed the sliver of a view. I pushed my cap back on my forehead and cupped my hands to shield my eyes from the blowing sand.

The woman sat on the green chair that had been on the porch. She was alone. The chair was the only piece of furniture in the empty room. Her bare left shoulder angled toward my window. A skylight directly overhead encircled her with a narrow stream of honeyed light. The rest of her body drifted in shadow. My eyes adjusted. Her raised left elbow revealed the soft curve of a breast. She appeared to be vaguely Asian, though her skin looked too white. She was clearly naked. Her fingers moved rhythmically along the slender neck of a musical instrument.

The wind died. Silence took its place. I held my breath. What was about to happen was rare, though I had experienced it a few times in my years on 117.

The setting sun burned into a layer of advancing high red clouds that swirled with sand. Propelled by the wind, the clouds picked up speed and rushed across the flatlands, where they broke against the mesa cliffs and splintered like a giant wave. The backwash of wind roared toward me across the miles of desert shore driving sand ahead of it. My hands glowed from the intense approaching light.

I was caught in a blinding red flash. The air around me crackled with electricity. I fought the impulse to close my eyes. The skylight above the woman filled the room with a pulsing pink glow like the inside of a beating heart. In the unnatural light, the fingertips of her left hand flew over the absent strings. Her right hand grasped nothing as it sawed the air. The soundless instrument rocked side to side with music only she could hear and I could only imagine.

The light in the room transformed into deepening shades of

the spectrum. I tried to recall the name of the instrument the woman played. Its name was lost in the curve of her bare shoulder and half oval of breast, seamless yet distinct against the instrument. The woman and the instrument were a cameo in the empty room.

She stopped playing. I felt shame. I had no right to be there. It was wrong.

Too late, I realized the light had slipped behind me. A misshapen silhouette of my head was cast through the newspaper and across the floor in front of her. She turned toward the window where I stood. She returned her attention to her instrument. Her chin dropped to her chest. She was lost again in her private music. I felt shame but was helpless to turn away. I continued to listen.

The sun dropped below the mountains. It only took a few minutes. She played on until I could no longer separate her from the darkness. I walked from the house into the dusk and remembered the name of the instrument—a cello. I sat in the cab with the engine idling and thought about the woman and the cello and the red room and the haunting music I didn't hear. I whispered to myself, "Go home, Ben."

The headlights wrangled the soft darkness in front of me. I stared but didn't see. She might have been standing there for some time. The sleeveless flowered print dress she now wore was loose fitting and fell to her knees. A slight wind fluttered its hemline. Her coal eyes were intent upon me. She moved only to push wild strands of her long dark hair away from her face. There was little chance she could see me with the headlights shining in her eyes, though I felt as if she could. Maybe I wanted her to see me through glass the way I had seen her.

I opened the door and slid out from behind the wheel until I felt the chrome running board under my boots. The interior lights flashed on and off. She reached up again and brushed the hair from her face. I stepped out in front of the headlights. She took a step backward to the very edge of light.

She didn't shout. Her voice lifted itself without effort over the rise and fall of the gently fluctuating rpms of the Detroit diesel.

"Are you a music lover or just a pervert?" she asked.

There were only two ways to answer that question. I wasn't pleased that the question so precisely limited my response. "Are those my only choices?" I asked. When she didn't say anything, I said, "I guess I'm a music lover."

"Go ahead, then," she said, her voice breaking this time. "Take it and go."

"Take what and go?" I asked.

Instead of answering me she turned and disappeared into the darkness. The faint sound of her footsteps stopped. From out of sight, she asked, "Did the owner send you?"

I didn't know what she was talking about. "No one sent me," I answered, aiming my voice up and out into the night.

"Then why are you here?"

"I just wanted to apologize again for what happened this morning."

Her own laughter caught her by surprise. It erupted from her throat in choking hiccups before it exploded into a brief howl. A coyote answered her call. She howled back in a long, high-pitched response that made me shiver. I tossed my head back and let loose a howl of my own. My effort fetched only silence.

There was no way for me to know if she was still nearby.

"I'm a truck driver," I said. I turned back to the cab and stepped up on the running board. I stood there high and small beneath the first shy desert stars. "I'm sorry I bothered you, ma'am," I said. "Thanks for the loan of the wall."

I already had one leg inside the cab when her clear voice drifted down out of the darkness: "You're welcome."

I listened hard for more and wished for another hiccup of laughter or a tender howl. All I could hear was the rhythmic fall of her shoes on sand that told me she was moving farther away up the slope. The coyote let loose again while I was closing the door.

As I backed up to turn around, my headlights rose slowly toward the entrance. She stood on top of the hill beneath the arch, her arms wrapped around herself against the chilly breeze. In the desert, the line between what is dead and what is alive often gets blurred. She appeared to me as a vaporous feminine spirit guarding the gate of a cemetery. I confess, as my headlights aimed toward Price, there was an odd sting of homesickness inside me, though for what exactly, I couldn't have said.

5

I felt the comfort of moonlight on my face. The glow from a small digital clock next to my bed marked the long moments of waiting for sleep, moments thinking of her face and the questions that came and went unanswered, questions and answers that were none of my business. Who was she? Where did she come from? How had she come to an abandoned housing development with a cello—a cello without strings? What was she doing for food? Water? Was she alone? How long would she stay, or was she already gone? Did she need my help? I remembered a definition of chivalry I'd heard once: a man protecting a woman against every man but himself.

Using my toes, I manipulated the moonlight to make shadow puppets on the wall. As entertaining as this exercise was, I had another option.

After midnight I pulled my ancient Toyota 4×4 pickup onto the asphalt ranchlands of Walmart parking. I was determined to find a CD of cello music, though part of me actually preferred the phantom music the woman had shared with me in silence. Price had just one Walmart and it was open 24/7. During most of the day it was a popular place. The next nearest Walmart was a hundred miles west through the mountains, in Spanish Fork, a sprawling satellite of Salt Lake City along the I-15 corridor. Somewhere in the endless aisles of car batteries, tank tops, and Hostess

Twinkies there had to be a CD of cello music. I wasn't convinced of this, merely hopeful.

The night-shift workers were busy restocking the shelves under the high artificial lights. No one paid any attention to me as I made my way through the maze of products that filled the aisles. In an ocean of busy blue vests I heard little English or anything else being spoken. Lost in this desert, I was Moses searching for the Promised Land. I located it in a far corner behind a wall of technology.

A plump young woman in a blue vest with a silver ring in her nose dozed peacefully as she leaned against a display rack of last season's DVDs. I didn't want to wake her. She looked like she could use all the sleep she could get. Her face appeared almost childlike.

The CDs were neatly arranged in categories, each category divided by artist and each artist divided alphabetically. About the only thing that seemed familiar to me was the alphabet. There was no category for cello. There was a category for classical that held only five CDs, four of which were compilations beginning with *The Best of.* I had my choice of the best of Beethoven, Mozart, Brahms, and Chopin. The fifth CD was *Johnny Mathis Sings the Classics.*

"Hi, Ben."

I was startled to hear my name. I turned to see that the young woman had awakened. She exhumed a tired smile. She wore an unborn child around her waist that had previously escaped my notice.

She placed her hands on her hips and stretched backward. "You don't remember me, do you?"

I subtracted the nose ring and the heavy bags beneath her violet eyes. Then I took away the pregnancy and finally the orange streaks in her short black hair. What was left was the daughter of a woman I had dated maybe five or six years before. She had been just a little girl then—just a girl now, even with the nose ring and the rest of life's additions. The ring in her nose was the only ring in sight.

"Ginny," I said, pleased to see her again, or as pleased as I could be given the circumstances. "You've grown up." Innocently, though not sincerely, I inquired after her mother.

"My mom is a piece of shit."

"I wouldn't go that far."

"C'mon, Ben. After what she did to you? You're disagreeing with me? Or are we just deciding on the size of the piece?"

This was the kind of conversation made worse by the glare of indirect lighting and the time of night, the bright floors, sterile air-conditioning, and minimum-wage work. Was she seventeen? Eighteen? Maybe it had been closer to ten years since I'd last seen Ginny and Nadine, her mother.

"Let it go, Ginny," I said. "Please?"

"Fine," she said. Among the few constants in life is the certainty that when a female uses the word *fine* to a man, things are about as far from fine as they can get. "What brings you to Walmart in the middle of the night?"

I told her what I wanted. She stepped around me and surveyed the bins of CDs. "Cello?" she asked, as if maybe she had misunderstood me.

"Cello," I repeated.

"I can look, I guess. Unless George Strait or some rapper has taken up the cello, it's a waste of time."

I thanked her.

She asked me if I had an MP3 player, and the look on my face answered her question. "Same Ben, huh? No cell phone or GPS, either, I'll bet."

"I have a computer now," I said proudly.

"If that's true," she said, "which I doubt, I'm guessing it was made before I was born. Maybe before *you* were born." She was just messing with me now, and we were both enjoying the change-up. "I've got a break coming. Let me see what I can do."

We agreed to meet at my pickup before her break was over.

When my passenger door opened I knew I had fallen asleep. In a couple of hours I would be at the transfer warehouse beginning my day. Ginny sat in the passenger seat and handed me two silver-colored CDs. "You do have a CD player, don't you?"

I nodded. It came with the new truck. I left out the part about never having actually used it.

Satisfied her time wasn't wasted, she said, "I downloaded some random stuff off the Internet, mostly Yo-Yo Ma, and used my laptop to burn you a CD. My break is over. I got in a hurry. I'm not sure which one has what you want. One is probably some mix left over from my youth. Most people my age are pretty digital these days."

I saw no trace of humor on her face. To her way of thinking, her youth was over and all she had now were souvenirs.

"So who's the woman, Ben?"

I was still half asleep. "Woman?"

"Yeah," she said, "woman. Maybe I'm only seventeen and knocked up, but I'm not an idiot."

I saw the sharp, playful little girl I remembered, so wise beyond her years, and now years beyond her wisdom. I also saw a silver stud in her tongue.

"It's the middle of the night at the Walmart in Price, Utah. A truck driver I haven't seen in years walks in and asks for cello music. Yeah, woman. If she's into the cello, then I already know you've upgraded from the likes of my mom. I've always figured you for a romantic."

"That's not saying much," I said. "These days anyone who believes the sun will rise in the morning could qualify as a romantic."

I thanked her again for the CDs.

"When's the baby due?"

This was my clever way of changing the subject. It worked perfectly. Ginny burst into tears.

The simple answer, the one I expected but wasn't all that interested in, was one, maybe two months, give or take. Between sobs and in quick order I also learned that the baby's father was thirty-eight and her mother's unemployed live-in boyfriend. He said he loved Ginny. When she could no longer hide the pregnancy, she confessed both the pregnancy and their "bad love" to her mother. The boyfriend denied his love and everything else. Her mother responded by kicking her out and telling Ginny she had gotten herself into this mess and she could damn well get herself out. The mother and the boyfriend moved to Salt Lake City to start over. That had been four months ago. Since then Ginny had quit high school and got her GED and had been living with friends and in her car. She concluded by asking me for a job, a second job, so she could afford her own place when the baby came.

I hated to disappoint her. I explained that I was pretty much a one-man operation. It then occurred to me that there was a third thing a man alone in bed can do and if I'd done that instead, maybe I would be alone and asleep and not sitting next to a distraught pregnant teenager in a Walmart parking lot in the middle of the night.

When Ginny reached for the door handle, I said, "Let me ask around. Maybe I can find something for you."

She leaned over and kissed my cheek. The nose ring felt

strange and cold against my skin. She struggled with her bulk and cursed my worn seat before she managed to get out of the truck.

Before she closed the door, I said, "I think we've settled that question about your mother. She is a piece of shit. A big piece."

The night had slipped away. At home I took a long hot shower and had a good sad laugh about Nadine.

Nadine and I had only been together a few months when I surprised her and a UPS driver late one night. They were inside the cab of my tractor-trailer that I was allowed to park behind a locked gate with the UPS vehicles. I asked them what in the hell they thought they were doing. Stupid, since clearly there wasn't any thinking going on. Besides, an answer was out of the question. Both their mouths were full. Quite an amazing bit of circus contortionism considering the confines of my truck cab. Had the event taken place another time in another place with other people, I might have broken into well-deserved applause.

A woman I met in a bar once told me she might have taken her husband back after he cheated with a neighbor, if only he hadn't done the deed in her kitchen—her room, the center of her family. For her, the kitchen was a more sacred place than their bedroom. My guess was she hadn't seen the inside of either one for quite some time. She had been making slow and steady progress toward emptying a bottle of Seagram's and filling an ashtray.

After I settled down, I discovered that the only true anger that remained came not from the cheating but from where Nadine chose to do it—the cab of my truck. Sometimes the smallest things are so damn unforgivable. Maybe because they aren't small—they only seem that way to someone else. You never know what someone holds sacred until it's too late.

Loading up at the transfer warehouse went quickly. I used the extra time on the dispatch office computer to search for information about cellos and cello music. The woman and the cello were linked in my mind in a way I couldn't explain. Knowing something about cellos seemed like the only way to get to know the woman. And, given the opportunity, however unlikely, for her to get to know me. It seemed an innocent enough way to pass a little bit of time. Maybe a little pathetic. After all, I had told her I was a music lover.

When my time was up, I still didn't know much about cellos or the people who played them. The cello was just an overgrown violin. In Italian *cello* meant "violin for the leg." From its origin in the late 1500s, the cello had become more and more popular. Someone once said that the sound of a cello was closer to the voice of a human male than any other musical instrument. Remembering the woman playing the cello, I tried to imagine a man's voice, singing maybe, just below the wail of the wind and blowing sand. But it wasn't a man's voice I heard—it was her voice.

The most expensive musical instrument ever sold was a cello—over eighteen million dollars. It was made by someone named del Gesù in the 1700s. A window popped up. It asked me if I wanted additional information about that cello. Another pop-up offered me the chance to be put on a mailing list or to join a chamber music appreciation club. I have never willingly consented to be on anyone's mailing list. The woman with the cello was the only club I was interested in joining, and the odds of being asked seemed depressingly small, even if I were a luthier, one who, so the Internet informed me, made stringed instruments like violins and cellos.

6

I took on fuel and glanced at my delivery schedule to plan my stops. My mind took an unplanned siesta at the turnout to Desert Home and didn't want to go any farther. I roared out of the truck stop and onto 191 determined I wouldn't stop there. The traffic was sparse, and I reached 117 in record time, not that I was in any kind of hurry.

Ahead in the distance I saw John's ten-foot wooden cross bobbing along the shoulder just as my rig wound around the curve. John's appearance meant spring had officially arrived on 117. He was just coming up on the turnout to Desert Home, so I pulled in front of him. With a cold bottle of water in hand, I waited a few minutes for him to arrive. He kept a strict schedule. If he had time he would stop and rest the cross.

Spring through fall John lugged his wooden cross up and down 117. He had a church of sorts in Rockmuse, the First Church of the Desert Cross. Denomination unknown and unimportant. It had once been a True Value hardware store. He left the door open twenty-four hours a day whether or not he was in town. If anyone showed up to sit in one of the few rickety deck chairs, he would deliver a sermon as if the hardware store held a congregation of hundreds.

Early on in his ministry I had attended his church. My atten-

dance was due less to hearing the Word of God and more to need-
ing a half-inch drive socket and being inside the True Value store
before I realized it had become a church. Once inside the door, I
was too embarrassed to admit my mistake and leave. People gen-
erally referred to John as Preach. I always called him by his first
name. No last name.

John moved toward my truck at a good steady pace. He had
attached a bracket and tire from a wheelbarrow to the road end of
his cross. It made the going easier, or as easy as dragging a cross
through scorching heat and wind can be. Other than the wheel,
John was a stickler for authenticity. The cross was solid wood,
rough-hewn from oak, and it was heavy. A small backpack that
contained a little food and water and some camping supplies was
strapped to the cross and made it even heavier.

John was a tall, lean man, six four or better. He kept his gray
hair cut short and let his beard go the way of God. In his late
fifties or maybe early sixties, John traveled approximately twelve
miles a day. He stopped near sunset at one of his unofficial Stations of the Cross camping sites along 117.

John set his cross down alongside my trailer and took the bottle of water. He thanked Jesus and drank, careful not to drip any
precious water into his long beard. When the bottle was empty he
raised both hands into the air. "Bless you, Ben."

We sat down next to each other on the ground in a spot of
shade provided by the trailer.

"How 'bout a smoke?" he said, and winked.

"Don't mind if I do," I answered. "I'm out. You?"

This was a ritual between us. I had quit smoking several
years earlier, and John had quit long before that, back when, as
he put it, "117 was a dirt road and I was on the expressway to

hell." He had mentioned once that he missed it. So did I. Our ritual began.

"Just so happens I do," he said, as he reached into his shirt pocket. "Got some new papers."

He licked the ends of the imaginary papers and pulled out a nonexistent drawstring pouch of tobacco. His fingers went through every motion until the cigarette was rolled and ready for fire. "Got a match?"

We always did it this way. I went through my pockets until I located an imaginary wooden Diamond match. I struck it against my whiskers, which was probably the bigger fantasy. God hadn't given me much of a beard. Imagination is one of the few things a man can count on if he's got the reality to feed it.

The match head popped, and I held the invisible flame under John's cigarette. We could smell the sulfur. He inhaled and handed me the cigarette.

Exhaling, he said, "Haven't seen you in church lately."

This was also part of the ritual. He had learned long ago why I had wandered into his church, though it didn't matter. There were no accidents or coincidences in John's world. Everything that happened was part of God's plan. Here I was at the turnout to Desert Home, where I had not planned to be. I wasn't sure I believed in God, but when my unspoken desires coincided with his plan I was more inclined to give his existence the benefit of the doubt.

"You know, Ben," he said, "God has lots of power tools for dealing with sin."

"Next time I'm in Rockmuse on a Sunday morning," I said, "I'll check out his inventory."

My stock answer, since in all my years on 117 I had been in Rockmuse on a Sunday morning exactly twice. Both times because of breakdowns. I took a drag and held on to the cigarette while we watched the smoke curl into the morning air.

"You know, Ben, you are the only person who calls me by name. I've been meaning to thank you for that. A man likes to hear his Christian name once in a while."

I passed him the cigarette. "What do other people call you?"

"Most people just call me Preach, which I don't mind."

"Most people call you Preach? No kidding? I thought most people called you Wacko."

"Not to my face," he said, with a hint of sadness. "Not that it matters when you're doing God's work."

It did matter and I knew it.

From where we sat I could see the slope that led up to the iron arch of Desert Home, though the arch was hidden from sight. I was upset with myself because I wanted to see her again. Though I wasn't planning to stop, I had stopped, because of John, which I conveniently told myself was God's plan. I was so close to her. John was getting the tailwind from my frustration.

My thoughts began to drift to the other side of the arch. I wondered if she might let me share some of my newly acquired appreciation of the cello. Thanks to the Internet, like everyone else, I could be an expert on anything in no time at all. I was just another Internet genius. The extent of my knowledge of the cello was next to nothing. I figured I'd picked up enough information to start a conversation. She might surprise me and say something besides *Go away*.

Ginny's comment about upgrading from the likes of her mother came back to me. I didn't really know any more about the woman than I did about cellos. I thought about the opposite of *upgrade* and about my financial situation. I was a truck driver who lived in a run-down rented duplex and was behind on the lease payments on his truck. My thoughts went downhill from there while John and I smoked.

I said, "Have you ever been interested in a woman you knew you shouldn't be interested in?"

"You mean married?"

John passed the cigarette to me for the final drag.

I took the cigarette. "No," I said, hoping I'd summoned the proper amount of indignation. "Someone who's so completely different from anyone you've ever known. Nothing in common. Out of your league."

"Every woman I've ever had in my life has been out of my league one way or another. I'm assuming you mean a good woman?"

"I don't know. Maybe."

"Then the truth is this: a good man can only *aspire* to be worthy of a good woman. She'll always be out of his league in ways he'll never understand. But he'll appreciate what he doesn't understand—if he's smart. You got someone in mind?"

"Nope," I said, even as I revisited her image in my headlights. "Why am I asking you, anyway? What would you know about women?"

I had hurt him. I snuffed out the cigarette in the dirt.

"You can be a mean son of a bitch, Ben."

There was some truth to that. The meanness seemed to jump out of me when I least expected it. When I was younger it took the form of fighting. Now nearing forty, instead of fighting I had a tendency to use harsh words and say unkind things. With money getting tight, the meanness was showing up more often.

I apologized to John. He looked past me down 117.

"I'm old," he began. "I live in a vacant hardware store and pull a cross back and forth along a desert highway. But I'm still a man, Ben. Good and bad," he added as he gazed down the road. "A man." It was as if he saw something on the roadside and was walking out to meet it. "There was a time before the Lord when I drank and drugged and whored—sometimes for years. The Lord gave me a better woman than any man ever deserved. I threw her away."

Whoever she was, maybe it was her that John saw somewhere on the highway ahead.

To lighten the moment, I said, "Years? You sure you're not bragging?"

He brought his eyes back from the road and put them on me. "Be careful," he warned. "I'm serious as sin." He had lost track of the cigarette and forgotten I had already put it out. "You're a better man than you know, Ben. Certainly better than you'll admit." He inhaled smoke and exhaled. He let the spent butt drop to his side. "It's time," he said, and stood up.

Without stretching, something he always did after our roadside smokes, John took up his cross and continued down 117 in the direction of Rockmuse. I wanted to say something to him. All I did was watch him go. His pace was slower and his back was more hunched, as if the cross had become heavier. Words to some hymn drifted back to me. He was singing.

7

John's singing merged into a thundering throaty growl that could have come from only one machine. I'd heard it several times. The sound was distinctive and unforgettable. Walt was flying down 117 toward me on his Vincent. He passed John, who was going the other way. I heard him gear down and thought he was going to stop. Instead, he revved the engine and picked up speed as he shot by me. He wore a white T-shirt and faded blue jeans. No helmet. A pair of aviator goggles held his flowing snowstorm of hair down against the wind. Out for a morning ride, I guessed.

Walt didn't wave or even look my way. In a second he was gone up the highway, accelerating into the turn with the controlled skill of a veteran rider and a youthful abandon and disregard for life and limb. At the top of the curve he must have exceeded a hundred miles an hour. The V twin-cam of the 998cc hand-built 1948 Vincent had more to give him if he asked. From the sound of the exhaust as he hit the straightaway on the other side, he was asking for everything the Vincent could give. When, or if, Walt Butterfield ever died, it wouldn't be from old age. There wouldn't be enough left of him to pick out of the sand with a pair of tweezers.

I turned and looked up the slope to the hidden arch and got in and out of the cab a few times while I tried to make a decision. Finally I walked to the arch and stood there, though only for a moment. Nothing had changed. Far to the south of Desert Home, on the other side of the tangle of empty streets, was the white shimmering ribbon of heat and glare of what people called a mirage. Since the first desert wanderer dying of thirst, mirages had appeared in the distance, promising water only to deliver more parched earth. The closer you came, the farther the promise retreated. This one looked like a long, cool lake.

The front door of the house opened and she stepped onto the porch. I took a few steps back from the arch. I could still see her. I hoped she couldn't see me. She was wearing the same sleeveless dress she had worn the night before. She was barefoot. In the daylight, even at a good distance, her dark hair caught the sun and sent it back to my eyes in brilliant flashes. She scratched herself like a major-league pitcher on the mound and reached her arms out as if she were about to take flight. She turned slowly in a complete circle, her fingers grasping at the sunlight. I thought for a second she might have seen me. She dropped her arms and went back inside. She returned almost immediately and stood motionless on the porch with her hands behind her back.

I took a deep breath and stepped into view. I waved. She did not return the wave. I shouted my hello, which also wasn't returned. I knew she could see and hear me. I began what seemed like a very long walk down to the house. Twenty yards from the porch I stopped and waited for her to acknowledge me. That was how visitors, friends and strangers alike, approached a residence in the desert. Not just good manners, it also kept the number of shootings down to those that were absolutely necessary.

Calmly, she removed her hands from behind her back. She rested her right hand against her right hip and let the revolver dangle there with its barrel pointed slightly downward yet still aimed in my general direction.

"I'm curious," she said. "Is this place the only rest stop on your highway?"

I reached up to take off my cap as a respectful gesture. She raised the barrel of the gun a couple inches without moving it off her hip.

It was a very nice hip. It matched the other one perfectly. I'd had guns pointed at me before. I knew she was capable of shooting me where I stood and exactly where she wanted. She had that kind of confidence, even, I suspected, without the gun. I didn't want to be shot, but if I had to be shot by someone, she would have been my first choice.

She kept her chin high. Her nose was wide with tiny brown freckles that disappeared into the skin across prominent cheekbones. I wondered if maybe she was part Native American. Again, her skin was too white. Indoor skin. She was part something, but she was all business.

"I'm sorry about yesterday," I said. "I didn't even know this place existed."

"So today you decided you'd just drop by and re-mark your new territory?"

I approached her carefully and put my business card, one of the rare remaining four hundred and eighty or so from the original batch of five hundred, on the lowest porch step. "You can call me if you need anything." Coming and going I never took my eyes off the gun, or her hips.

"I'll be sure to do that," she said. "I keep my cell phone right next to my flat-screen television and my laptop."

This wasn't how I saw our first real meeting taking place.

"So, what do you deliver?"

"Whatever people out here need."

"What do you think I need?"

"I don't know," I said. "Strings for your cello?"

Every muscle in her body popped and pulsed beneath her skin. We stood a long time. Through the whole long wait I expected a bullet. Mentioning the cello had been a big mistake.

"Truck driver?" she confirmed.

I nodded. My mouth was getting dry, and the sun was broiling the back of my neck.

She sat down on the porch. We baked in the sun a little longer until the sweat was pouring down my face and chest. There was something familiar about her. Maybe, after standing and looking at her and her gun for so long, she was just beginning to seem familiar.

Finally, she said, "Mr. Truck Driver, don't ever spy on me again. Do you understand?"

I croaked out an affirmative, then managed to add, "My name is Ben."

"Ben," she said, after a long pause, "I just left my husband. He's probably looking for me. I would really prefer you protect my privacy until I decide what to do. Will you do that?"

I said I would.

"Do you know who owns this property?" she asked.

When I said I didn't, all she said was, "Good." She took a quick glance at my card. "If I need anything, I'll let you know."

"Yes, ma'am," I said.

"Claire," she offered, though still as professional as a customer-service operator. "I'll consider that our understanding. You will not mention me or this place to anyone. One more thing. Consider it an addendum to our agreement. This is a difficult time for me. Don't try to deliver anything I do not ask for."

Her meanings, all of them, were clear. I didn't say anything.

"Thanks for not trying to charm me with chitchat. You're not one for chitchat, though, are you?"

"Yes." I hesitated and began again. "No, Claire, I'm all for talk. For the last forty-five minutes or so I've been talking like crazy—to myself."

"You know what they say about talking to yourself?"

"What's that?"

"It's fine as long as you don't answer. You don't answer, do you, Ben?"

"I would," I said, "if I knew what to say."

I mentioned the phone booth at the diner a few miles west. "Take some change," I advised her. "Believe it or not, that one still takes nickels."

"Nickels. Got it."

It seemed like I should probably warn her about Walt. "If you go to the diner, you might want to steer clear of the old man who owns the place. He doesn't like visitors. Keeps to himself more than most around here. To tell you the truth, he's a bit of an asshole."

The marvel of her smile was watching it travel toward her mouth, like a freight train picking up speed as it dropped down a mountain grade. It began with a slight wrinkle high on her forehead and then spread into her dark eyes. From there the smile descended to her lips, where it burst into full view with all the momentum of her body behind it.

"Really? An asshole who doesn't like visitors? The two of us should get along just fine."

"He's not a bad guy. Just old and set in his ways."

"Are you two friends?"

"I consider him a friend. I can't speak for him."

For the first time she lowered the revolver completely and seemed to relax. "Okay, then. We have an agreement."

The meeting had been adjourned. I had been dismissed and I was eager to be on my way. Halfway up the hill she called after me. "Ben!"

I stopped and turned in her direction.

"I scream," she shouted.

"What?"

She repeated herself. This time I understood. "Ice cream."

"Okay," I shouted back.

I didn't know what I had expected. I had a vague idea of what I'd hoped for, and that wasn't a woman running from her husband. The gun didn't bother me, not that I liked having it pointed at me. I was glad she had one and seemed to know how to use it.

The husband was another matter. There had been a time in my life when I had drunk from that tainted water. It was simple then: I was thirsty and there was water in front of me. Or maybe I found an attractive body of water and it made me thirsty. Perhaps I had grown up. Maybe it was just a matter of being able to see the consequences, not just for me, but also for everyone else involved. When a spouse was cheating, or worse, when both spouses were cheating, the list of the injured was always long. What had begun as a provisional warning to myself had gradually evolved into a rule.

In this case I didn't need the rule to tell me what to do. Claire, if that was really her name, had made herself clear. I admired her for that. Even though she didn't know me from Adam, she had told me her situation and how she felt. Directness, however unwelcome, is appreciated. *Mr. Truck Driver, you may deliver ice cream*. Claire hadn't specified a flavor. It just so happened that I had several cases of butter brickle in the small refrigerated cubicle that had been custom-installed at the front of my trailer.

Dan and Maureen McCauley had gotten pregnant again. The child would have been their fourth, but she miscarried. During Maureen's first pregnancy she went through several half gallons of various flavors, which I delivered one at a time along with other things they needed for their family and the reptile refuge they ran several miles outside Rockmuse. She was still experimenting with flavors during the second pregnancy, but she quickly developed a taste for butter brickle. The news of her third pregnancy was announced not by a home pregnancy kit or a doctor, but by a sudden craving for butter brickle ice cream. Dan had a big grin on his face when he told me it was time to start delivering butter brickle again. I congratulated him. The next day I thought I'd corner the butter brickle market. The bulk discount increased my profit margin.

Then the miscarriage. I couldn't return the ice cream to the wholesaler. I didn't have the heart to ask the McCauleys to pay and take the ice cream, or even bring the subject up. For the past two months $225 worth of butter brickle ice cream had been sitting in the fridge unit.

That $225 would buy a lot of diesel. It also happened to be exactly a quarter of a month's lease payment on my rig—I was currently in arrears on almost three months. Or two thirds of a month's rent on my shabby duplex—I was one month behind on that. Or one-tenth of my Visa balance. Or . . . I hoped to hell Claire liked butter brickle ice cream. It would be ideal if she considered it an essential food group. If that happened I might quit asking God to please help the McCauleys get a new bun in the oven.

As I hiked down from the arch, I saw Walt on the other side

of 117, arms folded, leaning against his Vincent. His goggles were up on his forehead. He might have seen me walking down the hill from the arch. I couldn't tell for sure if he had or hadn't. He was directly across from my tractor-trailer, which might have blocked his view.

I walked straight to my cab and opened the door. I had made a promise to the woman. If he had seen me and asked me what I was doing, I wasn't sure what I would tell him. My best bet was to just keep walking. I had planned on getting the ice cream and taking it straight back to the woman. Walt's appearance made me rethink that. It wasn't like Walt to stop and want to talk. Or ask questions.

The roadway was quiet. We were only fifty feet apart. Without moving from his motorcycle, Walt asked me if I had broken down.

I got into the cab. Through the open window, I shouted, "No. You?"

He answered that he hadn't.

I checked my mirrors and put my truck in gear. Walt hadn't moved an inch. I shouted at him above the engine. "You like butter brickle ice cream?"

"What?"

The truck crept forward onto 117. Walt started to walk across the highway. I revved the engine, double-clicked through two gears, and left him behind in a haze of diesel exhaust. A minute later I was cresting the hill. Walt was standing in the middle of the road staring after me.

The morning was half over and I hadn't even made my first delivery. My trailer held, in addition to the ice cream, a crated John Deere tractor engine, twenty-seven five-gallon containers of DuPont Santa Fe red paint, forty coloring books, fifteen packages of crayons, a new windshield for the one and only Rockmuse postal vehicle, and ten cases—one thousand to a case—of Trojan condoms for the vending machine in the men's room at the Rockmuse Shell station, a quantity I thought was overly optimistic on Hal's part. Other freight included a metal carport kit, a Craftmatic adjustable bed, and a huge black plastic tub from a women's apparel manufacturing company in St. Louis. The contents of the tub were identified as "Imaginative Clothing." It weighed 253 pounds, which I thought was an obscene amount of imagination. The recipient was the middle-aged owner of the Rockmuse Collision Repair Center. Maybe there was a connection between the ten thousand prophylactics and the imaginative clothing, if I cared to think about it. I didn't. Leave the mysteries alone. The only mystery I couldn't ignore was how Ben's Desert Moon Delivery Service was going to survive.

8

It was well into evening by the time I reached the turnout to Desert Home. Too late to deliver the ice cream. I didn't arrive back at the transfer station until nearly ten. By eleven I was asleep on my bed with my jeans and boots still on.

At 4:30 a.m. I began another long day, to be followed by a long Thursday of downtime getting some long overdue engine maintenance. Even though I wouldn't have the tractor much longer, I still didn't want it to break down somewhere on 117. The loss of a day would make Friday even longer and that would begin an excruciatingly full weekend going over my accounts and trying to come up with a way to make ends meet. Or at least get them into the same time zone.

Pulling the grade out of Price, I saw a new Ford sedan parked on the other side of 191, pointed west, toward town. The man inside was talking on his cell phone with his head turned away. The sunrise light flashed back to me off something in his ear. Probably an earring. He didn't look like he was in trouble. I didn't care if he was, especially since the outskirts of Price and a couple of gas stations were within fairly easy walking distance.

Truckers I've talked with think their bad press started with the movie *Thelma and Louise.* My opinion was it started long before that; the movie only confirmed what the public thought they knew—all truckers were menacing, violent degenerates and sexual predators. This didn't register with me until I came upon a disabled minivan ten years ago.

Four young children were playing dangerously close to the shoulder. Mom was behind the wheel and Dad had his head under the hood. It was 106 degrees. I never found out what the trouble was, or even got a chance to ask. No sooner had I pulled over and jumped down out of the cab, on a steep uphill grade no less, to see if I could lend them a hand than Mom let out a scream I could hear a hundred yards away. She kept screaming until the kids scrambled back into the van. I couldn't help but notice that Dad beat the kids into the van.

A good fifty miles from the nearest services, 106 degrees, and they sat behind locked doors and closed windows and watched me hike to their van. I felt sorry for them. One look at their frightened faces told me there was nothing I could do, nothing they would let me do. The other truth was I felt a bit sorry for myself that I did an honest job and people who didn't even know me were willing to die of heatstroke just to avoid me. After that incident, unless I recognized the vehicle or the driver, I passed by distressed motorists and hoped one of my good-hearted degenerate brethren with a radio or cell phone alerted the highway patrol.

At the bottom of the grade, the highway dropped onto a long straight stretch. I saw a car with its hood up. This one had its emergency flashers on. The driver was cute as a button, not that I have ever given buttons much thought. This button had a mountain bike hanging from the trunk of her car and was dressed in hiking shorts and a tight mesh athletic top. I wasn't going to stop. She, too, was within a healthy walk of Price, or a quick ride if she used her bicycle. She waved. When I didn't slow, she stepped up near the shoulder and waved again. She was so close to the shoulder a small, unexpected gust of wind might have resulted in a button tragedy. I passed her and then pulled over and set the brakes and turned on the emergency lights.

She was walking toward me as I walked toward her. When we were still a good way apart, she threw me a golly-gee-whiz smile and said, "I was afraid you weren't going to stop. Thank you."

A tanker honked as it passed us. Probably no one I knew. There isn't a lot of crossover between the over-the-roaders and short-haulers.

I asked her what the problem was as we walked to her car. She shrugged and paraded a pair of helpless blue eyes. "I'm a school-teacher," she said. "Elementary. Science. I know about dinosaurs and head lice. When it comes to cars, I know about gas, dinosaurs, and head lice." She had a pretty little laugh. "I just filled up back at the Conoco. This is a rental. I just got in from Salt Lake City."

When she made the remark about dinosaurs, I knew what had brought her out to my part of Utah. Some of the most important finds in the last century had been made in this desert, which had once been a huge freshwater lake before it became a swamp that reached from the mesa to the Wasatch Range. There were fossils almost everywhere. Just down the road she could have excavated Walt.

I got in and turned the key. All the lights and gauges jumped to attention. The tank was full. The engine didn't turn over. Nothing but the irritating seat-belt buzzer.

"I just pulled over for a few minutes to check my map," she volunteered. "When I went to start the car—this."

I told her I didn't know a lot about new cars. Or dinosaurs. Though I did know a good home remedy for head lice. Another trucker honked. She turned her head, and the rising sun lit her mesh top in a distracting way. I knew him a little, or rather I knew all I wanted to know.

There are Christian truckers, Muslim truckers, lesbian truckers, married-couple truckers, opposite-sex and same-sex. I don't know how it used to be. Now about every race and religion, age, and whatever else was represented on the roadways of America. As a group, they were probably more honest and morally upright than what you'd find in Congress or on Wall Street.

Then there was Larry. Some called him 1K Larry. All I really knew was why he was called 1K Larry. He was proud of his nickname. Every thousand miles he had to get his pipes tuned and he didn't care who or what tuned them: animal, vegetable, or mineral. I only saw him every couple of months, usually just in passing, at the truck stop I used outside Price. He hauled for a big OTR outfit that kept him between Salt Lake City and Chicago.

Larry thought everyone wanted to hear about his latest tune-up. In fact, very few did. Hero T-shirts were fairly popular, each made with a different photo. One driver had a photo of a small boy with no hair. The kid was his son who had been fighting cancer for two years. Larry often wore a T-shirt with a picture of Bill Clinton and the caption "My Hero." The last time I saw Larry I wondered if the former president had the same T-shirt with Larry's photo.

"You seem to have a lot of friends," she said. "You must drive this highway a lot."

"Not really. Just this short stretch," I said. "I drive State 117. Down the road at the next junction."

I first wiggled the automatic shifter to make certain it was in park and pressed my foot down hard on the brake. I turned the key again. The engine came to life. "Transmission in Park and Foot on Brake" was the automobile industry's answer to unintended acceleration. My old Toyota pickup had a difficult time accelerating even when it was intentional.

She was thrilled and so was I. "You did it!"

I was thrilled to be able to get on my way.

She thanked me twice as I extracted myself from her little rental.

"Can I buy you breakfast?" she asked. "Maybe you can recommend some good mountain biking trails?" She extended her hand. The fingers were slender and delicate. Her fingernails were manicured—long and shaped, with a fresh coat of red polish. "I'm Carrie."

I didn't know any mountain biking trails, good or otherwise, and my lack of knowledge wasn't going to change, and neither was my schedule, or my mood. I told her the only place to have breakfast was either ninety miles ahead in Green River or ten miles behind her back in Price.

She pointed up the road to the sign for The Well-Known Desert Diner. "How about there?" It was the south billboard, the one without the graffiti. I couldn't help but laugh.

"Did I say something funny?" she asked.

"No," I said. "It's just that diner is really never open anymore."

"It was open last night."

This was surprising news, and it must have shown on my face.

"Honest," she said. "It was. The lights were all on and I could see a man and a woman behind the blinds. They were dancing."

I couldn't help myself and forgot my manners. "No shit?" Maybe I didn't know Walt Butterfield quite as well as I thought. Strange cargo from New York. A trip out of town. The lights on at night. A woman. Dancing. "Are you sure?"

"Oh, yes." There was an earnest schoolteacher clip to her answer. "I even drove my car into the lot. The man pointed to the 'Closed' sign. I didn't get out of my car. It was pretty late. His wife or girlfriend must have switched off the lights. The place went dark. I could still hear the music playing. It must be open now. So, what do you say? Breakfast?"

At that moment I was so shocked I couldn't have said anything. I stared at the sign. It was a mystery I knew I would have a problem leaving alone. I smiled, thinking of Walt and the mystery woman dancing in the diner that had been in lockdown for so long.

She took the smile for a yes. "I'll just follow you," she said.

Before I could say anything, another truck slowed but did not blow its horn. Some trucks were equipped with a microphone and an external speaker, for safety reasons I guessed. I didn't have one. Even if I hadn't seen the turban and beard, I would have known the driver by his voice and greeting. The truck crept by. The loudspeaker screeched, the Indian accent unmistakable. "Truth is timeless being. Greetings to you, my brother, Ben. Tell me. Here are you in discomfort?"

"Truth is timeless being," I shouted back to him. "No discomfort. Just helping this lady."

"Very good. Very good." Manjit's tractor-trailer gradually picked up speed and merged back onto the highway.

If I ever decided to have a hero T-shirt made, I might use his photograph, with his turban and dense white beard. I'd been behind him on 191 several years back as a whole line of trucks were tiptoeing over an icy downgrade through blowing snow. The driver in front of Manjit lost control of his tractor-trailer and began a slow-motion jackknife.

Maybe one driver in a hundred could have avoided the skidding truck and kept us all from piling up. Manjit managed it with skill and lightning reflexes. He remained calm and threaded his double trailer around the jackknife without allowing himself to be forced into oncoming traffic. I didn't know much about the Sikh religion or what they believed. I didn't really care. If Manjit was an example, I had a good idea of how they lived—clean, tolerant, hardworking—which tells you a hell of a lot more about a man than knowing his religion.

"Who was that?"

"Manjit," I said. "He's a Sikh."

"A what?"

"An Indian," I answered, hoping to cut the discussion short.

"You mean Native American, don't you?"

I picked up a trace of condescension.

"Sure," I said. "Native American."

She got into her rental. "Well, we're off. I'm right behind you."

"I have to get going," I said.

"Just coffee, then?"

"No. Sorry."

She was persistent. "Maybe later, then?"

I knelt down by her open window. "Ma'am, I've already had coffee, with my wife. And tonight I'll have dinner with her and our three children."

More than anything she seemed startled. It wasn't the rejection. She appeared totally unprepared for the news of a wife and children. "Oh?" She glanced at my left hand. "Sorry. No ring."

"There's a ring, all right," I said. "She's having it engraved for our twentieth wedding anniversary."

With not much of a good-bye, and another quick thank-you, she sped back onto the highway. I sat in my cab a few minutes while my little lie worked on me. It had nothing to do with her. Saying I had a wife and kids at home almost made them a reality, and I missed them. I could imagine kids getting ready for school and running out the door of a place that was a lot like the model house. The happy voices disappeared into the empty, sand-covered streets of Desert Home.

9

Afternoon had slipped into early evening when I pulled into the turnout of Desert Home to deliver Claire's ice cream. I grabbed a half gallon of butter brickle out of the fridge unit and trudged up to the arch and stood there for a moment.

A storm was moving in. The sweet smell of rain came to me in a soft breeze. It might be a light rain or a hard rain that was coming, though in the desert the rain usually came down hard and all at once on parched earth that couldn't absorb so much rain so quickly. Arroyos filled with fast, churning water and mud following any gentle slope, gaining speed and volume until it was a raging torrent sweeping everything in its path to nowhere. That was how people got into trouble. Maybe they heard lightning and thunder a long way away and figured, well, it's raining over there, but not here. They didn't know they were in trouble until it was too late. I thought about the schoolteacher, Carrie, somewhere out in the desert on her mountain bike. I hoped she had sense enough to pedal like hell for higher ground.

Claire stepped out onto the porch, again with her hands behind her back. She seemed to be able to sense when I was nearby. I held the half-gallon carton above my head. She waved me forward with her left hand. She was wearing a man's checkered short-sleeved shirt and a long old-fashioned dress made from blue denim.

The air was still warm, but it was cooling fast. This was a de-livery I wanted to make quickly, a courtesy, and get back on the road before the sky opened up.

Spring through fall, stretches of 117 became flooded and im-passable for several hours at a time. For no good reason, I was eager to get to my weekend accounting, which had been filling most of my thoughts throughout the day, interspersed with vi-sions of Walt dancing in his diner. I knew the numbers were bad. Now I was filled with a morbid curiosity to know just how bad they were, to the penny.

Again, about twenty feet from the porch, I stopped and held out the carton of ice cream. "Ma'am," I said. "Your order."

Her right hand swung out from behind her back and the sun-light glinted off metal. I stumbled backward, instinctively closing my eyes. Somewhere inside a part of me welcomed a bullet from the crazy bitch.

When I heard her laughter I dared to open my eyes. She was holding a tablespoon. "Ben, Ben." She repeated my name several times before adding, "I'm so sorry!"

I wasn't laughing. That didn't stop her, though I could tell she was working on controlling herself. I thought I might laugh later, in a year or so. Her laughter. It was the answer to the age-old question, what attracts you most to someone? It was a question I hadn't considered much. I enjoyed Claire's laugh, even at my expense. I doubted there was ever just one thing about someone. For me her smile and her laughter highlighted everything else about her, set everything else on fire—her dark, slightly slanted eyes, the curve of her throat, the way she held her shoulders back with a gentle pride that made her breasts confident and under-stated at the same time.

Aware of the way I was looking at her, I dropped my gaze to

her feet, still bare. They definitely weren't elegant. They were wide, strong feet, with short toes—sturdy, beautiful feet built for balance.

"I've been waiting all day for this ice cream," she said.

I handed her the carton and backed up a few steps. She held the carton in one hand and the spoon in the other. "How much do I owe you?"

Without hesitation, I said, "Twenty thousand dollars." More or less it was the figure that had been bouncing around in my head all day. Probably more. It was what I needed to come even, and the sound of such an amount coming from my mouth almost hurt. It had the weight of "good-bye" behind it.

"Yikes!" she said. "That seems a little high, even for delivery in the desert."

"It's butter brickle. Plain vanilla is only ten thousand."

She sat down on the top step. "I guess I'll have a couple hundred worth. I only have one spoon to my name. If you don't have any trucker diseases, you can join me."

I told her I had all the usual trucker diseases. None of them was contagious. "Thanks, but no thanks," I said. "I have a rule against eating ice cream with married women. Especially married women whose jealous husbands are probably looking for them."

"You have a lot of rules, do you?" she asked.

"Not that many," I answered. "Just enough to remind me how complicated life can get when you don't have any."

She dug the spoon into the open carton. "Oh-o-o," she said, her mouth full. "Twenty thousand suddenly seems like a fair price. I could get used to this stuff."

"That would be good news," I said, "since I happen to have several cases of it."

"Please," she said, nodding to the space next to her on the

step. "I can't keep this frozen and I can't eat it all by myself." She took another bite. "Well, not in one sitting."

I declined again and took some pleasure watching her shovel the ice cream into her mouth. For a few seconds it was so enjoyable I forgot about my troubles. "A rule is a rule," I said.

"It's just ice cream," she said.

"It's just a rule," I said. "In my experience it could be coffee or a banana daiquiri. Husbands tend to get violent. Ice cream really tends to put a match to their fuses."

"Dennis doesn't have a violent bone in his body."

I assumed Dennis was the husband.

"He's a musician. An artist. As far as jealousy goes, I don't think so."

"You might be surprised how quickly such bones can grow," I said. "Some of the most violent fights I've ever seen were between men who would have told you they weren't violent just before they bashed someone's skull in. It's in all of us, men and women alike."

"You, too?"

"Except me," I said, and tried to smile.

"You're right, I guess," she said. "Thanks for the ice cream."

I told her she was welcome and turned to leave.

"How much, really?"

"This one is on the house," I said. "I'm like a heroin dealer. The first butter brickle fix is free. Once you get hooked, the sky's the limit."

"I'm hooked," she said. "When can I get another fix?"

"Monday," I answered. "I usually don't work weekends."

10

The rain started before I got back to my truck, just a few huge, round drops that cratered the sand and dirt with loud plops. As is often the case in the desert, the sky directly over my head was blue and clear. The heavy clouds, what there were of them, hugged the rim line of some distant hills. No thunder or lightning. These drops were the scouts, dispersed by wind, announcing the deluge that would arrive shortly. It took less time than I anticipated. A few minutes later the rain pelting my truck sounded like firecrackers. My wipers couldn't move the water off my windshield fast enough to allow me to drive more than thirty miles an hour.

This was the desert, everything all at once, whether it was needed or not. What survived had learned to save, live carefully, and keep a low profile, even appear to be dead for long periods. Perseverance and patience.

The rain subsided. I was picking up speed as I passed the diner. Walt's place looked as it always looked: perfect and closed, with no sign that anything out of the ordinary was going on. That was exactly what passers-by said in June 1972 when they learned that Bernice, Walt's wife, was being beaten and raped by three men inside the diner.

Though Walt's wife was Korean, she'd chosen to go by Bernice. The word that was used then was *savaged*. Bernice had been savaged by three men, though no one knew for sure if all three were involved, or if there might have been four. If only one had been involved and the others just watched from the sidelines, she was still savaged by all of them.

I'd first heard the story when I was a teenager. By then it had been handed down by at least one generation and embroidered. Now, forty years later, it was both transformed and forgotten in the way terrible events often are.

The last time I'd heard it mentioned the event had supposedly taken place in the 1950s, a hundred miles away at a small trading post at the summit of Soldier Pass. In that incarnation both the proprietor and his wife had been killed, and the murderers, escaped convicts with long prison records, recaptured and brought to justice. Maybe that was true, too. History has a way of chasing gravity just like water, feeding into other parts of itself to become something else, something larger and grander, until the one pure thing it was no longer exists.

The only eyewitness account of Bernice's rape, or at least part of it, came from a high school kid Walt had hired to clean up and wash dishes. What the kid saw came out in disjointed parts, like a jigsaw puzzle missing a lot of important pieces. There was a beginning of sorts, and an end, and just enough pieces of the middle to allow a good guess at what the middle had looked like.

Walt had driven into Price that afternoon to run some errands, leaving the high school kid and Bernice alone at the diner. She was cooking and waitressing, and the kid filled in where he could. There had been a dinnertime rush. Near sunset the place had cleared out. Dirty plates and utensils and half-empty cups and glasses were left on the tables and on the counter.

A fairly new Chevrolet Biscayne sedan pulled up to the pumps, and the kid went out to pump gas and clean the windshield. He later swore there were four men in the car. While he filled up the tank they went inside the diner, where Bernice was cleaning up.

How long did it take to pump fifteen or twenty gallons from one of those old glass pumps? Five minutes? Ten? It wasn't until he was finished with the gas and cleaning the windshield that he went inside. Only then did he hear Bernice's screams.

At least two of the men, all average-looking guys around thirty years old, had Bernice on the floor of the diner. Her white blouse had been ripped off and was already covered in blood from her head wounds. Her blue skirt was nowhere in sight. She was naked from the waist down. That was the last thing the kid saw until he came to behind the counter, paper napkins stuffed in his mouth, his right arm broken so badly the bones jutted out from the skin in two places. He could only see out of one eye. A butter knife had been jabbed into the other.

When he opened his one good eye he saw Walt kneeling over him and he could still hear Bernice screaming and what sounded like grunts—and laughter. Walt had come in, as usual, through the back entrance into the kitchen. He gently stroked the side of the kid's head with his hand. The kid said later that Walt kissed his forehead, maybe because he thought the boy was dead, or soon would be.

There might have been four men, but there were only three bodies. Maybe one got away and ran into the desert. Maybe he died there. Maybe he'd been living for years in someplace like Petaluma, California, with his wife and visited his grandchildren twice a year in Denver. No one knew. Maybe Walt knew, but he never said a word about what happened next—not to the highway patrol, not to the sheriff, not to the county attorney, not to anyone.

Bernice's screams stopped. Everything was silent. The kid heard something like a drain becoming unclogged, a gurgling.

Somehow, with the knife still in his eye, he crawled on the floor around the end of the counter, dragging his broken arm behind him. A ragged bloodstain on the linoleum tiles marked his path.

One of the men, the man nearest the kid, was just standing there, his back to the kid. A steak knife stuck out from the base of his skull. The gurgling sound came from a man on the floor. His throat had been cut. Walt stood over him with a butcher knife. The third man was on top of Bernice. He had his head turned and was looking up at Walt. The fourth man, if there was one, was sitting in one of the booths. The kid didn't see him but claimed he saw the man's shadow thrown across the floor by the setting sun coming through the front windows.

The kid passed out and survived. He probably lived somewhere with the memory of that evening. He'd be around fifty-seven or fifty-eight. Walt thrust the butcher knife so deep between the shoulder blades of the man on top of Bernice that it came out the man's chest and punctured Bernice's left lung. What had been up until then a stealthy and disciplined attack must have finally turned to wild rage.

Walt was experienced enough from his stint with the Marines in Korea not to try to remove the knife from the kid's eye. If he had, the boy would have bled to death within a few minutes.

Walt scooped up the boy and Bernice and put them in the back of the 1964 Willys station wagon they owned. He drove them to the hospital in Price. He called the boy's parents but through what had to have been a long, worried night he didn't call the authorities. The police learned about it early the next morning from a hysterical tourist calling from the phone booth outside the diner.

I can't imagine what that tourist saw when he or she walked into The Well-Known Desert Diner that morning. I've heard it said that some things are best left to the imagination. That might be true. Then again, maybe there are some things that shouldn't be.

No charges were ever filed against Walt, though for a time the families of the men were trying to stir up the county prosecutor. All of the men had been attacked from behind.

And these men, these three, or four, men, were they escaped convicts? Desperate men on a crime spree? Men with long, violent criminal histories? Crazy Vietnam vets, as was the fashion for blame in those days. Druggies? Charles Manson disciples or wannabes? People just wanted an explanation that would make sense, even if it made no sense.

The public got all there was. They were men with wives and families, upstanding citizens with mortgages and car payments. No criminal records of any kind. They were shoe salesmen, at least the three who were found, returning to Salt Lake City from a sales conference in Denver.

There were a few idiots who tried to say that Bernice had somehow provoked them, or wanted what she got. There were theories that Walt knew the men and there was bad blood, as if that would explain anything or even begin to justify what they did to Bernice. There were those who simply maintained that Walt had no right to kill the men no matter what they had done. All I ever pondered was the maybe ten minutes between a Chevy full of shoe salesmen saying, "Fill 'er up" to a young pump jockey, and a free-for-all on a defenseless thirty-five-year-old Korean waitress. Ten minutes. Tops.

Two events occurred in 1987. Either one of them might have signaled the end of the Well-Known Desert Diner, though together they sealed its fate. Bernice died, though almost everyone would have said she died a long time before that. And Lee Marvin, the actor, died. He had been Walt's closest friend since their

Marine Corps days in Korea. The two deaths took place within a week of each other. The month before, the exteriors were shot for the last film ever to use the diner. Oddly enough, it was different from every other film to feature the diner—it was a love story.

All of that had been way before my time on 117.

Bernice spent over two months in the hospital in Price recovering from the attack. There were some injuries the doctors couldn't repair. From the hospital she went to a sanitarium outside Logan, where she spent the next eight months. When she returned to Walt, she looked fine, but she never spoke another word. She sat in the end booth nearest the jukebox with a vacant smile on her face. She spent all day every day from 1974 until the day she died looking out the window across the road into the desert, her hands cradling a cup of coffee she never drank. Walt ran the diner with some help. There was always a red plastic placard on Bernice's table that said, "Reserved." It was still there the last time I was in the diner.

I didn't doubt any of this information, though I didn't hear it from Walt. Bernice died sitting in that booth. The diner stayed closed after that, even during those rare times when it was open.

If Walt had been dancing with a woman, I couldn't help but wonder if the woman the schoolteacher saw was Bernice. Knowing Walt the way I did, a ghost was the only thing that made sense to me. I would sooner believe a ghost than a live woman. If Walt were seeing a woman from around Price, I would have heard about it.

Not far down the road from the diner was the runaway wife, Claire, except she was way too young. And married. I was pretty sure she was just squatting at the model home. Perhaps she had found Desert Home the same way I had, by accident. It was a safe place for her because she didn't know anyone. If she knew someone in the area, it sure as hell wouldn't be Walt Butterfield.

No one really knew Walt anyway, even me. We only really knew *of* Walt. That was a fact and it hurt to admit it.

On Monday, or the week after, I expected to show up at Desert Home and find Claire gone. I would stand on the porch or sit on the chair and wish her well. Maybe I would hear the silent cello. She would become just another one of the mysteries I had to leave alone. She might become one of the mysteries I would find myself leaving alone for the rest of my life.

11

The rain hadn't slowed me down much. I arrived at the transfer station near the Price airport earlier than usual and parked my empty rig against the cyclone fence alongside the UPS trucks and vans. I returned tired waves from some of the guys I knew, including the one I had caught with Nadine. He'd been married and divorced twice since Nadine. No mystery there.

My hand was on the door handle of my pickup when my name came over the yard speaker telling me to come to the station supervisor's office. The last time a supervisor had called me to his office, some higher-ups had decided I should start paying a monthly fee to park my rig inside the secure gates of the transfer station. There was a good chance they had come up with a new fee to charge me. There was no chance I was going to pay it.

End-of-workday spirits were high as I walked past the drivers' lounge. It was one of the women, a day driver, who asked me about playing Boy Scout that morning on 191. Her route was clear on the other side of Price. I leaned inside the doorway. Mildly curious, I wanted to know how she knew what I was doing at that hour.

"1K Larry," she said. There was a round of laughter from the other drivers. "Everyone within a hundred miles heard about it. A nature girl." The way she said it you could almost hear her teeth grinding. "Healthy living. Mountain bike. It's not like you to stop,

Ben. You must be getting lonely. Or was she really in trouble or something?"

"Or something."

Another voice, this one male, had joined in from behind the main group. His comment brought forth another round of laughter. He was a big guy with a handlebar mustache. I don't mind joking around with people I know. I didn't know him.

"Who in the hell are you?" I asked.

The lounge became quiet. All the noise—diesel engines, voices, and the faint roar of a jet landing on a nearby runway—seeped in from the open loading docks down the hallway. Everyone had developed a sudden interest in the floor of the lounge while they waited for what might come next. I stepped inside in the doorway.

When he didn't say anything, I said to no one in particular, "I stopped for a stranded motorist. That's all there was to it. If anyone else has a comment, I'd be happy to hear it—outside."

Another page with my name filled the silence.

The handlebar mustache stepped through the other drivers and extended his hand. "I'd be happy to step outside. First I'd like to make my apology here and now." He introduced himself as Howard Purvis. "I started last year." I let his right hand hang in the air. He was maybe forty with a shaved head and biceps roughly the size of a hindquarter of beef. "I was out of line. I apologize. I'd like to be here next year. My wife and kids would like me to be here, too, bringing home a paycheck."

I shook his hand. The room began to breathe again. "Ben Jones," I said. "I'd like to be here next year, too." It occurred to me that probably wasn't in the cards.

"Can we step into the hallway?" Purvis asked.

We stepped into the hall. He rested his big shoulders against the wall. "About five thirty this morning I was headed south on 191. A quick side run to a ranch. That same woman was outside her car talking on a cell phone. I could tell from the exhaust the car was running. She didn't have her hood up or her flashers on, or I would have called the highway patrol. Like I said, she had a cell phone."

"So what?" I said.

"So I'd seen her yesterday. No disrespect intended, but yesterday she wasn't any nature girl."

"What was she?"

Some drivers filed by out of the lounge trying not to look at us. Purvis waited until they were out of earshot before he answered. "Here's the thing," he said. "I think she was waiting for you."

He let what he'd said sink in for a moment before he continued.

"Yesterday afternoon I saw her walk into Joe's Sporting Goods in the mall. I was making a delivery a few doors down. Joe's was my next stop. She was a blonde yesterday. Short dress. Red heels high enough to give you a nosebleed. Enough cleavage showing that old Joe saw them on their way toward his place and ran to the door to open it for her. She walked past him like she'd never opened a door for herself in her life." He let go of a small laugh. "To her Joe was nothing more than an automatic door opener."

"You sure? Same woman?"

"Same woman," he said. "Again, no disrespect intended, but she looked to me like a divorce that hadn't found a courtroom yet. You married?"

I shook my head. "Why would she be waiting for me?" I thought about how she had practically stepped into the highway to flag me down.

"Maybe she wasn't," he said. "Just seemed that way to me. When I got to Joe's he was way too busy with her to sign for his packages. I had to wait. She bought everything she was wearing this morning. Including the mountain bike and the bike rack. Paid cash. And I can tell you, she didn't know a mountain bike from a tricycle. She didn't seem to care. Boom boom," he said quietly. "Seemed strange to me then. Seemed even stranger to me this morning when I saw her decked out on the side of 191 looking like she just escaped from a granola commercial." He pushed himself away from the wall. "That's all I meant by 'or something.' Not suggesting anything, Mr. Jones. None of my business. I should have let it stay that way."

I put my hand out and he took it. "Normally, Mr. Purvis, I'd say it wasn't any of your business. But I'm glad you mentioned it. I'm obliged. Are you thinking what I'm thinking?"

"Hijack?" he ventured.

"Or just setting up the groundwork for one," I said. "What else? Except the most expensive piece of freight I've hauled in twenty years was the jawbone of a T. rex from a dig site off 117."

"Maybe they know of something coming your way worth jacking?" We both thought about that for a moment before he pointed out the obvious. "You're way out there on 117."

"Maybe. But I won't be stopping for her again. Or anyone else."

I thanked him again and continued on through the maze of hallways to the supervisor's office, thinking about a lot of things, her transformation mostly. From there I began to consider her story about seeing the diner open and Walt dancing with a woman. What in the hell did that have to do with anything? She said she had just arrived from Salt Lake City. If that was true, what was she doing on 117 the night before?

Whatever that schoolteacher was up to, I didn't plan to attend any more classes.

12

The station supervisor was a young guy with a salesman's smile that had so far served him well. Price was his second stop in two years on his way up the corporate ladder. When I walked into his outer office, his receptionist was paging me for the third time. She told me to go right inside his office even though I was already standing in front of his gleaming glass desk. He was on the phone and motioned for me to take a seat.

There were only three objects on his desk. Of the three, what interested me least was a photograph of him shaking hands with the president of the company. The photograph wasn't for him to look at; it was intended for me, and anyone else sitting in his office. The frame was strategically angled outward, away from where he sat. The second dealt with the unlikely prospect that anyone might forget his name and title; it was engraved in brass and stood guard next to the photograph. "Robert A. Fulwiler, Station Supervisor." He was a yes-man. All he said into the phone as I waited was, "Yes." He said it at least five times, each time with more conviction than the time before.

He was out of breath from all his yes-ing when he hung up and flashed his whitened smile at me. I was about to buy something I didn't need or want.

"Ben," he said, "I just have a quick question for you. I know you've been having a tough time of it and a certain opportunity for someone has come up. Interested?"

"No," I said, and lifted myself out of the chair. "But thanks for the thought. I'm doing good."

His smile only got larger. "You sure? It means some extra money. You wouldn't have to do anything you're not already doing."

I kept standing and told him again I wasn't interested.

"Close the door, Ben." When I didn't, he closed it himself. He sat down in the chair next to me. We were just two guys, two friends, equals having an equals chat. "Please sit down, Ben."

I sat down. He got straight to the point, or rather the on-ramp that merged onto the road that led to his point. "So you're doing good?" He glanced over his shoulder at the third thing on his desk, a white envelope with my name printed on it. He made no move to pick it up. "Do you know who that was on the phone just now?"

"Well," I said, "you're the station supervisor. My first guess would be Jesus."

He shook his head as if my answer had both offended and amused him. He polished his teeth with his tongue.

I took another guess. "God?"

He reached for the envelope and held it in his hands. "Ben, I'm trying to help you here." Reluctantly, he handed the envelope to me. "I think you have an idea of what this is."

"Who was on the phone?"

He perked up. I had been dangerously close in my guess. He couldn't wait to tell me whom he had been talking to. "That was the executive vice president for communications and public relations at corporate in Atlanta." He couldn't resist taking a peek at the phone on his desk. There was the chance that some of the power of the caller was still lingering there and could be snatched out of the air and stored for later, or simply inhaled. "We've spoken twice this afternoon."

"Wow," I said. "Twice." I folded the envelope and stuffed it into the back pocket of my jeans.

"You're not reading that because you know what it is," he said. "Ben, let's not waste any more time. I know what it says. The two men from the leasing company who dropped it by for you told me. It's a final thirty-day repossession notice on your truck and trailer."

"Well," I said, as if it weren't that big a deal, "times are a little lean for everyone. This is only my first final thirty-day repossession notice."

"They also served me with a property right-of-way release signed by a judge that allows them to come onto the property to take your rig. I can help you, Ben. If you'll let me." Any moment I expected him to put one of his delicate pink hands on my knee. "At least listen."

I listened and kept a close eye on his hands. If I'd had any money in my wallet I would have taken it out and put it in my boots. It was the opportunity of a lifetime. He didn't specify whose lifetime.

A television producer wanted to come and ride with a driver for a few days. If it worked out, he would come back with a small crew. They were willing to pay five hundred dollars. "That's just for starters," he said absently, as if imagining the hundred-dollar bills being counted out one by one into his palm instead of mine. "They're thinking of doing a cable TV series that would run every week next fall. If it works out, the drivers they use will get up to five thousand apiece."

"And what do you get?" I asked.

"Me?" He acted as if he had totally forgotten he was in the room. "Oh, me? I don't get anything. The company would get a lot of free publicity. It's going to happen, Ben. With or without you."

"Just a ride-along?"

"That's it."

"When would I get paid?"

"The day the producer climbs into your cab."

I reminded him that ride-alongs were expressly prohibited by insurance carriers.

"We'd take care of that," he assured me. "A full release, even covering gross negligence."

"The company vouches for him? This all checks out?"

"One hundred percent."

I couldn't keep myself from asking, "Why me? I'm not even really an employee. I'm a contractor, remember? And don't tell me it's because you like me and want to help me out."

Time for the earnest puppy. I had to resist looking at his ass to see if his tail was wagging.

"No one does quite what you do, Ben." He paused for effect and repeated, "No one."

I put on my best aw-shucks face.

"There isn't another place in the country with a driver who has the unique relationship you have with us, or you have with your customers. And I *am* thinking of you. Everyone here is on salary, except you." He knew he had me, or thought he did, and decided to toss all he had into the pot. "Your contract comes up for renewal next year, doesn't it?"

He knew damn well it did.

"If this goes well it might make renewing your contract a lock. Possibly get you a better contract. If you don't want the opportunity, just say so." He lowered his head and clasped his hands. "Hell, Ben, this will help all of us. You're all alone out there on 117."

That was the second time I'd heard that since entering the building. It made me think.

I waited. Better than Broadway. This was the big production finale. He raised his head and lowered his voice. "You and I both know there's a good chance you won't survive financially until the end of the year unless you get a miracle. Maybe not until the end of the month."

In case I might have forgotten, he reminded me I was about to lose my rig back to the leasing company.

"Here's your miracle, Ben. All you have to say right now is yes."

"No," I said, not quite believing what I heard coming out of my mouth.

He was so certain he had persuaded me, my refusal caught him in midsmile with his hand already reaching for mine to seal the deal. "What?"

"Let me think about it over the weekend. When do you have to know?"

"He'll be here Monday, but—"

"Then I'll let you know on Monday morning."

He stood up and walked back behind his desk. "Never mind. I'll just get someone else."

"Bullshit," I said, not moving from my chair. I let him examine *my* teeth for a change. "If they wanted someone else, you would have already talked to that person by now. Your headquarters VP asked for me, didn't he? You didn't have anything to do with it. I'll bet you tried to sell them on every driver but me. Right, Bob? It's okay to call you Bob now, isn't it?"

"You want more money?"

"No," I said. "I need more money. Five hundred won't save my ass. I won't do it for just a piece of a life raft. Let me tell you what I think. These television people want lonely roads and colorful characters with goddamn purple sagebrush and sunsets because they've done the amber waves of grain and ice roads to fucking death. Maybe the company volunteered me because I'm expendable. I can embarrass myself without embarrassing the company. If I don't play well they can say, he's not us. So, Bob, I need to think about it until at least Monday before deciding if I'm going to open up myself and all my customers to reality television— that's what we're talking about. Right, Bob? Parading us in front of America for some cheap laughs and cheaper tears."

The appearance of the woman on the highway started to make sense. Those perfect fingernails said something about her. What they said had nothing to do with dinosaurs and mountain biking. "And tell that television woman she better not step in front of my truck again," I said. "See you on Monday, Bob."

He dropped his ass into his ergonomically designed leather chair.

"On second thought," I added, "I'll call you. Just say yes, Bob."

"Okay," he said. "We'll do it your way. Stupid and stubborn. Just think about what you have to gain—and lose. You and 117 were made for each other."

While that might have been true, it wasn't what he meant. "Monday, then," I said, and headed toward the door.

"One more thing," he said. "Corporate sent in some IT guys. Were you on the company computer a few mornings ago? The one in dispatch?"

For the first time in our conversation, I raised my voice. "Don't start with me about the fucking computer, Bob. I can use it. It's in my contract."

He pushed his chair backward and raised his open palms. "Whoa, Ben. Take it easy. The IT guys were here. They were curious. I said I'd ask you. That system was installed five years ago. You've used it maybe twice before. I was just wondering if someone else had logged in with your user name and password. That's all."

"I was checking the weather report," I said. It was the first thing I thought of. I sure as hell wasn't going to tell him I had developed a passing interest in cellos that had already passed. Everyone would get a laugh out of that. "This time of year 117 can wash out," I said. "Simple. That okay with you, Bob?"

When he didn't say anything, I walked out the door and breezed by the receptionist. The look on her prissy little face told me she was two digits into dialing 911.

I was halfway down the hall. Bob shouted after me, "What woman?"

I walked by the drivers' lounge just as the handlebar mustache was coming out. "Do me a favor, Howard?"

He asked me what.

"You got a cell phone with a camera?"

He nodded. "Sure," he said.

"You see that woman again, will you take her picture?"

"Without her knowing? I guess I could do that. Why?"

"I think I have an idea what she was up to this morning. In case it's more serious than that, and something happens to me out on 117, show that photo to the highway patrol and tell them what we talked about."

He agreed.

We walked out into the transfer yard together without any further conversation.

13

It was dark by the time I reached my duplex. It had been a dark drive. The inside of my duplex was dark. If I had ever locked the place it would have been tough to find the keyhole. I'd lost the keys years before, back when I used to drink. Back then I couldn't get the key into the lock under a searchlight. I tried to remember the last time I had paid the electric bill. I held my breath while I fumbled for the light switch.

She was stretched out in my La-Z-Boy recliner snoring softly. The leg rest was up as high as it would go. There were small irregular holes on the worn bottoms of her pink high-top Converse Chuck Taylors. I concentrated on the shoes. I didn't care to extend my sight to her dark skirt, which was unfastened and hiked up in a bunch at her waist. The white tub of her belly was suspended beneath it. Below that were her laced fingers.

I covered her up with an old red Indian blanket off my bed and opened the refrigerator to see if the food fairy had stopped by. It hadn't. What few containers there were inside had reached the age of consent. I closed the door. She snuggled deeper under the blanket with a contented whimper.

The kitchen counter was littered with the signs of Ginny's foraging. She had gone through a mostly full jar of peanut butter and a whole box of saltines, and a cube of butter. My eyes followed the trail of white crumbs from the counter across the shabby carpet to the La-Z-Boy.

The last time that blanket had covered a baby, I was the infant. My mother abandoned me wrapped in that blanket at the clinic on the Warm Springs reservation in Oregon. It was the only possession I'd had my whole life, and it had held up well over the years, through two foster homes until I was six years old, then stayed with me when I was adopted. Now it covered two babies, one inside the other.

My living room, dining room, and kitchen were all one room. I took out a ruled tablet and hunted down a pencil before grabbing the cheap accordion folder with all my bills, past due notices, and accounts receivable. It was a thick, disorganized file. I reached into the folder and withdrew a random handful of papers and dropped them on the little kitchen table. Aces and eights. There was one unopened envelope from the IRS requesting payment for the last two quarters of estimated income tax, plus three threatening letters from the leasing company about my truck. I took the envelope I had received from Robert A. Fulwiler, Station Supervisor, and tossed it onto the pile. A busted flush.

Ginny moaned in her sleep. Her hands moved under the blanket, probably trying to lift her stomach for a little relief from the weight. That blanket, as far as I knew, hadn't been cleaned since it was made. I couldn't even guess when that had been. Mr. and Mrs. Jones, the older, childless couple who adopted me, had been savvy enough to never touch the blanket.

The subject of cleaning the blanket came up only once, at dinner a year or so after the adoption was final. Mrs. Jones said she would like to have my blanket cleaned for me. I told her something bad would happen to her if she ever touched that blanket.

The two of them just nodded. A threat from a seven-year-old was serious if not dangerous. I asked them if they were Indians, too. Mrs. Jones said she wasn't, that she was just an old woman. Mr. Jones, a quiet man who rarely spoke and never raised his voice, volunteered that it wasn't a question he ever thought about one way or the other.

They asked me if I thought about it much, being Indian. I don't think I had, at least until I left the reservation school and came to live with them in Utah. In no uncertain terms I told them never to forget I was an Indian. Something I thought only because I had been with Indians at an Indian school, though without any tribal affiliation. Not having a tribe, and with no parents, I was an outcast.

Years later, in my early twenties, I tried to find out something about my birth parents. A retired nurse's aide I'd reached by phone in Seattle told me she was at the clinic the morning they discovered me. There was no note. She did remember that someone thought they had seen a young female, a Jewish social worker or college student, on the porch early that morning. The young woman had been volunteering at a reservation mental health clinic several miles away.

The nurse's aide said, "One of the bucks probably had at her. Poor thing."

I asked her if anyone had ever tried to locate the young woman.

"No," she said, in a hurry to end the conversation. "Or if they did, I didn't know about it. No one kept real records of volunteers on the reservation in those days. Every young person and their bleeding-heart brother wanted to help the noble savages."

"So, you don't really know if I'm Indian or not?"

"There are no Indians anymore, Mr. Jones. Just Native Americans. You had a head of thick coarse black hair and black eyes and reddish skin. You were a big newborn. Over thirteen pounds as I recall. If your mother gave birth to you alone, as I suspect she did, she had a tough go of it. That's all I can tell you."

She hung up without saying good-bye or wishing me luck.

That was all I ever knew. Maybe my father was Indian and maybe my mother was Jewish, which I guessed meant white. Over the years my hair turned dark brown, though it was still coarse and thick, and my skin darkened into a perpetual tan. I grew to six foot three, an unnatural height for either Native American or Jew. To my way of thinking, the only thing left that made me an Indian, or Native American, was that red blanket, and it was, if only in that way, just an old red blanket to me. After that conversation with the retired nurse's aide, I just let it all alone.

Ginny was looking at me through one sleepy eye. "Sorry, Ben. Don't be mad at me, please?"

I told her I wasn't mad, but she couldn't stay with me. No discussion. I winked at her, and added, "But that kid of yours is going to be mad. Don't be surprised if he, or she, bears a strong resemblance to a Reese's peanut butter cup."

She opened both eyes and stretched. "What time is it?"

I told her it was about eight. "When do you have to be at work?"

She yawned and closed her eyes. "Pretty soon. Did you have a chance to talk to anyone about a second job for me?"

Before I could answer she was snoring again.

When she left for work I was asleep, my head on a pillow of papers strewn over the dining table. It was three o'clock in the morning and I was hungry enough to wish I'd kept some of the Lacey brothers' jalapeño corn bread birthday cake. Out of habit I opened the refrigerator door again, not expecting anything to be different. But it was. The food fairy had come after all, the pregnant teenage food fairy. While I had slept Ginny must have made a run to a grocery store. I had bread and eggs and four new cubes of butter. On the clean counter was a new jar of peanut butter and a bag of ground coffee. The saltine crumbs were nowhere to be seen, the knife was washed and put away, the sink scoured, and the empty jar of peanut butter thrown in the trash.

I turned and looked at the empty recliner. "I don't care," I said. "You can't stay here." Then I noticed the red blanket was gone. I found it in the bedroom, folded in thirds across the end of my bed. Within a minute I was also folded across the bed, still dressed and still hungry, but filled with the pleasant anticipation of a hot breakfast when I woke up, which I hoped wouldn't be for a long time. The appointment with the truck shop wasn't until ten a.m.

14

Almost all of Thursday was eaten up in the lounge of the shop as the mechanic divided his time between my maintenance job and the drop-ins with quick-fix emergencies. I drank coffee and thumbed through years'-old issues of *Vanity Fair, Guns & Ammo, Esquire, Easyriders,* and *People.* They all covered topics of great interest to someone else who had way more money than I ever would. Usually I spent my time stewing over my finances, which is mostly what I thought about all day Friday as I made deliveries along 117.

I left the duplex only twice during the weekend; once on Saturday to get a new pencil and once on Sunday to buy a cheap digital calculator. The first pencil hadn't been working for me. I did pretty well in my math classes in high school, but the figures that kept coming up didn't make any sense.

The calculator didn't help. The numbers only got worse. If everyone who owed me money paid me, I was still over $30,000 in debt: $32,963.18 by pencil; $33,102.03 by calculator. I needed over $22,000 just to come current. Strips of adding-machine tape and balls of wadded-up paper lay everywhere from the dining room to the bedroom. A few had even made it into the bathroom.

There was nothing I could do but give Robert A. Fulwiler his yes. It was like grabbing onto a life preserver that was attached to an anchor. The thought of sharing my life and the lives of the people on 117 with a film crew and a television audience made me ill. I couldn't do it. I had to. My customers wouldn't stand for it either. Most of them didn't own television sets or computers, though that wouldn't matter to them. They lived where they did and the way they did because they liked it that way. Whatever trust we shared would disappear the moment they saw a camera. I was calling from the phone booth outside the diner. "Let me put you on speakerphone," Bob said. "Mr. Arrons is here with me. Did I hear you say you'll do it?"

"Josh Arrons here." The voice sounded like it was coming from the other end of a tunnel. "We have a deal, then?"

"No," I said. "We don't have shit."

"Then why are we talking?"

"You can do the ride-along. With a signed release. And a thousand—a day. In cash."

"Can't do it, Mr. Jones."

Bob broke in. "Jesus, Ben. A thousand a day to sit in your damn truck?"

"No, Bob," I answered. "It's only a hundred a day to ride in my truck. But it's nine hundred to be sitting next to me while I drive it."

"Okay, Mr. Jones," the distant voice said, "I'll pay fifty for your truck and seven hundred for you. Take it or leave it."

I thought it over. "Okay," I said.

"Now do we have a deal?"

"No," I said. "Not yet. Three-day minimum. Four-day maximum. You stay inside the cab when I make my deliveries. You don't talk to my customers. You don't take anyone's photo but mine. But I'd prefer you didn't. You violate our agreement in any way, or just piss me off, I'll dump your television ass in the desert without so much as the sweat off my balls to drink."

No one said anything for several seconds. "All right," he said. "I don't like it, but I'll agree."

"Then write it up just like we agreed," I said. "Meet me at the transfer station at five a.m. tomorrow morning. If you're one minute late, I'll oil-spot you."

Mr. Arrons wanted clarification from Bob on what "oil-spotting" meant.

"That means if you're late he'll leave you behind like an oil spot."

"Agreed," he said. "Have you worked in television before?" He laughed immediately and Bob joined him.

I didn't know why Mr. Josh Arrons was laughing, and I would have bet that Robert A. Fulwiler, Station Supervisor, didn't either. It didn't matter to Bob that he didn't know what he was laughing at.

It mattered to me. I hung up.

I hadn't sold my soul. I had just agreed to accept a down payment for a test drive. No commitment. No promises. In all those stories about people who sold their souls to the devil, I never quite understood why the devil was the bad guy, or why it was okay to screw him out of his soul. They got what they wanted: fame, money, love, whatever—though usually it turned out not to be what they really wanted or expected. Was that the devil's fault? I never thought so. Like John Wayne said, "Life is tough. It's even tougher when you're stupid."

I had no intention of doing any more than taking money for a ride-along. When that was done, I was done. I was only buying time anyway. I would still be broke and out of business. At least I'd have a little cash in my pocket. Or, if I got real lucky, I would figure a way to keep Ben's Desert Moon Delivery Service going and also have some extra cash. Either way, I got to keep my soul.

I pulled away from the diner explaining it that way to myself with the hope that by the end of the week it would seem like it had been a smart decision. If it didn't work out that way, I promised myself there would be no blaming the devil. When we mortals pray for a miracle and get one, why do we always assume it came from God? Strings. That's why. We think there are no strings attached to a miracle from God. But God has more strings than the devil. The devil at least tells you up front what the strings are.

My trailer was as packed as I could get it. If I was fast and stayed on schedule I wouldn't make it back to the transfer station until after seven. There were a lot of deliveries that could have waited until later in the week. My plan was to take as much as I could. The next day, when the television man started his ride-along, he wouldn't have much to do but enjoy the scenery. It was after five when I parked my truck in the turnout and trudged up the hill to deliver Claire's butter brickle.

I stood beneath the arch of Desert Home. She appeared on the porch and waved her spoon in the air as I started down the hill. The sun had been behind a layer of dark clouds all day, letting the heat in but not allowing it to escape. Without a breeze to move it around, the heat was scorching dry. If I had thrown a glass of water into the air it would have evaporated before it hit the ground.

I handed Claire her ice cream. "No need to pay me," I said. "I'll just put it on your husband's account, ma'am."

She didn't waste a minute and sat down on the porch step.

The ice cream had been frozen solid five minutes earlier. Now it was the consistency of a milk shake. Three heaping spoonfuls had disappeared before she slowed down enough to talk.

"I pay my own bills, thank you." She took another bite. "I paid almost all of his while we were married. Correction. Even before we were married." The sweet ice cream had little effect on the bitterness when she spoke.

I apologized. "None of my business."

"This time I am going to pay you. No more charity. How much?"

"Ten dollars."

She pulled two twenty-dollar bills from the pocket of the same denim dress she had worn on Friday. "Here's twenty for this one and the first one. And another twenty in advance for the two you're going to deliver this week."

I handed one of the twenties back to her. "I can't make any more deliveries to you this week."

She took the twenty back and nibbled her lower lip. "Not worth it? Or tired of me?"

I debated with myself whether to tell her about the television producer and decided not to say anything. "Busy week," was all I said. "Maybe next week."

"I'll be dead from sugar withdrawal by then." She held the cold half-gallon container against her forehead. "Damn this heat today."

I hunkered down on my heels. We were a few feet apart and eye to eye. "I don't know if your name is really Claire, but let's assume it is. Claire," I said, "I don't know how long you've been here. I don't know how you've managed out here as long as you have. You have no running water. No electricity. As far as I know ice cream is what you've been living on. Any day now I figure you'll decide to move on, either back to your husband or to some-place with room service and air-conditioning."

She peeked out from behind the ice cream. "Is that what you figure?"

I stood up. "If you don't move on somewhere else soon, you'll die out here. Is that what you want? If it is, if he's hurt you that bad, you've come to the right place. Things aren't always as bad as they seem."

"Then again," she said, "sometimes they're worse." She placed the ice cream on the porch, got up, and reached inside the door. The porch light came on and off. "You're right about running water, though. But the reservoir is full. For a while longer any-way." She pointed to the south, to what I had thought had been a mirage. "Take a walk with me, Ben." She picked up her ice cream and started walking toward the mirage. I followed her, shaking my head, still baffled by the display of electricity.

It was a short, hot walk. Within a few minutes we had crested a small rise and looked out over a beautiful expanse of shimmer-ing blue water, two or three acres at least.

"It's a self-cleaning reservoir—fed by those hills over there." She pointed to a few bare spikes of earth a mile or so away. "When it rains the water fills the reservoir. The bottom is built at an angle so the dirt and sand wash out over there into a settling pond, and what's left is stored in an underground cistern."

I was stunned, both by the reservoir's existence and her knowledge of its design. "How do you know all that?" I asked.

"I just do."

We began the walk back to the house. "And the electricity?" I asked.

"It's run off an old-style solar array. There's a backup gas generator behind the house. It has a full tank. I try not to use it very much."

The ice cream was just a puddle by the time we got back to the house. She poured it out onto the dirt next to the porch. "As you can see, I have no intention of dying out here. I can't explain it, but I'm at home here. Sometimes I feel happier here than I've ever been in my life."

"Food?" I asked.

"Enough to last for a while. Except for ice cream. There's a refrigerator with a small freezer. I can keep things cool but not frozen."

"So you're going to be around for a while?"

"I could be. I don't know. When I leave, it will be my choice."

What she said about choice reminded me of one more obstacle she hadn't mentioned. "This place might be abandoned," I said, "but someone owns it. He—"

"Or she," Claire interrupted.

"Or she," I added, "could show up anytime. What then?"

"You think too much, Ben."

That was true. I usually waited until there was very little I could do, and then I gave the matter a lot of thought. I needed to think ahead, which was what I was trying to do for Claire.

"Suit yourself," I said. "If the owner shows up you won't be the one making the choice about leaving."

She still didn't appear concerned. "Well, that will be my problem, won't it?"

"Yes, ma'am."

We were both sweating from the heat and the walk. Perspiration had settled into the small wrinkles around her eyes. A dark object fluttered above us and squeaked before veering off. It was dead quiet. You could almost hear the sweat seeping through the pores of our skin as we stood beneath the oppressive sky. It was dusk and the surrounding hills had begun to fade into brown silhouettes. I wanted to kiss her, and I could feel myself beginning to lean helplessly toward her. The dark object returned and darted between us.

She jumped backward and swatted at the air. "What was that? A bird?"

"A bat."

She shivered. "Oh God!"

My urge to kiss her had been broken. I was suddenly relieved to be reminded of why I was there and why I was leaving. I began walking away. "Remember," I said. "You're happy here."

There was something in her that liked to wait until I was a safe distance away, as if she found joy in calling my name and seeing me turn toward her.

"Ben," she shouted. "I'll pay you a special delivery charge if you can bring me some ice cream on Saturday."

I shouted back that I would try. No promises.

"Ben," she called out again. "Don't make me go to your competitors."

I didn't respond to that. She shouted my name again.

When Claire was certain I was looking at her, she raised her arms wide as if to embrace the approaching evening. She was a small and indistinct figure, equal parts body and shadow, standing at the edge of the porch.

"Children of the night," she shouted in a terrible imitation of Bela Lugosi's *Dracula*. Her voice echoed across the sandy streets. "Children of the night, I love you little fuckers!"

The diner was dark when I drove by. There was no dancing going on, and I had begun to doubt there ever had been.

15

Josh Arrons was waiting for me when I arrived the next morning. I didn't have any idea what I thought a television producer would look like, but certainly over thirty, which he couldn't have been. His blond hair was combed straight back in a way that highlighted his diamond stud earrings and dark sunglasses. A wispy little goatee dangled from his chin. He was impossibly slender but appeared fit. My first impulse was to ask him where Scooby-Doo was these days, except he was dressed like he'd been Dumpster diving behind the local Eddie Bauer outlet store.

We took care of the release and the agreement. He counted out the $750 in fifties and I signed a receipt. Bob the Station Supervisor hovered over his shoulder, grinning.

"Climb in," I said. "We'll be on our way."

Bob, for some unknown reason, repeated exactly what I had just said.

"Are you going, too, Bob?" I asked. "If you are, the price just tripled."

He grinned at me. "No," he said, as if for a moment he had been considering it. "Just glad we all worked through the details." He slapped Josh on the back. "It was touch-and-go there, right, Josh?"

"Right, Bob," Josh answered. He glanced at Bob's hand on his shoulder. "But the touching part is over. This man has work to do."

Suddenly I was in danger of liking Josh.

Josh didn't say a word and sat in the cab while I fueled. I got the cash discount on top of the one I got with my CDL card. It wasn't until we had turned off 191 onto 117 that he reached into his pocket and took out his cell phone. "Mind if I take some notes?" he asked.

I answered that I didn't mind. He spoke into his cell phone for about five minutes. The date and time we left, the address of the transfer station, taking on diesel, even our average speed and the approximate time we turned onto 117. He ended with, "Driver, Ben Jones, owner and operator of Ben's Desert Moon Delivery Service, Price, Utah."

I admired his thoroughness.

As we passed the diner, he said, "That's an interesting place. Ever stop there?"

"When I have to," I said.

"It looks familiar."

I laughed. I figured there was no harm in telling him about the movie years. But that was all I told him, nothing about Walt, Bernice, or the motorcycles. He listened and, I noticed, so did his cell phone, which he had pointed discreetly in my direction.

"Any chance you might introduce me to the owner?"

"Nope," I said. "Even if I tried, he might not open his door. No story there. Just a cranky old man."

Josh wanted to know how old Walt was. I knew exactly how old Walt was but I took my time answering. "Somewhere between eighty and a hundred."

"Bet he has some stories to tell."

"Maybe," I said, "except no one will ever hear them. I expect his memory isn't too sharp. I wouldn't be surprised if he kicked off pretty soon."

Josh stuck to the letter of our deal. He didn't ask many questions and I answered even fewer.

The long miles ticked off through the desert while he made notes into his cell phone about things I had long since stopped noticing, like how the ground seems to reach outward in evenly spaced swells from the mesa to the Wasatch Range. He picked up on the fact that at a certain point the milepost markers disappeared and there were no telephone wires or utility poles along the shoulder. He was alert every minute of every mile. The few times we stopped to make a delivery, he not only stayed inside the cab, he pushed himself back in the seat so it would have been hard for anyone on the ground to see him.

Toward the end of our morning Josh stared out his window for a long time. From time to time he would shake his head. I could tell something was gnawing at him.

"What do you see out there?" I asked.

"It's what I don't see."

"Go ahead," I said. "Ask."

"No road signs. No utility poles. And—"

I finished for him. "No mailboxes."

Josh nodded. "Isn't there mail service out here?"

He was an observant little bastard. "Yes," I answered, "there is. All the way from Rockmuse to the junction with U.S. 191. But no one uses it. Or wants it."

"No one?"

"A few, close to Rockmuse. None that I can think of this far out."

"Why is that?"

There wasn't any harm in explaining, though what I could provide was far from an explanation.

People on 117 needed me. And I needed them. That was simple enough. What wasn't simple was exactly why they felt they needed me when a lot of what I delivered, at a fair but significant expense, could be obtained free or at a much lower cost through the U.S. Postal Service.

I shrugged. "No one knows why."

"There has to be a reason," Josh said.

"You would think so," I said. "It must make a kind of sense to them, if not to anyone else. It's like they're all related, which they aren't. They do share a stubborn nature and a perverse distrust of any and all government institutions."

"You mean they're anti-government?"

I laughed. "Hell, no. They don't even talk to one another. They sure as hell don't agree on anything except a desire to be left alone. They're anti-everything."

"There's got to be more to it," Josh said.

"If there is more I don't know what it is," I said. "It's best just to say they prefer it that way and try to leave it at that. Every damn one of them steadfastly refuses to put up a mailbox of any size or description. Without a mailbox the U.S. Postal Service will not, cannot by law, deliver mail."

Josh was convinced I was playing with him. "Come on, Mr. Jones," he said. "I'm not falling for it."

"Then don't," I said. "Of course, there is general delivery."

"I thought so."

"Think again," I said.

Josh listened, periodically shaking his head. I might have done the same thing if I hadn't long ago accepted things as they were.

General delivery mail was held by name at the small post office in Rockmuse. Predictably, if irrationally, such mail was only infrequently claimed. The infrequency had, in some cases, stretched to decades, even when the postmaster knew the recipient was alive because he or she walked or drove by the post office, sometimes several times a year.

Though I didn't tell Josh, this preference, or game, if that's what it was, included Walt Butterfield. The Well-Known Desert Diner was forced to have an address for the business license, which Walt faithfully and inexplicably renewed annually and displayed on the wall of the diner. No mailbox or mail slot in the door. The diner had a Rockmuse address despite the fact that it was closer to Price than to Rockmuse.

"Maybe," I continued, "in some dark, desert past, there was a good reason for such nonsense. No one knows or remembers what that reason is anymore. Like a lot of things in the world that defy explanation, if they go on long enough, you just give up and accept it. Out here we acknowledge such a mystery by referring to it as a 'tradition.'" I winked at Josh. "The desert is lousy with traditions." I added, "And here's a bit of free advice: don't ever screw with traditions. Especially out here."

Josh didn't ask any more questions about mail service. He did appear to go on thinking about it. Every few minutes for the next hour he would stare out his window, slowly shake his head, and smile. For my part, I did what I could to make his day as boring as possible. Eventually I realized that I didn't have to work so hard at it. To most people my days were boring. Sometimes they bored me.

At three thirty we were already on our way back to Price.

"You never asked me how I got my start," I said.

"Okay," he said, looking out the window. He made no move to get out his cell phone to record my story. "How did you get your start?"

"Showing is better than telling. I'll do both," I answered. "In a few miles we'll pull over and I'll give you the grand tour. You should be ready to stretch your legs."

"I wouldn't know," he said. "I lost the feeling in them about ten this morning."

I eased the truck and trailer along the narrow shoulder, careful not to grab too much ditch in the process. There was barely enough room to park safely. Josh waited for my nod and hopped out of the cab. The wind blew some sagebrush to his feet, where it attached itself to the laces of his fancy new hiking boots. He stood there as if a wild but loving animal were harassing him.

"This is where you got your start as a desert trucker?"

I asked him to follow me. Every few steps he paused and tried to shake the sagebrush loose. "Right there." I pointed to a cross sticking up out of a pile of rocks.

"Someone died here?" he asked.

"Two men died here." For the sake of accuracy, I added, "They died over there." I pointed ahead of us to the northeast. "About a half mile away, on an access road that doesn't access a damn thing except a steep ditch and a hundred miles of nothing."

I explained that Rockmuse had once been a viable little town until the coal mine shut down. "Fresh out of high school, I drove back and forth from Price to Rockmuse for Utah Express Provisioners. I did that for about five years. Every day, five days a week. I hauled everything from a baby mule to a wedding cake. When the mine closed, the trucking company pulled out and let me go. People on 117 would phone me or flag me down and ask me to deliver this or that. I used my little Toyota pickup and pulled a small trailer—mostly on weekends for about six months."

"The men who died were truck drivers?" Josh asked.

"Not exactly," I said. "One drove for UPS and the other for FedEx. They got lost in a snowstorm the December after the mine closed. When they couldn't find anything else they managed to find each other. They froze to death in each other's arms in the UPS van. It took search and rescue over a month to find them."

"That seems like a long time."

"Think so?" I asked. "Look at your phone. Got a signal?"

Josh checked and shook his head.

"Spotty reception at best. GPS and homing beacons aren't much better. Same with radios. Even satellite phones. This desert is like a Bermuda Triangle of sand and rock. I heard once it had something to do with the mesa and a weird magnetic iron content. Someone else told me it was sunspots. Personally, I think aliens have a secret base out here somewhere, and they jam everything."

Josh nodded, caught himself, and smiled sideways at me. "Makes sense to me."

"Makes as much sense as anything else in this world," I said. "All I know is I've gotten along okay with nothing more than common sense and a lucky star. Almost twenty years now.

"Those two Mormon boys couldn't be thawed so they could be separated. It was minus ten degrees the afternoon search and rescue located them. It was night by the time the Guard helicopter came. They had to be airlifted in one piece suspended from a cargo net like an ice-blue statue of reconciling lovers. A lot of folks in Price still remember that night, seeing the copter coming in low over town with its grisly cargo swinging in front of a full moon."

Josh cringed. "God, that's terrible."

I couldn't help smiling. "Except for one thing," I said. "There wasn't any moon that night. You can't argue when tragedy collides with a bored population's power of imagination. Around Price it's like JFK's assassination or 9/11. People can tell you exactly where they were and what they were doing when they saw that copter. One more thing."

Josh glanced at me. "What?"

"The copter never flew over Price at all. It landed at the small airfield outside of town. The bodies were thawed in a hangar and taken separately in ambulances to the hospital morgue—two days later."

I started to laugh. Josh joined in. "Crazy. Is that behind the logo on your truck?"

The sides of my trailer had a drawing of a full moon with a helicopter dangling a cargo net. "About a week later both FedEx and UPS came and offered me an annual contract to deliver for them. I get a flat monthly fee. Not much. A little cushion. The 117 route wasn't profitable for them by a long shot. With the driver deaths, no one was in a hurry to take it on. My logo is just my way of keeping my job. I don't want UPS and FedEx, or anyone else, to forget. The area out here had a reputation for strange occurrences long before that."

"Like?" Josh asked.

"An entire Boy Scout troop vanished for a week. The boys all eventually showed up in good condition, though with no memory of what happened. The adult leaders were never found. Various tourists and campers have been reported missing and never found. Trucks and their drivers. A deputy sheriff disappeared. All that was found of him was the red and blue bubble light off his cruiser. Of course there are the UFO sightings. Those usually come from one person."

Josh was catching on. "Let me guess. You?"

"There was another reason why UPS and FedEx offered me contracts."

Josh raised his eyebrows. "Because you know the area and the people?"

"Because," I said, "I have no family and no one gives a shit what happens to me, out here or anywhere else. I'm not a Mormon, either, which is the same as having family in Utah. If I disappeared, the search would last about a minute. No helicopter would be sent for my body. Guaranteed."

Josh didn't have anything more to say. Neither did I. We stood in front of the roadside marker in silence for a few moments.

"Nice of you to remember them with this little monument," he said.

"Mine was nicer," I said. "Unfortunately, it didn't meet with the approval of one of the widows. I saw a woman out here one day about six months after they were found. It was spring, like it is now, some green—desert flowers getting a foothold before summer. I figured she might be one of the widows. I stopped to pay my respects. I assumed she might be grateful and thank me for the roadside shrine I had built to the memory of the drivers. Took me hours one weekend. Found a beautiful cross at a secondhand store in Price. Not a cross, exactly, but I liked it."

Josh walked over to the cross and put his fingers to the wood. "This is a nice cross," he said.

"That's not the one I put up. Instead of thanking me, she read me the riot act for the better part of a half hour. Turned out I had chosen something called a Star of David. It was a pretty thing, but it wasn't a cross. She gave me a lecture I didn't want or need about how her husband was Mormon, and the differences between crosses and stars."

"Wow," Josh said. "She did that?"

"She did. Then she kicked over my star and broke the hell out of the mortar-and-rock base I'd made. You know much about Mormons?" I asked.

"Not much," he said. "I know more about Jews." He patted the cross affectionately. "I should probably know more than I do."

"You're Jewish?" I asked. When he nodded, I volunteered that my mother was Jewish. "At least that's what they tell me."

This was a subject that held some interest for him. "Technically," he said, "since your mother was Jewish, that makes you Jewish. I don't think there are many Jewish truckers."

"Why not?"

He seemed either unwilling or unable to answer my question.

"You know," I said, warming to my point, "Mormons don't get married till death. A lot of people don't know that."

He admitted he didn't.

"They get married for eternity. Can you imagine that? Eternity. Whenever I pass this cross, I think of that poor Mormon bastard. Not so much how he died here, but his widow. What a bitch she was about that marker I put up. I think he must be in Mormon heaven trying his best to enjoy himself before she shows up and ruins eternity."

Josh laughed. "According to my mother and father, some marriages just seem like an eternity."

"Difficult marriage?"

"To hear them tell it, pure hell." Josh laughed. "Not mine, of course."

"Of course," I said.

We were quiet on the short hike back to the truck. Inside the cab Josh turned to me. "Eternity? Damn. And I thought *Jews* were masochistic." He hadn't taken any photographs of the monument. I liked him for that, assuming it was out of respect. Then he asked, "You know what *masochistic* means?"

I told him I probably might if I'd taken the sixth grade again like they'd suggested.

"Sorry," he said. His apology only made me angrier.

He shut up the rest of the way back to the transfer station. It occurred to me that he might have been so moved by the shrine, he'd simply forgotten to take a photo. The easy truth was probably the case: he just hadn't been all that interested. Either way, it didn't matter to me. We said our good-byes with only a wave.

Bob was waiting for him. I overheard the offer of a steak dinner and a "meet the missus" invitation. Josh looked tired after his day of checking out shades of brown and squinting into the road glare. My guess was that he'd be facedown in his baked potato within a couple of hours.

I put my hand in my jeans pocket and caressed the lion's share of the fifties. Tomorrow's plan included more of the same, with whatever dash of excitement might come with a tractor-trailer wash. Josh might make it another day or two before he ran screaming back to Los Angeles, taking his opportunity and his money with him.

I had a nice dinner out, alone, at a large cheap restaurant filled with rowdy children and parents staring blankly at one another. There was no one in the restaurant I knew. The place setting across from me dared me to engage in conversation. I resisted. I pulled the rumpled bills from my pocket and counted and recounted the money as if it might eventually come to an amount that could change my future.

The place cleared out and the waitstaff joked near the kitchen door while I picked at my dinner. A small Hispanic man ran a noisy vacuum cleaner over and over the dirty carpet that refused to give up its stains.

Feeling small, I left a big tip.

16

Josh climbed into the cab the next morning looking dead tired. He held a flimsy cardboard tray with two big foam cups of coffee. "What's going on today?"

I took the coffee. It was a small gesture, maybe even a trivial one. It meant more to me than perhaps it should have. "Nothing's going on," I said. "Not until I get my money."

He passed me an envelope that I didn't inspect and threw on the dash. "To answer your question," I said, "not much." The truck lurched slowly out of the yard into the predawn darkness. "Sometimes the fun never starts."

Josh closed his eyes. "Do you always have to be such an asshole?"

"I'm not being an asshole. I'm being colorful."

From behind his closed eyelids, Josh said, "Yeah? Well, you're a colorful asshole."

"How'd your dinner with Bob and Missus Bob go last night?"

He moaned and blindly guided the coffee to his lips. After a sip, he swallowed hard. "Excruciating. Do you know how much genuine hardwood floors cost? I do. I will never forget. He told me three times. He told me everything three times while his wife just smiled. She has to be on some serious drugs."

"I didn't know she was ill."

"Anti-Bob drugs. Or should be. When I get home the first thing

I'm going to do is fall on my knees and kiss my wife's feet. Then I'm going to kiss our little boy's feet. I hate this fucking job."

"I imagine you have to travel a lot."

Neither one of us said anything for a minute or two. The coffee was listing dangerously to one side in his hand. He looked as if he might have fallen asleep. I lifted the cup from his hand and put it into the holder.

Sleepily, he continued. "I almost never have to travel. I stay in my shop and people come to me. I don't know how I got talked into this. Never again."

"You're quitting show business?" I asked.

"What?"

"Whatever you call it. Television. The entertainment industry."

Josh's head jerked forward. He opened his eyes. "What?" He had the scared, disoriented expression of someone who has awakened suddenly in a public place. "Did I fall asleep?"

I didn't know if he had or not. "You said something about staying in your shop. I guess that's what you call your office? Oh, and you were kissing your wife's feet," I said. "You were slowly working your way up her dress while a choir of angels sang."

He leaned back again and closed his eyes. "Fuck you, Ben."

"Don't piss me off," I warned him. "Or I'll throw your ass out in the desert."

A minute or two passed before he answered. "Any time." His breathing became regular and his head dropped to one side.

Mr. Josh Arrons, television producer, slept through fueling and the truck wash and went on sleeping through my first delivery. The truck was gaining speed on a long, straight piece of 117 when he awoke and stretched. "I think this will be my last day," he said.

"Three-day minimum," I reminded him.

"Right now I'd give you my kid and his college fund to never get into this truck again."

"I'd have to pass on the kid," I said. "You have any photos?"

He pulled his cell phone out of his pocket and held it out in front of me. "Sometimes a man just gets lucky. Married eight years next month."

The screen held a photo of a petite brunette in jeans and a powder-blue sweater. She was holding a small child, who had his fingers in her hair, and the two of them were laughing. They shared the same blue eyes that matched the mother's sweater. Behind them an ocean sparkled. Josh took the phone away.

John and his cross appeared in the distance. We were closing on them fast. The bright eastern sun threw a disfigured shadow from the cross back toward us. Josh leaned slightly forward into the windshield, uncertain what he saw, or if he was seeing anything at all. We sped past John and his mobile cross. Josh's head whipped around. "What the hell was that?"

"What?"

Josh's eyes were fixed on his side mirror. "That!"

"What?" I said. We dropped into a slight hollow and began rising onto another straightaway. I made a big deal of looking into my side mirror. "I don't see anything. What did you see?"

"Okay," Josh said. "If that's the way you want to play it. But when a Jew starts seeing Jesus carrying his cross through the desert, I'm telling you the apocalypse can't be far off."

A little ways down the road, I gave in. "It wasn't Jesus," I said.

Josh said he was relieved to hear it. "I didn't think so. For one thing, Jesus is shorter and his hair is longer. That's the way it is with all celebrities. They just don't look the same when you meet them on the street." Josh grinned at me. "So, who was the stunt double for Jesus?"

I had to give that one some thought. In a way, my telling him
it wasn't Jesus was enough. It was enough for me. As far as I knew,
no one knew John's last name, or his story. He had a past, as we
all did, but it didn't matter much. If it did matter, sooner or later
such curiosity would end badly. What could I say about John and
his cross and his seasonal wandering up and down 117?

Finally, I said all I could. "He's just a religious nut."

"That cross is huge!"

"It's heavy, too," I offered. "Solid oak."

Josh thought for a moment. "What makes a man do something like that?"

It was another question that couldn't be answered. I'd heard
rumors, and the little bits and pieces John had volunteered during our imaginary roadside smokes. Even if I knew the details, I
doubted they could sufficiently answer the question. That was the
thing about curiosity, especially about people: the real questions
never had answers that meant anything for very long. Pretty soon
you had a batch of new questions.

"Leave him alone," I said. "Even if you come back here. If
you're a decent man, it's the decent thing to do."

Josh nursed his cold coffee the rest of the morning without
saying much. He wasn't as alert as he had been the first day. His
cell phone didn't appear once. With my permission, he got out of
the cab at the Rockmuse Shell.

We sat at a picnic table beneath a lone cottonwood and
lunched on barbecued rattlesnake subs. It was all for the tourists,
the few who wandered down 117. It was really chicken, which
explained why so many people said, "It tastes like chicken." Josh
looked a little squeamish. It made him feel like an insider when I
told him the truth. We washed the sandwiches down with venom
punch, which was really Mountain Dew and Hawaiian Punch.

The taste was appropriately terrible and as such seemed genuine enough.

Again it was only midafternoon when I finished my last delivery. Josh had been napping on and off since lunch. When he was awake he stared out at the passing desert, probably not thinking about the desert at all but the end of the day and returning to his son and wife.

The wind had kicked up. Tumbleweeds bounced across the road, and the sun baked the tar into sticky black ribbons. A particularly hard gust shook the trailer. I swerved over the centerline. It woke Josh up.

"Are we there yet?"

"This is the desert," I said. "There is no there here."

Once again, the cross loomed ahead on the highway. It wasn't moving. Something didn't look right.

Josh straightened up in his seat as I slowed. "What's going on?"

I didn't answer him. The cross was propped up at an odd angle far off the shoulder. A blue plastic tarp had been pulled over part of it to form a rough tent. The tarp's ragged corners whipped back and forth in the wind. Protruding from beneath the tent were two pairs of legs. In quick order I had my rig off the road and was setting the brake even as I jumped from the cab. If there had been another vehicle on the road I would have been struck and killed in my haste to get to the cross. I couldn't take my eyes off the legs.

My knees hit the hard dirt of the shoulder. I yanked the tarp back, afraid of what I might see. The feet of one set of legs were bare and bleeding, the socks nothing more than rags around the ankles. They were the feet of Duncan Lacey, though I recognized him by the calico hair and the red suspenders. Duncan's face was burned by wind and sun into blistering sores. John was cradling

Duncan's head against his shoulder, trying to get him to drink from an old army canteen.

John held up his free left hand to keep me from speaking. Duncan opened his swollen eyelids. He acknowledged me with a smile, though considering the condition his face was in, particularly his lips, it would have been difficult to identify it as a smile. In a hoarse, guttural croak he began to sing "Happy Birthday." John shook his head but didn't try to stop him. When Duncan got to the part where he should have said my name, he paused and stumbled again into "Happy Birthday." John coaxed him into taking a couple of sips of water and Duncan closed his eyes.

"What the hell happened?" I whispered.

John scooted out from around Duncan and gently positioned his shoulders against the cross before he motioned for me to back out from beneath the tarp.

"It's Duncan Lacey," he said. "Or what's left of him. He came wandering out of the desert from the north. I couldn't believe my eyes. God was looking after him, all right. Another few hours and he would have died."

"I know who he is. How'd he get way out here? We have to be thirty miles from their place. How do you know who he is?"

John rubbed his big arms. "Last winter he and Fergus came to church a few times. They drove that old Jeep of theirs through the snow and icy wind."

"Church?"

"Don't look so surprised. We all feel a need to come before the Lord, Ben. And I got the feeling they had a greater need than most. Particularly Duncan. And that's all I'm going to say." John tipped his head toward Josh. "Who's that?"

Josh was standing behind me. "I'm Josh Arrons." Josh put out his hand and John took it in his. "Ben's letting me ride along with him for a couple of days to see if I might like to try driving a truck."

John raised a wild gray eyebrow, looking at me for confirmation.

"Something like that," I said. I barked at Josh to get back to the truck.

"No," John said. "We'll need his help getting Duncan into your cab and back to his place. Fergus needs to look after him."

Josh couldn't hide his pleasure at having an ally, especially the man he'd seen hauling the cross. I was stuck.

"What about you?" I said to John.

"I'll be fine. I can still get a few more miles in before nightfall. The sooner you get Duncan home, the better. I'm just glad the Lord gave me some of his work to do."

John and I moved Duncan out from under the tarp and to his feet. His knees buckled and John threw him over his shoulders like so much sacked feed and carried him across the highway to the truck. I was tall and John was taller. I had a clear sense of just how tall John was as he towered above Duncan and steadied him with one big hand on his shoulder. He said a short prayer and made the sign of a cross above Duncan's head.

"Okay, Ben," he said, "let's get him in."

It took all three of us to get Duncan up and into the front seat of my truck. Duncan was short of stature, but dense with muscle. John soaked some rags in water and wrapped Duncan's head and feet. He resembled a sleeping mummy by the time Josh squeezed by him and perched on the console.

"Shouldn't we get him to a hospital?" Josh asked.

Maybe we should have. That wouldn't be what either of the brothers would want. Duncan was suffering from exposure and heat exhaustion, if not heatstroke. The old saying about what doesn't kill you makes you stronger is a nice sentiment, but it isn't true, not on 117. Out in the desert what doesn't kill you just pisses you off and will probably kill you the next time.

There were endless opportunities for injury and death. Rock-muse hadn't had a doctor since the mine closed, which left a few folks dead and a lot more pissed off, and nobody stronger. Gener-ally, no one had health insurance or much money to pay for treat-ment, especially in a hospital. Only one of the McCauley kids had arrived in a hospital, and that was because Maureen went into labor during a rare family trip into Price. Self-reliance was the true faith on 117.

"No," I said. "We shouldn't."

Josh didn't say a word during the drive to the Lacey brothers' place. He sprinkled water on the rags and a couple of times tried to get Duncan to sip from a water bottle.

Duncan's jeans were torn out at the knees as if he'd been crawling, which I knew he had. His fingers were dirty and raw. I counted back the days since I had seen them both and calculated how long he might have been out in the desert. My best guess was no more than three days.

Contrary to popular opinion, without water, a few days is all you'll have, and the third day you can't tell your toes from your nose. Without water your muscles stop working and you can't walk even if you have the energy. I was afraid of what we might find at the Lacey brothers' place. Whatever had happened to Duncan might have also happened to Fergus. For all I knew, Duncan was the lucky one.

Josh tended Duncan. When Duncan moaned, he winced as if he could feel the pain himself. The edge of the water bottle against Duncan's raw lips drew blood a couple of times. Josh patted the red away and moistened his lips. I'd seen people in worse shape than Duncan, but none better or more tenderly cared for. Though I wouldn't have said so, I was grateful to have Josh along.

The truck bucked and banged along over the ruts on the road to the Lacey place. Josh did his best to keep Duncan comfortable. He put his arm around Duncan and held him close to absorb the blows.

I saw Fergus on horseback galloping at an intersecting course to ours. He pulled up next to the window and glanced past me to his brother. He did a quick double take when he saw Josh. He didn't bother to speak. He rode alongside the truck the last couple hundred yards into their turnaround.

Fergus dismounted. "How bad is he?"

"Bad enough," I answered. "He'll probably live. You can thank the preacher for that. John just happened to be on 117 when he saw Duncan."

It was my turn to hoist the man over my shoulder. Maybe Fergus could have done it, except that he didn't appear to be in much better condition than his brother. I doubted he had eaten or slept much since his brother had disappeared. No doubt he'd been out searching day and night. I didn't have to tell Josh to stay put. He slipped down into the passenger seat and pulled the door shut with only a nod to Fergus. Fergus took no notice of him. His concern for his brother outweighed anything else, even the presence of a stranger.

I'd never been inside the boxcars before. I was surprised. I'd been in contemporary tract homes that weren't as comfortable, or as spacious. The interior had the feel of one of those cartoon Arab tents that held tennis courts and a swimming pool.

Fergus pointed me toward one of two twin beds at the far end of the boxcars. I walked past two tinted panoramic windows that had been cut out of the metal side of one of the boxcars. A sliding glass door had also been added. The view was north, out over a nice wooden deck and into unobstructed miles of desert filled with the slanting golden light of late afternoon. An awning covered most of the deck and helped to keep the heat down.

I lowered Duncan onto one of the twin beds. "You know what to do?"

Fergus stood quietly over his brother and didn't answer me. I went back to my truck and brought back my first-aid kit. Fergus was sitting on the edge of his bed. Tears streamed down his sunburned cheeks.

"You need to rehydrate him," I began. "Do it slowly. Warm water, not cold. If the water is too cold you could send him into shock. You have something to take his temperature with?"

Fergus stared at his brother and nodded.

"Take his temperature. Put him in a tub of tepid water. When you get his temperature back to near normal, then you can worry about the burns and blisters." I set a tube of antibiotic and bandages on the nightstand between the two beds. "It's going to take a while. Afterward he's going to have a hell of a headache and a lot of pain. You got something for the pain?" I put a mostly full bottle with the supplies on the nightstand. "Here's some ibuprofen."

"Where are his boots?" he asked.

"He wasn't wearing any when John found him."

"Preach?" he asked.

"One and only," I said.

He seemed relieved that it had been John and not someone else who had found his brother. "I woke up early in the morning a couple of days ago. He wasn't in his bed. I waited until noon to start searching. He's been acting strangely lately, but . . ." His voice caught and he turned his head away from me and coughed. "We can't go to a doctor."

"Can't," I said, "or won't?"

I didn't wait for him to answer. I didn't really expect him to. I turned to leave. "Just stick close by him. If he gets away from you again, you won't need a doctor."

Fergus came suddenly to his feet and took my hand in a jerky shake. He was saying thank you, or trying his best.

I told him to tie a rope to one of Duncan's belt loops. "And tie the other one to yourself. You need to get some sleep, too."

Fergus found his voice. "You take credit cards?"

"What?"

Fergus twisted his own swollen lips into a painful smile.

I told him I'd check back in a day or two.

As I passed the windows again the angle gave me a clear view of a bright patch of close-cropped green grass. I turned back to Fergus. "Is that a putting green?"

Fergus looked up from his brother with an embarrassed smile. "It is. You know," he said, "these days there are some prisons that have them." He glanced down at his brother's bandaged head. "It helps keep the inmates from going crazy."

17

Josh wasn't expecting me back so soon. The sound of my door opening spooked him. The silver discs tumbled out of his hands to the floor. "You scared the shit out of me."

The center console was open. So was my glove box. Josh had turned the air-conditioning to high. Pieces of paper and dust were circulating around the cab. I felt as if I'd just caught someone with his hands in my pants. There was a guilty expression on his face.

I got behind the wheel. "What the fuck are you doing?" The good feeling I'd had about him had vanished.

Josh picked the CDs up off the floor. "Relax. You've got this fine Bose sound system. I thought you might have some music. I was bored."

"Don't you have music in your i-fuck or whatever you carry? I thought all you dizzy little punks carried your lives in your phones."

What I said seemed to catch him off guard, as if he was shocked I knew phones could be loaded with music.

He shook his head. "My i-fuck?"

"You know what I mean."

There had never been a CD in the player. It had come with the truck. I didn't even know how to operate it. The two CDs were the ones that Ginny had made for me that night at Walmart. I'd forgotten about them after my brief but passionate interest in the cello had passed.

I pulled back onto 117. My heart rate was returning to normal. Josh was cowering against his door with the two CDs in his hand.

I apologized. "It's been a long day."

"You mean it's only been one day?"

"Go ahead," I said. "Put them in."

He asked me how to work the sound system.

I told him I was busy driving. "It's easy. You can figure it out."

It only took a minute for him to get the music going. A man's voice asked, "Are we rolling?" The notes of a guitar began. I drove and we listened. Josh smiled. "I never would have figured you for a Nirvana fan. 'Heart-Shaped Box.' A classic."

It must have been one of the songs from Ginny's not-so-distant youth. I gathered from the lyrics that the guy was in love with someone and neither one of them was very happy about it.

"Yeah," I said, "I'm a big fan. It's practically all I listen to." This was partly true. I hadn't listened to any music in a long, long time.

For a moment I was returned to that evening at Desert Home and Claire naked in the pink light with her silent cello. I couldn't say I'd heard music, though I knew I had somehow felt it.

Josh hummed along for several bars. "That surprises me. I figured you for a George Jones or Clint Black aficionado. But Nirvana? Some of the best songs from the worst musicians I've ever heard."

"You know a lot about music?"

Josh seemed to be shaken by my question. "Me? No. I mean, I took piano lessons as a kid. Didn't everyone?"

"I took lessons on the bagpipe for a while."

Josh looked out the window. "Okay, now that really surprises me. Were you any good?"

"Nope," I said.

Mr. and Mrs. Jones had kindly offered me lessons on any instrument I wanted. I'd never mentioned my love of bagpipes to anyone before. A Jewish Native American half-breed orphan playing bagpipes wasn't the sort of impression I ever wanted to make.

"Didn't stick with it. No one in the neighborhood was sorry when I gave it up. Most of the pets took off. Some never came back."

I had gone on playing a little. When I was a teenager I would ride my bicycle or drive the Joneses' old pickup out into the desert at night and play to my heart's content. With the certainty that only a kid can have, I was certain I was alone.

The shrill wail of the pipes beat back the darkness. I walked and played the only two songs I knew, "Amazing Grace" and "Loch Lomond." Up and down trails and into small canyons, I blew and blew. The pipes seemed to echo in all directions when I stopped. One Saturday night I took a girl out to the desert and played for her. She laughed for five minutes. I refused to go to school for a week.

We listened to the songs on the rest of the CD. A few he skipped through. None of the songs was familiar to me. They did give me a glimpse of Ginny—innocent, gritty, and filled with a teenage cynic's love of disillusion and failure. She didn't have to listen to it anymore. She had to live it now and, hopefully, get through it. With any luck it might drive her into country music or gospel, though I doubted it. Maybe it would drive her into a love of silence, which, with a baby, she wouldn't be getting much of, or sleep.

I didn't see Josh switch out one CD for the other. When it began, I started to say something. The words stopped on the inside of my mouth. The instrument we heard was a cello, just the cello, a line of quiet notes, some short and some long, vibrating with a sadness I hoped Ginny would never know, or her child. What stopped me cold was the expression on Josh's face, as if he had quit breathing. The fingers on his left hand began to twitch.

He punched the eject button and muttered something about hating classical crap. I didn't buy it. There was the recognition of something in the sound of the cello that drove him deep into himself. He didn't say another word all the way back into Price.

If the first CD surprised him, why didn't the second? That was the point. The second CD surprised him so much that he couldn't even say he was surprised. I told myself it was nothing. But it was something, something that wasn't good. All I knew for certain was that the cello music connected with Josh. The only other person I knew it connected with was Claire, who was hiding out from her husband.

Josh was in a hurry to get back to his family, or so he said. He kept his hand on the door handle the entire time I was backing my rig up against the cyclone fence.

Before I set the brakes, he pulled the handle. I reached over and gently gripped his left arm. "Hold up, Josh."

He looked at my hand on his arm and did his best to stare me down.

"Why are you in such a hurry?" I asked.

"I'm not," he answered. He was doing his best to sound casual, and he was failing. He was distracted, and defensive. "Thinking of home. You know."

I let go of his arm.

Josh said, "I know. I know. You want tomorrow's payment, right? Well, you're going to have to trust me to drop it by Bob's office before I leave town."

"How about dinner?" I didn't really want to eat dinner with him. I wanted to hear how he responded to my offer, or maybe just see the look on his face.

"Can't."

"Yeah," I said, "you're tired and probably want to get a good night's sleep at the hotel before you leave. Call the wife. Discuss your day, that sort of thing."

He wasn't sure what I was getting at, if anything. He put his shoulder into the door. "That's pretty much it."

"How about a photo, Josh? You and me and the truck? Something to remember our adventure? Little boys love trucks. Your son would get a kick out of seeing Daddy and a big truck and trailer. Wouldn't he?"

He hopped down out of the cab. "Maybe," he said. "No camera."

"How about your phone? Let me take it. What do you say? Dad behind the wheel?"

Josh walked quickly away and threw his regrets back at me from over his shoulder. "Just don't have the time, Ben. Thanks for the offer. And thanks for an interesting couple of days."

I watched him cross the yard, moving fast but not too fast, dodging the trucks coming and going. He got into a compact Ford rental and wasted no time getting on his way. There were only two car-rental agencies in Price—one rented Chevys and the other Fords. You had your choice of an SUV or a compact. If he hadn't turned to give me a halfhearted wave as he exited the gate, I never would have identified Josh as the man I had noticed

parked on the shoulder just minutes before the stranded elementary schoolteacher flagged me down. Two compact Fords.

And something else.

Light doesn't reflect off people, only objects. I hadn't seen the
man's face that same morning the schoolteacher flagged me down,
but I remembered the light catching something. I knew what that
something was—a diamond stud earring. It was the same flash I
saw as Josh waved good-bye to me. He was the man sitting in the
Ford along the grade going up out of Price—the man on the cell
phone, the man calling the schoolteacher a few miles ahead to
tell her I was headed in her direction. Whatever they were up to,
they were up to it together.

18

Thursday morning was overcast and cold. A heavy dew rested everywhere around the silent yard. It wasn't until I got behind the wheel that I saw the white envelope beneath my wipers. I reached around and grabbed it and threw it on the passenger seat. I figured it was the final payment from Josh, though I had pretty much come to the conclusion during a long, sleepless night that his name probably wasn't Josh and he sure as hell wasn't a television producer any more than Carrie was a schoolteacher. He seemed too young to be Claire's searching husband. He probably worked for the husband. I didn't know if Bob was in on the bullshit. Every time I was about to fall asleep I'd see or hear something, like the cello, or Josh's fingers twitching. I was fifteen hundred dollars to the good and none the worse for it.

The envelope hadn't felt like it contained cash. Maybe the son of a bitch had written me a reader, the kind of check that was only good for reading. I opened the envelope. Inside were a short handwritten note and a photo. The note said: *Wednesday morning. 10:16 a.m. Returning the costume to Joe's. HP.* A Walmart receipt for two four-by-six prints was taped to the back of the photo: one for me and one for him, just in case.

Howard Purvis had done what I had asked him to do. I was grateful. The photo had been taken at a distance. It was clear enough. There was no mistaking that she was the schoolteacher who had waved me down on 191. Her hair was the same and that was about all. She was buffed and polished. In her high heels she towered over the mountain bike she was wheeling into the front door of Joe's Sporting Goods. Joe was holding the door open, and he didn't look happy. She was happy enough, though. She was gazing past Joe at her reflection in the door glass.

I put the note back into the envelope and the photo in my wallet. On a hunch, I opened the glove box. Then the center console. I checked the CD player and the floor. One of the CDs was gone. I didn't need to guess which one it was.

At the truck stop I assumed I wouldn't see another cash payment from Josh. I decided to use my Visa card. The little gray screen flashed its message while I thought about all the freight I had been letting back up during my two days with Josh. It was going to be a long, full day.

The message on the screen meant more than it said. *Declined.* I canceled the transaction and tried again. *Declined.* I went inside to pay in cash. This had happened before, but not often. There was something about that word that sucked the self-respect out of your soul. This time it sucked out all my hope as well.

I had sixteen deliveries to make. I started driving, and my thoughts took over. The road time and the miles ticked off until I had reached the end of 117 with no memory of anything between the truck stop and the mesa wall a few hundred yards ahead of me. It was only the second time I had driven to the end of the road.

For a long time I sat inside the cab and stared up through the windshield at the red-flaked wall. It was after eleven. I needed a plan and to start lining up possibilities for a new job, maybe working for a big OTR interstate outfit. Independents went under all the time. I wasn't going to be the first, and I wouldn't be the last to have to live his life at cents on the mile. As much as that prospect bothered me, it wasn't what bothered me most. Highway 117 had been my life and as much a calling as John's was to haul his cross, not that either of us was going to make the cover of *Time*. When John got too old or died, who would miss him? Who would miss me?

I turned around and began what would be the first leg of my farewell tour. Ben's Desert Moon Delivery Service would survive through Monday. Maybe into the middle of the following week. Certainly not beyond that.

My tractor-trailer crept down the hot empty main street of Rockmuse, idling at the two stoplights. Everything I saw was sharp and etched with the bright enamel of nostalgia. I took in the few shops—the grocery, where Mildred Danner, owner of the Rock Dock Bed-and-Breakfast, was unloading a cart into the back of her battered old Dodge minivan. Two young boys in dark blue Cub Scout shirts with yellow scarves drank cans of Coca-Cola with their legs wrapped around parking meters in front of John's True Value First Church of the Desert Cross storefront. An old man whose name I never knew sat in a canvas chair on the sidewalk and watched me like I was a one-man parade on a national holiday.

When the mine closed, things had gotten bad; then the economy slumped, sending things further downhill. Still, it was home to these folks, and they found a way to hang on, though they were hanging on to less and less.

At the second light a brown ball of tumbleweed bounced through the intersection and came to a stop in front of me. As my truck moved forward, so did the tumbleweed. I followed it out of town past the Rockmuse Shell, where it finally slipped beneath my front bumper. In my sideview mirror I watched as it disappeared behind me.

Midway through my deliveries I took the turn to the Lacey

brothers' place to check on Duncan. I waited in the turnout for a few minutes before deciding to walk around to the deck. The sliding door was open, and I peeked inside. They were both on their beds asleep in their underwear. A piece of thin cord was stretched between them, the ends tied to their wrists.

Fergus had cleaned up Duncan. The blisters had been dressed, and his raw fingertips and feet were bandaged. His matted red and gray chest hair rose and fell with his breathing. From where I stood I could see several circular white scars exposed through his chest hair. They could have been caused by any number of objects. I could think of just one: bullets. I had a matching scar just below my rib cage on my left side. Duncan had at least six.

Outside I knelt on the cool putting green and felt a smile form on my lips. The smell of the grass in the sunlight made me sleepy. It was all I could do to get myself up and moving. The sun was high above the awning, leaving the grass partly shaded. The low desert hills rolled northward into a brown horizon that married itself to a deep blue sky.

Duncan would heal. I was sure of that. I wasn't sure if he would survive whatever else was wrong with him, or if Fergus would survive long without Duncan.

I passed the turnout to Desert Home and thought of Walt and the Lacey brothers, Claire and her cello. It was a relief, almost a pleasant distraction, to think of them. Maybe I was attached to them a little, like a satellite was attached to Earth by gravity.

Whatever their problems were, they weren't really mine. Soon even my small attachment would be severed without as much as a nod to mark my exit from their lives. Earth's gravity was a necessity; without gravity everything spins out into emptiness.

At the transfer station I got into my Toyota pickup no longer caring what Josh and the woman were up to. It wasn't a hijack, though a part of me wished it were. I had given my word to Claire not to mention her, and I had honored my word. If Josh and his lady friend wanted to find Claire through me, then they had failed.

Claire was just part of another little nasty domestic mess that filled hospitals, drunk tanks, and courtrooms every day all over the world. Maybe she and her husband would kiss and make up, until the next time. When he finally found her, maybe she would be happy to be found. Maybe instead of hearing the cello, I'd hear her moaning softly beneath him.

I fell asleep thinking about what I was going to do next, and the painful details of how the last days of Ben's Desert Moon Delivery Service were going to play out.

19

Well after midnight I awoke to a gentle tapping on my bedroom window. In my sleep a woodpecker was searching for insects in the dark-grained wood of Claire's cello. I lay in bed and listened to the *tap-tap-tap*, a pause, and then more tapping on the glass. The window was open a few inches, enough to let in a loud whisper.

"Ben," the voice said. "Ben. Open up."

I went to the window, drowsy with sleep, without thinking about who might be calling my name from the alley. The voice was female. It had been a long time since I'd heard a female voice at my bedroom window in the middle of the night. In fact, never.

"Is that you, Ginny?"

Ginny's head popped up on the other side of the glass. "Who else would it be?"

"I don't know," I whispered. "It shouldn't even be you."

I opened the window. The night breeze slipped over my bare chest. We argued a minute about why she was there and why she wanted me to let her in. I told her I would come to the front door.

A hand came through the window and slapped at my bare legs. A few inches higher and the hand would have slapped something more important. It suddenly seemed like a lucky coincidence that I was wearing boxer shorts.

"No!" she said, straining to keep her voice low. "Stay away

from the front door. And don't turn on the lights. I'm coming in. It's important."

When you're a single, thirty-eight-year-old man and a pregnant teenage girl arrives at your house after midnight, wanting to crawl through your bedroom window, you should take a moment to think about it. I took a moment and said, "The hell you are."

"Please, Ben," she begged.

I asked her if she was in trouble. She said that was a funny question considering the condition she was in. "No," she hissed, "you are. Now let me in!"

I took a couple of steps back. The bottom of the window was probably only three feet at most above the alleyway. Ginny was at least five foot six. She threw her arms over the sill and tried to hoist herself through.

While Ginny struggled I was reminded of a cat the Joneses had when I was a boy. For a year I had watched the big female tabby jump effortlessly from the floor onto the kitchen counter. She had put on weight, and Mrs. Jones informed me that the cat was "expecting." The cat made the leap as always until one day she jumped and hung suspended in the air well short of the counter. Cats aren't supposed to fall. The tabby fell. In that split second, the cat wore the same startled expression I saw on Ginny's face. Ginny realized she was no longer a scrappy little girl. She had been transformed midair into a heavy, awkward, pregnant young woman. There were tears in her eyes as I reached down and helped her swollen belly clear the windowsill.

She lay on the floor beneath the window huffing like a little steam locomotive that had jumped its tracks. I returned to the end of my bed and stood there.

"What's so important?" I asked.

Ginny rolled to her knees and used the windowsill to pull herself upright. She stuck her head out the window and looked both ways down the alley. Apparently satisfied, she pushed the window shut and drew the shade. Without moonlight, the bedroom was almost totally dark. She closed my bedroom door. I switched on the night lamp.

"Okay," she said, leaning against my dresser.

"Okay," I said. "What's so important?"

The carpet was still covered with white balls of ruled paper and adding-machine tape from my attempts to plumb the depths of my financial coffin. Ginny kicked a ball of paper with the side of her foot and watched it roll to my bare feet. She slowly raised her eyes from the floor and gave me a shamelessly obvious appraisal.

"Gee, Ben," she said, "not bad for an old guy. You're buff. No tattoos?"

"No," I said. "Why are you here?"

"Really? Not even one?"

"Not a one! Get to it, kid."

She laughed softly. "You're a disgrace to your profession. Do you work out?"

Annoyed, I said, "Yes, Ginny, I work out. I get up every morning and go out to work." I grabbed the red blanket and wrapped it around myself.

She began in earnest. "I think you're in deep shit. A cop and some old guy paid me a visit at work last night. They asked me all kinds of questions about you. The old guy did most of the asking."

What was old to Ginny might not be old to anyone else over the age of twenty-one. I thought immediately of Josh. "Describe him," I said.

"Under six feet, kind of a gut. Has this skinny little mustache. Oh, yeah, and he wore these tiny round glasses. He acted like he was all nice but he wasn't, not really. He creeped me out."

I sat down on the bed, and Ginny came over and sat next to me. She was still sweating heavily. After a couple of false starts she got the story out.

The night manager had called her into the break room. She thought she was going to be fired. The only thing the cop did was instruct her to cooperate. The man first asked her when the baby was due and made a big deal about what an exciting time it was for her. He showed her photos of his daughter and grandson. She started to relax. Then he asked if she knew Ben Jones. When she said she didn't, he showed her a blurred photo from a Walmart parking lot surveillance camera. It was clear enough to show Ginny sitting next to me in my pickup.

Ginny nibbled at her lip, or around the metal ring in her lip. "They had already gone back and reviewed the surveillance by the time they came to talk to me. No biggie. So I told him I really didn't know you, just that you had dated my mom a long time ago. He pulls out another picture of me! On your porch the other night! I thought I was going into labor, Ben."

I asked her what she had said.

"I told him the truth."

"Good girl," I said.

"I told them you had said you'd check around and see if you could find me a second job. I went to see you because your phone is disconnected."

"My phone is disconnected?"

"Yeah," she said. "Didn't you know?"

I shook my head. I didn't know. I wasn't surprised. It never did ring all that much. I just thought no one was calling. "Was that it?"

"You wish," she said. "He wanted to know what you were after in the store." She shrugged. "At that point, I told him you wanted a CD of cello music. Since we didn't have any, I went on the Internet and downloaded some and burned you a CD. That's what we were doing in your pickup." Ginny rested her head on my shoulder. "Ben, you're the nicest guy my mother ever went with, but . . ."

"But what?"

"But I think you're mixed up in something bad. Maybe you don't even know it. But you are, aren't you?"

I told her I didn't think I was. Even as I said what I thought was the truth, the wisdom of her words, that maybe I didn't even know about it, began to sink in. "If they come back, tell them the truth," I said. "You haven't done anything wrong."

"The man told me it might be best to stay away from you."

"Good advice," I said. "Take it."

"What if he knows I'm here tonight?"

"Tell him the truth."

Ginny nodded and stood up. She kicked at the balls of wadded paper again. "What is all this on the floor? Looks like it's been raining Hostess Snow Balls. Maybe I'm just hungry. I'm always hungry. Could you sneak into the kitchen and make me a sandwich?"

"In the dark?"

"Yeah." Ginny reached around me and switched off the lamp. "And hurry. I'm double-parked."

For reasons unknown to me I began to crawl toward the door, shedding the blanket as I went. "What do you mean you're double-parked?"

"I thought they might be watching me. I borrowed a bicycle from my friend Lalo in the display assembly department."

I was beginning to love that kid. "You rode a bicycle?"

Even in the dark she might have seen me smiling as I crawled into the kitchen. Eight months pregnant, and she rode a bicycle through the dark streets of Price to warn me. It was two or three miles each way, at least.

She must have thought I was dawdling. "Hurry," she whispered. "I have to be back to work in half an hour."

Life always brings new challenges. Making a sandwich in the dark, however useful a skill it might be, was not a learning curve worth much to a soon-to-be unemployed truck driver. I grabbed a knife, the loaf of bread, butter, and peanut butter while coming to the conclusion I was not going to skulk around my own house on all fours like a dog. Arms loaded, I walked upright and, with as much dignity as I could muster in my underwear, back into the bedroom.

Ginny approved of my solution. She made herself a quick sandwich for the road. With her mouth full, she asked, "So what is the deal with all the paper on the floor?"

I wanted to tell her to mind her own business. Instead I told her how I had spent the previous weekend and about the imminent demise of my little company. She would have found out sooner or later. Besides, I needed practice telling people Ben's Desert Moon Delivery Service was belly-up.

"Sorry," she said. "How about getting a smaller truck?" she suggested.

"How much do you know about men?" I asked.

Ginny patted her big stomach, leaving a tan streak of peanut butter across her dark sweater. "Not much," she replied. "But I'm learning."

"Then here's a lesson. No man ever wants a smaller truck."

In the middle of a chew she managed a garbled "Ha-ha." In two more bites the sandwich was gone, and she announced her imminent departure with a loud belch. She lifted the shade and then the window.

"What was the name of the guy who questioned you?"

"He said his name was Doc something. No last name I can remember."

I said that was okay, and reminded her to tell him anything he asked if she saw him again.

I was still convinced that whoever he was he had to be working with Josh, and Carrie the schoolteacher. That meant there were three. There might be more. What wife is worth that kind of payroll? I kissed Ginny's forehead and thanked her.

"You know what that asshole asked me? He was being all nicey-nice and then he says, 'Is Jones the baby's father?'"

That question angered me. Her having to answer that question made me even angrier. "I'm sorry," I said.

"I flipped the fucker off. I told him next time he went to the toilet he should wipe his ass with the photos of his grandson. He just smiled. I think he's been told that before."

"Go," I said. "Be careful. You're riding for two."

I eased her out the window to the ground.

"Ben," she said, "do you mind if I come back and take a look at your business records? I'm taking a business class at the University of Utah extension and I have to do a final term project. You could be my project."

"I thought you were *my* project?" I said.

She said please, and I figured it couldn't hurt, though I knew it wouldn't help either. I told her where I kept the file. "You're welcome to whatever is on the floor, or in the cupboards. You know where the door is." I added, "And the window."

I watched her take off wobbling down the dim alley. She looked like a black pumpkin riding a kid's bike. Working at Walmart. Pregnant. Alone. Broke. Homeless. And taking a college class. Half the parents in America would have killed to have a daughter with her kind of sand. I felt like a lucky son of a bitch just to have her as a friend.

After twenty minutes or so of sitting on my bed in the dark, I turned on the lamp again. I got dressed and turned on every light in my duplex, including the porch light. I scanned the street from one end to the other. I wasn't shy about what I was doing. The street was dark and empty, or looked dark and empty. I couldn't be sure that I wasn't being watched. I made some coffee, went back out to my porch, and sat on the steps for a long time in the cool night air.

If Josh paid me the money as he agreed, I would have about two thousand in cash. The leasing company would take my truck and trailer within the next couple of weeks. It didn't matter since, even with the cash, I would be unable to keep my company going for more than a handful of days. If I could land a job with an OTR outfit, I might be able to pull down forty or fifty thousand a year. After taxes I would probably be able to pay off my debts in three or four years.

It amazed me that a runaway wife was worth all the time and money and people that Claire's husband was investing in getting her back. Maybe she was worth it. Maybe they were rich. Rich people, what I knew of them, had a way of overreacting to life's speed bumps. Get in a beef with a neighbor, hire an attorney; lose some money in the stock market, file a lawsuit; your wife runs away, hire a bunch of private investigators and track her wayward ass down, damn the expense.

Ginny had said the man who had questioned her had a cop with him. The cop kept quiet. He was there just for show and to lend a false impression of authority to the man named Doc. That took not just money, but power, though if you had the first you usually had the second. Rich people always had someone to call who could arrange something that the average guy couldn't get done, no matter how right or wrong. The only call the poor man could make was to Jesus. If Jesus didn't answer, Smith and Wesson always did.

The husband would find Claire—of that I was certain. It was none of my business. I was certain of that, too. It pissed me off that all of their petty bullshit had to involve Ginny and me. I needed to tell Claire, purely as a courtesy, that her husband had called out the cavalry and, in any event, the ice cream man wouldn't be making any more rounds. Until then, I just had to do my best to keep the cavalry galloping in circles out in the desert and away from Claire. After I told her what was what, it was up to her, and my promise to her now had an expiration date. I had enough of my own problems.

In case I was being watched, I recycled my coffee off the front porch in full view of the street, going for distance and sending as much of a message as a broke and lowly Jew Injun truck driver could send.

20

I didn't leave the gates of the transfer station until full daylight. If I was going to be followed, I wanted to see whoever was doing the following. It occurred to me that there could be a device of some kind attached to my tractor-trailer, except that by now the runaway-wife posse should have figured out that technology was unreliable on 117.

I knew money was no object to them. After all, they had blown at least fifteen hundred to sell me a load of reality television bullshit. That didn't mean they weren't tracking me, only that they would have to somehow follow me in person. They didn't know I wouldn't lead them to Claire. Not today at least. So, who would it be, the schoolteacher? The man called Doc? Josh? Variety being the spice of life, I hoped for someone new.

I kept my speed not too fast and not too slow, and I used my turn signals well in advance of turns. Following me should be possible, but not easy. While waiting for a break in a stream of oncoming traffic in order to make my usual left turn off U.S. 191 onto SR 117, I began to wonder why Claire's search party was so convinced that I could lead them to her.

By my rough estimate, 117 cut right through the heart of about five hundred square miles of Utah's high desert. If they had traced her to the area around Price, Carbon and Emery Counties, there were a lot of roads, small towns, isolated ranches, and sparsely populated wide patches where she could hide out. I only drove 117. Everyone knew that.

If they had taken all that money and all their contacts and connections and simply asked me, maybe brought a bit of pressure to bear, which they could easily have done, I might have given her up. I'm not a coward, but I'm not a fool either. They could have threatened to pull strings here or there to mess with my commercial license, insurance, or even my contract with the corporate boys. What they did was screw with me, and then scare the shit out of a pregnant teenager.

Why don't people with money and power realize that when they screw around with the little guy when they don't have to—especially when it's a little guy like me with not a damn thing to lose—sometimes the little guy is just going to get pissed off and stubborn up? It was all I could do, and I was sure as hell going to do it. Whoever had drawn the short straw was in for a long, damned day of driving bad roads and sucking dust—all for nothing.

I dropped off two heavy crates at Walt's place without knocking on his door. I no longer cared if there had been dancing at the diner. There were three access roads between the diner and the Lacey brothers. None of them was fit for a fat snake to slither on and they led absolutely nowhere, with ninety-degree turns, narrow canyons and road cuts, and ruts so deep it took every ounce of driving skill I had, the right speed and load balance, to keep the tires rubber-side down. I took each one. A couple of times I headed out roadless, cross-country over hard rock that left no tracks. Each time I rejoined 117 I would check my mirrors for signs of anyone following me. Each time I saw nothing but a lot of my own dust and diesel smoke drifting back the way I had come.

For the whole day I was the most sociable son of a bitch on

the map, paying unscheduled visits to abandoned ranches as well as customers I hadn't seen in weeks, in some cases months. I was on a first-name basis with every deer and jackrabbit, snake, prairie dog, and sagebrush that came my way.

There were discoveries along the way. Up a sandstone canyon so narrow I didn't have more than a few inches' clearance on either side, the road came to an abrupt end. There was nowhere to turn around, which meant I had to back down the narrow, steep grade maybe a half mile or more. It was going to be a bit of slow, tricky, and dangerous driving. I got out and walked ahead into the end of the canyon to stretch my legs.

What I found left me weak at the knees with surprise. Spiraling out of the rock was a series of mini-waterfalls, each emptying into a plum-colored stone goblet and finally into a deep, clear pool of water. The canyon walls were maybe forty feet high and only ten feet across at the top, leaving the waterfalls and pool in perpetual shadow.

A small herd of some kind of dwarf deer I'd never seen or heard of before drank from the pool with barely a nod of recognition to mark my presence. The pool, no more than fifteen feet across, disappeared into itself, down into the bedrock, refusing to trickle away its beauty and life into just another dry wash or sandy-bottomed arroyo. It began and ended where it was, without any ambition to go anywhere or do anything else. There wasn't a beer can or a cigarette butt in sight, or even the remnants of a long-ago campfire.

I didn't turn around to walk out. I backed up, placing my feet in the prints I had made coming in, holding my breath like a father leaving the room of a sleeping child.

I hiked back down the road several hundred feet and came to the conclusion that it was not a road at all, but a ledge of slough from the ridgetop above that simply resembled a road with a tight turn and a hundred-foot drop on one side. One miscalculation, and my truck and trailer and maybe I would come to a very loud and twisted end.

The position I'd gotten myself into was foolish, but part of me welcomed the challenge. Inch by inch I backed down the ledge, knowing that even if I had my trailer and cab perfectly centered, the lip could give way under the weight at any time. Over an hour later I was safely back down to the desert floor, drenched in sweat and, oddly, never happier. I had been enjoying the hell out of myself the whole damn day, running my tractor-trailer over lost roads, half roads, nonroads, and dry lake beds off 117. It was the most fun I'd had in months.

For a while I'd forgotten why I was tooling around the desert in five tons of truck, trailer, and cargo, most of which I had still not delivered by the time the sun began to set. On the desert floor I climbed on top of my trailer and did a slow three-hundred-sixty-degree circle looking for signs that I had been followed. The result was disappointing, unless they were better than I was willing to give them credit for. My feelings were mixed. I was also damn glad no human being had witnessed the mess I'd gotten myself into driving onto a slough ledge. That relief was mixed with regret that no one, friend or foe, had seen me back my rig down that treacherous piece of rockslide. I was a damn good driver.

It was past nine when I got home. The pregnant teenage punk fairy had paid me a visit. All the wads of paper were gone and the carpet vacuumed. My bed was made. The accordion file was gone.

On my dresser was a note. *Dear Ben, You old farts sure know how to show a young girl a good time. I made another sandwich. Took a nap. Hope you don't mind. Meeting with my professor about our project this afternoon.*

Above her name she had made a crude drawing of a skull and crossbones that I supposed was meant to convey affection in some youthful way I would never understand, and probably wasn't meant to. The skull did seem to be sporting a lopsided smile. I got the message. Whatever character flaws Ginny had, lack of loyalty and follow-through were not among them.

21

If no one had attempted to follow me the day before, someone was at it bright and early on Saturday morning. Moab was pretty much a day's drive and back. For a reasonable price you can rent a stripped-down Jeep to go four-wheeling, or use it to carry your mountain bike into the canyons.

Most of the rental Jeeps are fire-engine red or bright white. All the Jeeps come equipped with a GPS and a homing beacon. The Jeeps announced to the world that you had no clue where you were going or if you'd know when you'd arrived—but you had a Jeep with four-wheel drive. Everything else was just a detail. The GPSs and homing beacons regularly saved lives. Common sense was usually one of the details that didn't seem to matter when you had the overwhelming false confidence brought on by four-wheel drive. In the steady stream of early-morning truck traffic leaving Price, I was the only one being paced by an infected four-wheel-drive pimple.

I took my sweet, careful time making certain that all the oncoming traffic on 191 had cleared before taking my left onto 117. Whether the red Jeep passed me or waited behind me in traffic with the other vehicles didn't matter. Once I got on 117, I'd know. The Jeep waited with the other five or six vehicles behind me. It continued south on 191 after I made my turn. The driver was wearing a cap and sunglasses.

While I waited for traffic to clear, I thought about how much

expensive fuel I had burned the day before, and about the limita-
tions of the truck and trailer. I thought about Ginny and Claire.
I thought about Walt and his motorcycles. By the time I reached
the diner I had finished most of my thinking for the day. For the
first time, instead of parking off the shoulder along the gravel
drive, I backed my trailer up along the side of the diner to within
twenty yards of the Quonset. The nose of the cab jutted out from
beside the diner, where eastbound drivers could see it, though not
until they were almost directly in front of the diner.

I stood at the rear of the trailer and waited. Only one vehicle
passed the diner headed east. It was a red Jeep, moving fast. Its
brake lights flashed when the nose of my cab became visible. Josh
was at the wheel. The driver's head was turned away. It was Josh,
though.

"What the hell are you doing?" Walt's snarl was in top form.

I jumped. "Got some freight," I said.

"I asked you a question."

"I gave you an answer."

Sometimes a conversation with Walt went that way. He was
upset that I'd parked my trailer beside the diner. It really didn't
matter, except Walt was always at war with any kind of change.
It was always possible that he might take a swing at me, though
it had never happened. His muscles twitched under his white
T-shirt, and his jaw was set on his face like a piece of steel. He
was only slightly shorter than me, and I outweighed him by maybe
five or ten pounds. Overall, we were evenly matched, if you didn't
factor in his age. Doing so would be foolish. He had the wide
chest and long reach of a gorilla. It occurred to me there might be
a first time coming my way.

Walt locked his pale eyes on me. When I didn't blink, he
turned and walked toward his workshop. "Don't park here again."

After unloading the boxes, all of them damn heavy, and setting them on the hand truck, I wheeled them to the door of the Quonset, which he had left open. He shouted for me to leave them just inside the doorway. The inside was as black as a cave, and a cool breeze blew by me.

"The union," I said, "says not to bring freight indoors. Or into unsafe areas that might result in injury." I didn't belong to any union. We both knew it.

Walt switched on a small light at his workbench. "You and Jimmy Hoffa can kiss my ass."

I took the stuff in and dropped it where he pointed.

"Why'd you park that way, Ben? I want a straight answer. When a man does or says something he's never done before, either he's gone crazy or he has a damn good reason. Has suckling all those losers on 117 made you crazy?"

Given his mood, I decided to forgo mentioning that Walt's place was on 117. He offered me a crate to sit on next to his stool in front of the workbench. Off to the side, stretching to the rear of the workshop, the motorcycles were dimly lit and arranged in the shape of a chevron. In spite of his years, Walt looked healthier and happier than I had ever seen him. It seemed there might be some truth in what I'd heard about his love life.

"I need a favor," I said. "A big one."

In all the years I'd known him, I had never asked Walt for anything, even a glass of water. Whatever he had given or done for me had been offered, not requested. I was curious how he would react.

"What do you need it for?" he asked.

"What?"

"The motorcycle." I hadn't told him what the favor was, but he guessed. "Tell me straight, Ben." This was a demand as well as a warning. I took heed of both.

He sat on his stool, bolt upright, and listened to every word. Every word was the truth, or as much as I knew of it. There was no sign on his face that he was concerned in any way. He listened and said nothing until I was done.

Finally, after a moment, he said in response, and by way of summary, "You made a promise to a woman you do not know. You owe her nothing, except that promise." Walt stood and switched on an overhead light above his collection of motorcycles. "I take it that once you ditch your shadow you intend to tell her the jig is up and it's time to either skedaddle or go home to her husband. Does that about cover it?"

That was exactly what I intended to do, and I said so. Until Walt said it plainly I hadn't realized, no matter how little sense it made, that I would miss Claire. "Yes," I agreed. "All I'm doing is buying her a little time. After that it's up to her."

Walt strolled up and down and between his motorcycles and then straddled one. "This is a 1966 BSA Victor 441. In the history of motorcycles, this might be the worst one ever made."

Knowing Walt's love of fine machinery, I had to wonder not only why he had one, but why he thought this one would fit my needs.

"Because," he said, examining the throttle linkage, "in my opinion it is the finest example of a piece of shit. It is the gold standard of shit." He caressed the yellow gas tank with an obvious tenderness. "This bike is everything the Vincent isn't. It is poorly designed and poorly manufactured from the poorest-quality materials available at the time. Every expense was spared. It's not a road bike and it's not a dirt bike. It won't stay tuned for longer than an hour. It handles about as well as your truck without power steering. Even on a smooth stretch of road the ride is so rough you might shake loose a filling or two. But," he added, "if you're going off road, the only other choice is that little 200cc Tiger Cub over there." He pointed to a small dirt bike. "But that is the bike Lee raced for a while. He gave it to me the year before he died."

The message was clear. Walt would rather send me out into the desert on a perfect piece of shit than risk lending me a reliable dirt bike that had sentimental value because of his lifelong friendship with Lee Marvin. If accused of sentimentality, Walt would have certainly denied it, though his motorcycles and the diner, especially the way he kept them up, were a shrine to a life and lives that no longer existed. Not only was the message clear, but I appreciated it. Given the same set of circumstances, I might have done the same.

He filled the tank of the BSA and gave me a few quick instructions. He kicked it over. The engine crackled to life. "Don't," he said, "expect it to start like that when you need it to. The Victors were cruel and capricious British bastards."

The two of us rolled it into the back of my trailer, which was almost full of cargo. We secured it with bungee cords to keep it upright, and then covered it with a thick blanket.

Walt wished me luck. "You are going to need every bit of it," he added grimly. "And if that old rattler quits on you out there, and it probably will, you drag, push, or pull the son of a bitch back to me. You understand?"

I told him I understood.

"If that bike makes it back without you," he said, "then I'll be sorry. You come back without that bike, you'll be sorry."

There wasn't much I could say. I gave him my best solemn

nod. Just as I was putting my truck into gear, Walt jumped up on my running board. He flat-handed the roof of the cab hard enough to startle me, again.

"Be at the diner tonight at seven," he shouted over the engine. "I'll feed you. If the Victor doesn't strand or kill you."

He didn't wait for an answer. He jumped down with the nimble light-footedness of a man one third his age and disappeared behind my trailer.

22

I went about my deliveries knowing Josh was nearby, if not close enough to see. He did a respectably good job staying out of sight. The motorcycle was always in my way. Walt was right. Even in silence it was a heavy, cumbersome pain in the ass. Over the course of the morning I lost track of how often I had to unfasten it and move it out of the way and then tie it down and cover it again. I wasn't ready to fire up the Victor yet, assuming it would start. Josh's extreme desert adventure wouldn't begin until I was ready, which wasn't until late afternoon.

Oddly, I was looking forward to dinner with Walt. I needed to, though I didn't particularly want to, tell him about my impending retirement from suckling the losers on 117. He'd predicted as much for years. That he didn't consider himself a loser wasn't surprising.

For one thing, Walt owned a business, even though it was closed most of the time. For another, his place was the closest to Price—to his way of thinking, closest to civilization, though every few months he went into Rockmuse to pick up his mail. He even shopped there once in a while. Walt also seemed to have a pretty good income. The diner had done well for a long time. The company that handled Lee Marvin's investments had managed Walt's movie dollars. The number one reason, though, was raw-assed pride.

Walt Butterfield was *the* Walt Butterfield the same way his café was *the* Well-Known Desert Diner. To hear him tell it, he had never failed, though from time to time, he'd had to wait longer or work harder before he succeeded. The single biggest burden everyone else suffered from was that none of them was Walt Butterfield. Sometimes I had to agree, though only to myself. It also crossed my mind that Walt Butterfield's single greatest failing was that he was *the* Walt Butterfield. He was vital and strong, and when he got ready to die, he would tell God when, not the other way around.

Once in a while I even wondered, especially after Bernice died, why he hadn't put God on notice. Beyond his motorcycle collection, I couldn't guess what kept him going, except for a determination not to fail in, at, or because of life, even if most of that life was gone.

I made my deliveries. It was a fine morning and a fine afternoon. A peacefulness came over me once I accepted that a part of my life was about to end. From that peace came strength to finally just stare down the tracks as the train approached. Everywhere I made a delivery I gave out a free half gallon of butter brickle. I got a few thank-yous. Usually I got a nod, and the icy container went immediately against a sunburned cheek or to the back of a neck.

My fit of ice cream charity hardly put a dent in my supply. I couldn't bring myself to tell any of the folks that I wouldn't be seeing them much longer. Not to give them notice wasn't fair, but given who they were, and the lives they had chosen to lead, *fair* wasn't a word in the vocabulary of 117.

Josh and his red Jeep were on my mind as I headed west on 117. My trailer, thanks to several bags of feed, a brace of Schedule 40 galvanized pipe, and other odds and ends—including a portable cement mixer—was still a third full. Maybe I'd deliver on Sunday, or just hold off until Monday, when I could make it another full load.

At three o'clock sharp I pulled off on the shoulder and took a nap. Josh had to be parked somewhere behind me. I knew he was baking in his red metal Jeep with the high sun beating down on him and no air-conditioning. I thought of it as a kind of aging process, like what was done to gourmet steaks in fancy restaurants.

While he aged he'd drink the little water he had brought with him, if he'd thought to bring any at all. He'd sweat, and wait, and pray, and finally curse me to start moving again. His mouth would be so dry he couldn't produce a thimble full of spit. Maybe he would run his engine just to feel the fan stir up the hot, stagnant air in his face. Maybe he would use more gas than he should. Sometime after that, I would get on the move.

I checked my mirrors for any sign of the red Jeep. About four thirty I released the brake and crept along the shoulder for a mile. As I crested a small rise, I was pretty sure I saw the Jeep behind me, keeping a steady distance between us.

I remembered a side road. It was deceptive. It began like a smooth macadam and gradually changed and worsened as it wound its way north toward an abandoned ranch. By the time the rotting timbers over the ranch entrance appeared, the road had become deeply rutted with nasty horizontal slashes up to a foot or more deep caused by years of erosion from spring washouts. In five or six places the road forked into different directions. Two of them dead-ended in arroyos. At least one piddled out into the sands. Where and how the others ended was a mystery to me. From the entrance onward to the burned-out ranch house, the road was a wide trail.

Early on, when I was working for Utah Express Provisioners, I had made deliveries there. One day I showed up and the place had burned to the ground, its charred rock chimney leaning like a drunk against a lone cottonwood tree. Belongings lay scattered everywhere—a broken table, miscellaneous clothing. No sign of the old couple who had lived there.

I parked in the ranch turnaround and stood on the running board scanning the horizon back the way I had come. I didn't see the Jeep, but I saw a wisp of dust. When and if Josh got back onto the road it would be a dark and treacherous drive. My guess was that he would run out of gas long before that, even if he used the five-gallon emergency can all the rental Jeeps sported on their rear bumpers. Taking my time, I unloaded the Victor and buttoned up the truck in case some drunken coyotes decided to take it for a joy ride.

The Victor started right up. I idled it around the debris in the ranch yard and in and out of surviving outbuildings to get the feel of it, and it me. About the time I estimated Josh was no more than a half mile away, I gunned the Victor to announce my departure and headed cross-country to the northeast, where there was even less hospitable ground. Bless his lying little bull-dog Hollywood ass, Josh followed, probably watching the dust I was none too careful about keeping down. And I watched his.

My plan was to take him out about ten miles from 117 as the crow flies, and then double back to my truck just before dark. He'd make it back to 117 eventually, even on foot, but it would take at least that night and part of the next day. If worse came to worst, maybe the Jeep's GPS homing beacon might work and the rental company would send someone out to find him. For all I knew, he might even get cell service, but only if he climbed to the top of one of the piles of rocks that sprouted up here and there like twenty-foot warts.

Dead reckoning was all I had to go on. Walt had put some

fear into me about the Victor's reliability. My heart rate jacked up a few times when the engine sputtered. Its 441cc power plant and road gears took a lot of patience—sluggish on inclines, but a rocket on the flat stretches. It was easy for me to keep the sun to my back and always the red mesa far to my right.

To be certain, Josh stayed on his toes. I stopped a couple of times and took a few cuts north, once almost crossing his path as he wound his way up an arroyo full of granite boulders. For a moment or two I almost felt guilty. The mesa was beginning to catch the full rays of the setting sun. Too often I took the spectacle for granted. I lifted my eyes skyward. The layers of blue upon bluer faded into darkness. The blue reminded me of the photograph of Josh's wife in her blue sweater and the blue of their son's eyes. They probably weren't even his wife and kid.

That was the end of it for me. I made a long lazy turn south and eventually west into a fast-setting and blinding sun, in a hurry to get back to the burned-out ranch and my truck, and on to Walt's for dinner. Maybe I was struggling with an unexpected change of heart about what I was doing and wanted to put as many miles as I could between me and Josh. A couple of times I thought I was about to pull into the ranch, only to discover more dirt and rocks. It occurred to me that I might have overshot it, gone too far south, then maybe too far west. Without so much as a fart or a giggle of warning, the Victor lurched forward, stalled, caught again, and died. After five minutes of fooling with the prehistoric Amal carburetor and giving the fuel line the blow job of a lifetime, I knew it was no use and gave up. Pushing the Victor uphill for a hundred feet stole my breath and left me drenched in sweat. The shame of waiting for Josh to show up to give me a ride in the Jeep settled over me.

I leaned against the Victor at the crest of the hill and looked back over the terrain I'd covered. Dusk was settling between the low hills. The first shadows wound themselves through and around each other. In the far distance Josh's headlights came on. Up and down, the beams bumped the darkness and then disappeared as he zigzagged in my general direction. All I could do was wait. I turned west to glimpse the last long streaks of the sunset and saw the cottonwood tree and chimney of the ranch, perhaps no more than a hundred yards away. It was a piece of good luck that I had started back when I did.

I loaded and tied down the Victor and decided to climb on top of the trailer to get a final fix on Josh's progress. I saw no headlights. Either he had stopped for the night, or he was in a gulley, or he had run out of gas. It didn't matter. A forlorn wind was beginning to wail through the charred slats of the ranch house walls. There wouldn't be much of a moon. Josh Arrons, or whoever he was, could count on a long damn night. Claire would get her head start. That was all I had signed up for and all I cared about. What I'd done was nothing more than perform a mean duty on a young man who, if pressed, I might have to admit I liked.

It was closer to eight than seven when I parked my truck at the diner. Walt was probably pissed off at me and, for no particular reason, I was pissed off at him, which I knew was just a way of avoiding the truth that I was pissed off at myself for leaving Josh stranded in the desert.

The blinds were drawn on the diner's windows. A soft yellow glow spilled out into the drive. My footsteps were heavy as I made my way toward the diner. The "Closed" sign was hanging in the door as usual. I didn't feel hungry. If Walt was in a mood,

I figured I'd skip dinner and backtrack to Desert Home to warn Claire. With my hand on the doorknob, I paused. Walt had the Wurlitzer jukebox cranked up playing some old tune from the 1940s or 1950s. He'd played it before. I was smiling as I opened the door. Walt was wearing a much bigger smile. He was dancing with Claire.

23

Claire had her back to the door. Her long black hair was tied in a ponytail with a red ribbon. A frown crossed Walt's face. He shook his head slightly from side to side to tell me not even to think of cutting in, or interrupting in any fashion.

I wasn't thinking of cutting in. For one thing, I'm not much of a dancer. For another, I was using all my energy trying to remember how to breathe. I just stood there watching them dance.

Claire was short, perhaps just over five feet, even in what looked like new turquoise cowboy boots. Walt was as graceful and light on his feet as a feather on a wire. I found my breath and lost it just as quickly. They were beautiful together, like they'd been dancing together their entire lives. Not quite intending to, I began to back up through the open door. If I could have, I might have run out into the desert night filled with envy.

The ending of the song was slow, its final notes drawn out into the loud rhythmic scratches of the phonograph needle. I was almost through the door when Claire noticed me. She lowered her hands from Walt's shoulders and rested her head against his chest for a moment without ever taking her dark eyes from mine. There was a tenderness in her gesture that any man would have given his life to feel, if only once, for a few precious seconds.

Claire saw the shocked expression on my face. She put her hands on her hips and began to laugh. I just stood where I was.

Walt turned to face me and joined her. "Look, honey," he said, "our dinner guest has finally arrived."

Claire rushed to me as if we were old friends, or perhaps more. She hugged me briefly, wrapped her right arm under my left, and led me toward Walt. One of the booths had been set up for dinner, three place settings, one across from two. There was a small flower in a vase. I remembered the name of the song: "Blue Moon." The flower was a nice touch, fragile and exotic, though that wasn't what caught my attention.

The flower took the place of something else. I was thinking of what that something might be when Walt, in an odd act of formality, took my right hand and shook it as if we were old friends who hadn't seen each other in years, or as if he were meeting me for the first time. Maybe both were true. It was Bernice's table. The red "Reserved" placard was gone.

Walt clapped his hands, and I supposed that meant it was time to get dinner going. Claire kept her arm folded in mine. We watched him go into the kitchen and listened to the clatter of pans. She sat in the booth and asked me to sit across from her.

"It won't take him long. We've been waiting for a while. Everything is ready. He thought you might be late for some reason."

"Did he tell you why I might be late?"

"No," she said, "just that you might be."

"Nice boots," I said. The bright turquoise blue boots were obviously hand tooled and made for impossibly small feet. Expensive. "They look new."

"They were a gift from Walt. But they're not new. They're old. Just not worn much."

My guess was that they had belonged to Bernice. It wasn't like Walt to keep something like that. It was even more unlike him to give them away as a present to someone he hardly knew.

I didn't feel like sitting. I didn't feel like standing either. I hesitated next to the booth. "I guess everything is ready," I said, "except me." I looked past her at the flower, which was as good a way as any to avoid meeting her eyes.

"Please, Ben," she whispered, "sit down."

"I think I should go."

"I think you should stay." It was her turn to look at the flower. "It's an orchid," she said. "My mother used to raise them. Isn't it lovely?" When I didn't say anything, she said, "Walt knew my mother. I'm half Korean."

"It's beautiful," I said, thinking of my own mother, who didn't raise me, even as a hobby. "I have something in my truck I need to return to Walt. It'll only take a few minutes."

She guessed I was considering not returning for dinner. "You can go, if that's what you want." She took my hand in hers. "I wish you would stay. If you don't, you might regret it. It's up to you."

I excused myself and went outside to unload the motorcycle. After I leaned the Victor against the side of the Quonset hut, I looked up at the stars and remembered Josh. He was in for a cold night. As for regrets, I couldn't make up my mind what I would regret more, leaving or staying. I still had to tell her about Josh and his employer, the husband I assumed, though a husband seemed like the farthest thing from her mind, and Walt's.

Still undecided, I walked along the back of the diner and past a small, high kitchen window. Inside, Walt was performing like a short-order cook—no wasted movement, everything in its place, or on its way to being in its place. He was totally involved in what had once been his life's work. He was whistling.

Skillfully, he took a large knife from a rack and sliced three pieces of meat, wiped the blade against his white apron in one swift motion, and tossed the knife end over end, where it caught on a magnet mounted on the wall. The knife, the kitchen, and Walt brought to mind Bernice, and that tragic evening forty years ago.

I went back into the diner and told Claire I needed to clean up—an understatement. It would take more than a few minutes in the men's room to get off the caked dirt and sweat. Arranging Josh's adventure had been dirty work. I did the best I could, then returned to Claire and took my seat at the single place setting. Walt was still busy in the kitchen.

"You're Walt's daughter," I said, as casually as I could manage. I didn't know how or why, but I knew it was true as deeply as I had ever known anything. I was kind of proud of myself. It didn't last.

She grimaced, more with her eyes than her mouth. Unlike her smile, the grimace didn't travel; it was simply there. "Not exactly."

Walt arrived with the plates positioned expertly down his left arm. One by one he set them down, first Claire, then himself, and then me. While he did this she slipped farther along the bench seat to make room for Walt. She shook her head a little to let me know the discussion we had just been having was, at least for the time being, over.

Walt stood back and admired the food. "A feast for my two favorite people. Enjoy."

He might have meant Claire and me, but I think he meant himself and Claire. He was smiling at her when he said it. If I had been him, looking at her, I might have meant the same thing. In this set of three, I was the crowd. True, I had been invited. I just wasn't sure why. I didn't have much to say or do during dinner. I moved the food around on my plate instead of eating it.

What Walt had prepared for us didn't matter. It wasn't the usual roadside diner fare. There was soup, red meat with a sauce, a vegetable, and a few other dishes I didn't touch. The main course was watching and listening to the two of them consume each other. Claire spoke of her mother with a strange reverence. Walt told one story after another about Bernice as if she were still alive and might soon be the fourth to my third. A few times he paused in midsentence as if he had forgotten what he was saying.

Claire waited patiently for him to continue. She rested her head on his shoulder. I realized it wasn't a struggle for him to remember some small incident or habit of Bernice's; it was a struggle for him to forget. Eventually the food became cold. The pauses in the conversation grew longer.

Walt looked directly at me for the first time since the meal had begun. I was the leftover. I didn't mind. Being the witness was easy work. It gave me a chance to see someone I cared for happy, and someone I was trying hard not to care for just as happy.

Walt reached down with his big right hand and gripped the edge of the table. "Bernice was Claire's mother." He was talking to me, though he seemed to be talking to himself, saying something important that he needed to say out loud. It certainly wasn't news to me.

She spoke quickly to fill the silence. "What's for dessert?"

Walt gave her a disheartened shrug. "I'm sorry." His shoulders fell. Anyone might have thought he had been found guilty of a terrible crime. "I'm not much of a dessert man. I should have been thinking about you."

It was my cue. "It just so happens I brought dessert."

Claire smacked her lips and leaned across the table. "Whatever can it be?"

Walt didn't care what it was, as long as it didn't come from me. "Venison jerky is not a dessert." To Claire, he said, "You don't want anything that's been rolling around in the back of that pigsty."

Claire ignored him with a small laugh. I just plain ignored him and politely excused myself. A couple of minutes later I returned with a half gallon of butter brickle ice cream. Walt examined it briefly. "Is Maureen McCauley pregnant again?"

"Nope," I answered. "You interested?"

Walt definitely was not interested. Claire definitely was, and announced her interest with zest. Walt sulked on his way to the kitchen to get bowls and spoons.

He came back carrying one bowl and one spoon and set it in front of Claire. "I have to clean up. You two will have to find something to talk about."

That something had become clear midway through dinner. Claire's "not exactly" in answer to my guess that she was Walt's daughter meant she had to be Bernice's daughter, but not Walt's. All the possible explanations had gone through my head while they talked. Most were quickly dismissed. Claire was Bernice's daughter from before she met Walt? Wrong age. Bernice and Walt had a daughter they had given up for some reason? Not possible. Bernice had had an affair while married to Walt and Claire was the result? Absolutely possible, but knowing Walt Butterfield, if that were the case, we wouldn't be sitting around having dinner together. Walt wasn't the forgiving type, even if Claire had no choice in the matter.

Only one explanation remained and it was an ugly reach, though on some level it meant maybe Walt was the forgiving type after all, but only after a few years had passed—almost forty of them. It certainly wasn't the kind of thing I was about to bring up during dessert. If ever there was a mystery I was prepared to leave alone, this was it. Claire and I sat in silence.

Claire shouted for Walt to bring another bowl and spoon for me. Walt shouted back, "Ben knows where the crockery is kept."

True, I did know where the dishes and silverware were kept. I told Claire I didn't want any.

She made a big deal of rolling her eyes. "What was the quaint word you used to describe him?"

"Cranky," I volunteered.

"No," she said, watching him make more noise than necessary in the kitchen. "I believe the word was 'asshole.'" She smiled at me as if my description of Walt was a secret we shared. She took a few bites of ice cream and pushed the bowl away. "We thought you should know we're acquainted."

"Acquainted?" I repeated.

"He likes you, Ben. You know he does. And you like him. You told me so. You might be his only friend."

I admitted I could nearly guarantee that. "Though accidentally running across you in the desert seems to be putting a strain on my—what did you call him—friend? I don't know why he bothered to invite me for dinner."

"My idea," she said. "A few days ago after our walk around Desert Home."

"Okay," I said. "Makes sense, sort of." I paused while I figured out how to word what I wanted to say without actually saying it. "You could have just told me who Walt is to you and left it at that. I know how to keep my mouth shut."

She thought about what I had said. "That's what I was going to do. Except . . ."

"Except what?"

"I don't know how to explain it. I guess I just thought someone needed to see us together. Someone else needed to know. Maybe having someone see us and listen to us made it more real. Make any sense?"

"Yes," I said, "it does. I figured I was a witness. Glad to oblige."

"You're angry."

"No, I'm not," I said, honestly, I hoped. "Is there really a husband out looking for you?"

"Sort of."

"Sort of? Either there is or there isn't. And don't worry, whether there is or isn't doesn't change anything."

Now it was her turn. With a sly smile she repeated, "Change anything?"

Walt had finished cleaning up. He returned for Claire's bowl and spoon. "Change what?"

Neither of us acted as if we had heard him.

"You can take the rest of that ice cream with you," Walt said. He hadn't meant it exactly as a suggestion. It was an offer more in the vein of *Don't let the door hit you in the ass on your way out with your damn ice cream.*

I suggested he keep it, though the word I was thinking of involved shoving rather than keeping. "If Claire wants more, she can come back to the diner. Your freezer works, doesn't it?"

Even the vaguest of hints that anything to do with the diner or Walt Butterfield might not be in perfect twenty-four-hour working order would never be taken kindly.

Walt bent down. He was so close to me I could smell his breath. "What do you mean by that?"

He was determined to use up my meager store of self-control. Claire's head swiveled between us.

"Nothing," I said. "Nothing at all. If Claire wants ice cream, she can come over and visit. That's all."

That wasn't all for Walt. Fortunately he decided to let it end there. I thanked him for dinner and nodded at Claire. He made me wait until he was ready to move out of my way so I could scoot out of the booth.

Walt grumbled a thank-you. He left with the bowl and spoon, and the carton of ice cream.

Claire whispered, "Walk me home?"

The invitation struck me funny. I stifled a laugh at the idea of telling or even suggesting to Walt that I might walk Claire home. "Are you crazy?"

"I need to talk to you." She glanced at the kitchen. "But I know what you mean."

"I'd like to have a brief talk with you," I said. "The sooner the better."

"I know you have a lot of questions."

"No, Claire," I said, "I don't. I have a few options for you."

"I'll wait for you at the house." She looked sideways toward the kitchen again and lowered her voice. "If you'll let me, I can tell you the answers to the questions you don't want to ask."

"It's six miles," I said. "That's a hell of a walk."

"It's six miles to you," she said. "For me it's less than a mile. There's another entrance to Desert Home just across the highway. To keep things civil, maybe you'd better drive the usual way. It's up to you."

I hadn't seen another entrance to anywhere across from the diner. Maybe it had been obscured by time like the other entrance. More likely, I just hadn't noticed. Like everyone else, I never looked anywhere but at the diner.

Claire called out to Walt. "See you tomorrow."

He walked quickly from the kitchen, wiping his hands on a towel, and brushed by me like I was stale air. "Let me walk you home."

I wasn't a man for praying. I prayed Walt didn't see the little smile in Claire's eyes. "I'll be fine," she assured him. "I need a walk alone in the desert. Okay?"

Walt agreed, though his heart wasn't in it. "Maybe Ben and I will have a quick cup of coffee."

"You do that," she said. She gave Walt a hug and stood on her toes to kiss his cheek.

Walt and I stood in the open doorway of the diner and watched her cross the dark highway into the desert. I stood behind him thinking the last thing I wanted was a cup of coffee. When she was safely out of sight and earshot, I said, "I think I'll pass on the coffee, Walt. It's late and I'm tired."

He closed the door. He was polite enough to let me finish talking.

24

If Walt had wanted to be especially polite, he might have softened me up with a little left jab or a rabbit punch to the gut. Walt Butterfield wasn't much for pleasantries. He led with all of his best, a right fist launched as if it had come out of a missile silo. He intended every knuckle to connect with every part of my face from my chin to my forehead. The pain radiated from my nose through my jaw. The damage might have been worse if some instinct in me hadn't half expected it. My head was turned to the side an inch before the punch landed, or my nose would have been as flat as last week's roadkill.

He was ready with another swing. He glanced down at the floor. That was where he expected me to be. He was momentarily annoyed to see me in front of him, wobbling but still upright. He bounced a left off my shoulder. This bought him the time he needed to bring his right elbow up under my jaw. A left reappeared out of nowhere and tagged me on my right ear. The earlobe popped like a water balloon full of blood. I went down so fast I didn't even stagger.

Walt stood over me. His fists quivered at his sides. He kicked me three times with the steel-toed tip of a motorcycle boot. A little too hard for my taste.

"She's not for you," he said, before placing a fourth and even harder kick, this one aimed for my left kidney.

The ear I could hear out of was ringing. I heard him loud and clear. He almost had a grin on his face. The exertion released beads of sweat that plastered some strands of white hair to his forehead. "Did you hear me?"

I mumbled incoherently and tried gamely to raise myself up on my elbows, failed, and fell back down. Walt hunched over me with his face just inches from mine, or what was left of it. He began to ask me again if I understood. I snapped my head up into his mouth. The impact loosened his teeth and tore part of his upper lip into a jagged flap. It was his turn to land on his ass.

I stood up and spit blood on his perfect floor. I liked to think I jumped to my feet. The truth is, I rolled like an amputee turtle.

"I didn't quite get that, Walt," I said. "Tell me again."

Walt almost did jump to his feet. It was demoralizing. He began to throw wild punches one after another. They were easy to deflect, though at great expense to the bones in my arms. I calmly and charitably asked him if he'd like to take a little rest. It had the effect I wanted. The next flurry of punches sapped his strength. He had trouble holding his fists up. The motorcycle boots he wore were spit-shined. I had a good look at the right one when he surprised me with a kick at my groin. It was only a surprise because I thought he'd have tried it sooner. I pivoted. All he got was leg.

At that point I could have just pushed him over like a cheap toy. I didn't want to do that to him. I made a big mistake. I did nothing. With his last ounce of strength he brought the heel of his right boot down on my left foot. I saw it coming out of my one good eye. I was too late. I thought I could hear my toes breaking like dry chicken bones. I returned the favor by driving my heel onto Walt's right instep, where his boots provided the least protection. The reflex bent him forward, head down, just as my aching right fist came up to meet his chin. His dentures flew out of his mouth and skittered across the floor. I thought he was tracking them as they went. It turned out to be his eyes rolling back in his head. Walt was down. I hoped out.

I wasn't going to make the same mistake he'd made with me. I kept my distance. Walt was out for less than a minute. The dirt he had knocked off and out of me combined with our blood to make a dark, slippery mud on the linoleum floor. I waited and listened. His breathing was steady and not labored. I resisted the urge to go check on him.

His face looked shrunken without his teeth. Somehow, though, even without Claire in the room, he looked younger and almost happy with his gray tongue lolling out the side of his mouth. I would have bet Walt looked better on his back than I did standing.

His eyes snapped open. He got himself upright. For a long minute he stared at me as if he couldn't quite believe what had just happened. Truth be told, it could have gone either way. I sat down on one of the stools and propped an elbow on the counter to keep from falling off. One of us needed to say something. I knew it wouldn't be Walt.

"She's not your daughter," I said.

Walt took a slow inventory and made sure he was still in working order. He felt his face and stretched his neck as if the previous few minutes had involved nothing more strenuous than a morning shave. When he bent over to retrieve his dentures, he turned his head away before slipping them inside his mouth. It was an odd bit of vanity. He was a vain man. Over the years I'd known him he seemed to grow more vain. It wasn't a garden-variety vanity. Walt's vanity was constant and intense as a coal-fired furnace, fueled by sheer willpower to vanquish change. He was determined to keep not only himself but the diner as it always had been—as it was when Bernice was alive.

"No," he answered. "She's not my daughter. But she's as much of her mother as I will ever have again. Good night."

Walt flipped the switches for the overheads and walked into the kitchen without the smallest hitch in his giddyap. The kitchen lights went out. The door of his apartment shut. I sat in the dark diner. At the far end of the room the neon of the jukebox still buzzed, spelling out the words *Today's Hit Parade* in pink and purple.

The longer I sat on the stool the more I began to hurt and the less I felt like moving. The headlights of a single car swept over the drawn blinds. Claire had said it was less than a mile from the diner to her house. There didn't seem to be much purpose in the ruse of driving my truck. The kicks and punches I had taken were working their magic. I had some doubt that I would be able to get up into the cab and still more doubt that I could move my arms and legs well enough to drive.

It didn't seem urgent to tell Claire about Josh, though it did seem important. There was a clock running on his adventure. I was also morbidly curious to see if I could walk that far. Maybe Josh and I would both end up sleeping in the desert. The way things had turned out, I was certain his night would be the more comfortable.

≡

25

Directly across 117 were two dirt mounds. Between them was an opening that appeared as if it had once been a road, though time and wind had reduced it to a wide trail. Given the size of Desert Home, it made sense that there would be more than one entrance. A long time ago it might have been more than a trail, and it might have accommodated a large vehicle. Now it only allowed for a small car.

The other side of the mounds opened onto a trail that eventually became a winding lane that descended onto the desert floor. Ahead I could see the lights of Claire's house blinking yellow in the distance. In a desert night a light always seemed closer than it actually was. Sad experience had taught me a light in the desert was like a mirage, impossible to judge and dangerous to rely upon, often withering into nothing as you approached, desperate for warmth and protection.

I dragged myself along. Claire's light stayed constant. I attempted to be honest with myself about why it was so important to see her so late at night. Walt had seen to it that I felt every one of his objections on my body. Not far from the house I tripped and fell. A short side path led off into a hillside. At the top I could see the silhouette of a low cyclone fence surrounding a rough cactus garden. I lay on the ground willing myself to get up.

"I see you've found it." Claire was standing above me, her round face hidden in shadow.

"Found what?"

"My mother's grave. Walt tends to it almost every day. Seems like a strange place to take a nap. Are you that tired?"

"Yes," I answered, still on my back, "I am. There's something so restful about a cemetery, don't you think?"

Claire extended her hand. She helped me to my feet. "I saw you fall. I've done it a couple times myself. Walt put in some stone steps here that lead up to her grave. They're hard to see at night, even if there's a moon."

Claire didn't let go of my arm. I was happy to leave it right where it was. "Walt owns all this, doesn't he?"

"He does," she answered. "They planned it together. My mom took night classes when she wasn't working in the diner. She designed everything you see. She even built some of it with her own hands." Claire turned and looked out over the Desert Home I could only imagine. "The watershed reservoir, the streets, all the solar power. Even how the streets were laid out. A few things didn't even exist. She invented them way ahead of their time. She designed the model house I'm living in. It's where they were going to retire. She was an amazing woman. Walt was so proud of her."

Though Desert Home had come to nothing, Walt wasn't the only person who was proud of Bernice and what she had accomplished in her all-too-brief life. Claire's pride in her mother was contagious. That pride was all the more heartbreaking as we stood surrounded by what was left of Bernice's plans and the long-ago events that ended those plans.

Claire started us toward the house. There wasn't a muscle or bone in my body that didn't ache. My back and legs moved with all the freedom of Dorothy's Tin Man after the rain shower. Claire noticed and wrapped her arm in mine for more support. Like any other red-blooded American male leaning on a small, beautiful woman, I gladly let her.

"You must have really taken a tumble," she said. "Do you think you broke anything?"

"Everything," I said, and placed my arm around her waist.

It wasn't until we got inside the house that she got a good look at me. From her expression she might have been considering burying me next to her mother. "That must have been a terrible fall!"

"It was," I assured her. "I must have hit my head on a rock."

Claire gently caressed the side of my face with the back of her hand. I winced.

"Just out of curiosity," she said, "was it a seventy-nine-year-old rock?"

It hurt to smile. "As a matter of fact," I said, "it was. Some rocks only get harder with age."

Claire sat me down in the metal chair, the only chair, and went about expertly cleaning my wounds with water and antiseptic. "I was afraid of this," she said. "Walt is not so different in person than in his letters. Just two letters. One word each."

She had first contacted Walt when she was eighteen. That was the earliest she was legally allowed to examine her adoption records. Her mother's name was there. No father. Walter Butterfield was listed as her mother's next of kin. There were two Walter Butterfields in Utah at the time. She had written to both asking if they were related to Bernice Butterfield. She received two answers. One was an attempt to sell her some Amway products. The second letter simply said, *Yes*. She wrote back and asked if he knew her father. Two years later she got an answer. *No*.

Claire suggested we move outside to the porch. "It's such a beautiful night. I'll bring a blanket."

I hesitated in the chair. "I might need your assistance, ma'am," I said in my most injured but brave voice.

"I bet Walt wouldn't need any assistance."

"Yes," I answered, "he would." It occurred to me that at that moment Walt was sleeping like a healthy toddler who had been allowed to play past his bedtime. "He just wouldn't ask for it. I'm not proud, just needy. How about some understanding?" I joked. "You do realize a seventy-nine-year-old man just kicked the shit out of me?"

Claire sighed. "You're right. The best way to deal with that humiliation is to whine to a woman."

"I'm glad you understand," I said.

We sat on the front porch. She covered us with an old quilt. I wondered if maybe her mother had made it. I recalled the old red blanket that my own mother had wrapped around me when she abandoned me on the reservation. It seemed as good a time as any to tell her about Josh. She listened the same way Walt did. When I'd finished she asked, "You lost him in the desert?"

I nodded.

"I'm surprised it took them as long as it has."

"Them?" I said. "You mean your husband, don't you? Or you mean the people he hired to find you?"

She didn't answer. In the long silence I dozed off.

My head was in Claire's lap when I woke. The quilt was damp with dew. She had draped it over her shoulder and my chest. She was asleep with her back against the door, her head tilted uncomfortably to one side. It was cold. I would have been happy to spend the rest of my life exactly where I was and then spend eternity boring every soul I met about how good it felt.

I willed myself to move and bundled Claire up as best I could in the quilt without waking her. I'd done what I'd come to do. I had been rewarded beyond my dreams—small, common dreams that they were. Judging from the sky, I guessed the time to be around five, give or take. What Claire did now and when she did it was up to her.

I knelt near her and watched her sleep for longer than I should have but not as long as I wanted. This was good-bye. Walt would, if I was lucky, give me updates every few years. They seemed so close now it was unimaginable that they wouldn't stay in touch. Walt, of course, was right. Claire wasn't really for me. I didn't know about Dennis, the musician husband. Maybe she wasn't for him either. She was, for however long in whatever way possible, for Walt, and in some minor way I couldn't think about, for me, too. Knowing better and not caring, I kissed Claire on her forehead. I began the long walk up the slope to the entrance arch of Desert Home.

Halfway to the top I heard Claire call out, "Ben!" Her voice was strong and carried in the crisp early-morning air.

I kept going, not looking back.

She shouted my name again, and again. Under the arch I turned. She was running up the slope through the half darkness, unsteady in her new cowboy boots, her black hair loose and wild, catching the first rays of the desert sunrise. She stumbled the last few steps. I caught her just as she began to fall. Breathlessly, she said, "You're going the wrong way. You left your truck at Walt's."

I kissed her. I went on kissing her as the sun began to rise in earnest over the mesa. My hands reached beneath Claire's skirt and I raised her to my hips and buried my sore face in the dense hair around her neck. She wrapped her bare legs around me and tore open my denim work shirt. She kissed my chest. I carried her that way, kissing my lips and my chest, down the slope to the house, my hands cupped beneath her skirt, pressing against her warm skin. The heels of her new cowboy boots dug into the small of my back. She removed her blouse as we approached the house and let it drop in the sandy street. A moment later her bra dangled from one finger before it, too, fell to the ground.

I eased her down on the quilt as my mouth found her breasts. She put both hands against my bare chest and lightly pushed me away. "Wait a minute, Ben. What about your rule? This isn't ice cream."

She was right. I groaned and tried to roll away from her. She held me fast around the neck. My rule had gotten lost, as a man's rules sometimes do, on their journey between his brain and his pants. I hadn't broken the rule yet.

I said, "Right now all I can think about is the exception."

She kissed me. "I'm the exception?"

I returned her kiss. "You're both," I said.

At first my answer seemed to confuse her. She laughed. She touched my lips with her fingers and searched my face. "Ben Jones, who *are* you?"

It wasn't a question I could answer.

Claire threw her head back and shouted, "Damn! Damn! Damn!" Her words echoed across the empty streets of Desert Home.

We made love on the porch in the cold. Afterward we lay naked and sweating, tangled together beneath the dawn.

26

I felt like a man who hadn't noticed his heart had stopped beating until it had begun again. The thought sounded foolish. My heart had started beating again, and the feeling was something brand-new and frightening.

Claire kissed me. "Ben," she said, keeping her lips close to mine, "I have something I need to say to you."

"Okay."

"I don't think I believe in happy endings anymore."

"I'm not sure I ever did," I answered. "But I always wanted to."

"You think it's okay if maybe, just for now, I believe in happy presents?"

"I think it's fine," I said, "as long as you're always in the present."

For the next hour we were in every moment of the present, making love again, slowly, until the sun was full and hot and we lay completely spent and sweating again. We sat naked together on the steps holding hands and did our best to stare down the morning sun until we were almost blind.

I saw him then, up high and far to the north, not hiding, just standing between some dwarf juniper and sagebrush. I didn't say anything to Claire, or allow myself to be angry or even embarrassed. I truly didn't care if Walt was watching us or for how long or what he thought about us, or me. Claire kissed my shoulder.

I kept an eye on Walt. He disappeared. I wondered if once, maybe a long time ago, he and Bernice had made love on this same porch. When he looked down on us, did he see himself and Bernice? Was the dream of Desert Home alive again? Was he alive again? It was the best I could hope for him. Maybe it was the best I could hope for Claire and myself.

Claire asked me what I was thinking. I didn't want to tell her. "I would tell you," I said, "except it's too embarrassing."

"How embarrassing can it be?" She pointed to the trail of her clothing leading from the walkway out into the street. She pointed to her feet and the only article of clothing between us, one white sock that had slipped below her left heel.

I hesitated. I started again. Finally, I succeeded in telling her about being a man who didn't realize his heart had stopped until it had started beating again. It sounded even worse with my voice behind it, but no less true. I didn't say anything about imagining Walt and Bernice on the porch.

Claire was silent. She raised my hand to her lips and kept her eyes on the empty desert streets in front of us. "Oh God, that *is* embarrassing. Thank you," she whispered.

"For what? Embarrassing myself?"

"Yes," she said, "for embarrassing yourself. You did it for both of us. Now I don't have to. I don't think I could have embarrassed myself as well. You're actually quite good at it." She flashed me a grin. "You've forever changed the world of kitchen window treatments for me."

"Ma'am," I said, "do you suppose you could find it in yourself to never mention that again?"

"Can't," she answered. "I couldn't even if I wanted to. It's a dear moment. I consider it our first date."

I dropped my head. "Congratulations," I said. "You just made it worse."

"You're a brave man, Ben Jones. There aren't many men who would take the risk you did in telling me how you felt. I'm not talking about being embarrassed. There's rejection. And losing your . . ."

"Self-respect?"

"Yes. That's as good a word as any."

"Only if it wasn't true."

We were quiet for a while. Then Claire said, "Remember when you told me you considered Walt a friend, but you couldn't speak for him?"

I answered that I remembered.

"That's the moment I started to like you. You accept Walt the way he is. You understand him in ways I'm just beginning to. He does like you."

I pointed to my face.

Claire smiled. "Yes. I know. You said yourself he was an old asshole who was set in his ways. He's old-fashioned."

I caught her glancing over my head up toward the arch.

"Is he still there?" I asked.

"No," she said. "He's gone now. He was up there before dawn."

I hadn't been aware of him as early as Claire had. It was that sixth sense she had. "It didn't bother you?"

"No. He was just checking on me. And you. You know he had to fight you, Ben. I bet he ordered you to stay away from me."

"He did. In fact, for Walt, he was quite vocal about it."

"He was testing you. Seeing how serious you were. If you gave up, he wouldn't have respected you. If you asked him to explain it, he'd probably say something about 'honorable intentions.'"

"You think so? That would mean he's thinking like ..."

Claire finished for me. "A father? That I'm here with him is proof that while his bite is the same as his bark, he's changing, trying to change. His daughter or not, I'm Bernice's daughter. I'm a part of the woman he loved, still loves. What happened to my mother ... losing her, it still causes him pain."

This was territory I knew had to be difficult for her. I'd been hoping it could remain unspoken. Claire's eyes began to fill. I didn't know what to say. There was nothing I could say. I squeezed her hand. She pulled it away with the rest of herself. "Don't. You don't understand."

My instinct told me that she didn't want me to understand. What she felt and lived with couldn't be shared or understood by anyone else. I knew she was right.

Her jaw set. She raised her knees up under her chin and held herself close. She would speak of it or not. The best I could do was shut up.

There had never been a time when she reminded me more of Walt. Perhaps, if I had known Bernice, Claire might have reminded me of her mother. Maybe I understood better than anyone. It was possible that I had also been the child of a rape. Mercifully, that was something I would never know. Claire knew. Walt knew. And now I knew. But only Claire lived with the seed of knowledge that she had been conceived not in love, not even in pleasure, but in violence and inconceivable pain, and she owed her life to that terrible event.

The moment for Claire to speak of it passed. I watched her thoughts move like a spirit through her small body. Her shoulders relaxed. She shivered briefly, though the cold of the morning had lifted long before.

"I told you I met Dennis in high school?"

I couldn't remember if she had or not, but just the mention of her husband almost made me wish for the subject we had just avoided.

I nodded and she continued.

"He was the only person I'd ever met who loved the cello, who loved music, as much as I did. We were constantly battling for first chair in the school orchestra. We made love for the first time in a practice room at our school. I had just turned seventeen. The school was empty and quiet. It was dark outside. The only lights in the room came from the shaded bulbs on our music stands.

"We had been playing our cellos for hours, not talking, just playing and playing, rehearsing for our senior recitals. I honestly don't know how we got from our practice to making love. I've thought a lot about that evening these past few years. For me, at least, it was natural, as if one led seamlessly to the other, like related movements in a symphony." She laughed at herself. "Now it's my turn to be embarrassed. But that's the way it seemed to me then. It wasn't just raging hormones and teenage sex. Not for me anyway. Some girls I knew got drunk or high and had sex with some guy and blamed it on alcohol or drugs. Not me. Sweet little Claire was undone by the cello. After that, Dennis and I started having sex every time we practiced together. It's a miracle I didn't get pregnant. The four got mixed up together somehow—Dennis and me, the cello and sex. Of course, over time, I thought of the four as Dennis and me, the cello and love."

I smiled thinking of sweet little Claire.

"What?"

I apologized. "I was just imagining sweet little Claire."

She dug an elbow into the one rib that might not have been broken or bruised by Walt's boot tip. "I was always small. Not so sweet sometimes. My mother took me into a music store when I was five. She only left me alone for a couple of minutes. The next thing she knew I had a bow in my hands. My parents had me try the violin for a year. I was only interested in the cello. I would throw tantrums like you wouldn't believe. I started taking lessons on the cello—a kid's scaled-down cello. I still had to sit on pillows until they had a special stool made. Did you ever play an instrument?"

I admitted I had. I refused to tell her what it was.

"Come on," she begged. "Percussion? Saxophone? I've got it! Clarinet."

The idea of me playing a saxophone or a clarinet was too much. "Bagpipes," I said.

Claire didn't laugh. "Really?"

"Really."

"I've always rather liked them. They're kind of supernatural. Whenever I've heard one it's made me feel strange. Haunted. Do you still play?"

I told her I didn't. She seemed to know that in some way, if only in my mind and for myself, I still played.

"Yo-Yo Ma did a duet with a bagpipe. Do you know who he is?"

It was not a name that could be easily forgotten. I remembered it from the night in the Walmart parking lot with Ginny. "Yes," I said, "I do. He's a cellist." I was proud of myself. The combination of bagpipes and cello was something hard for me to imagine.

"You're making that up," I said. "Bagpipes and cello?"

Claire shook her head. "No, I'm not. It's wonderful. Sometimes instruments that you'd think shouldn't go together just do." She giggled like a little girl. "My turn," she said. "I just had an image of boy Ben tramping around with these big bagpipes. I'll bet you went out into the desert all alone and played your little heart out."

It took a lot of effort to resist meeting her eyes with mine. Sure, it was a wild guess. Maybe a not-so-wild guess. She barely knew me. Still, we knew things about each other that were more than what could ever be told.

Claire wondered what she had said. I shrugged and began to think about the end of my company. Ben's Desert Moon Delivery Service was now officially one day closer to going the way that so many small companies had gone, especially in the past few years. I needed to say something about it to Claire. In her case, I really couldn't fail to show up one day. Josh came to mind. She didn't seem worried, but I was. I had always been prepared for her to suddenly be gone from Desert Home. Now that possibility had become part of saying good-bye to 117.

"What?" she asked. "Jesus, Ben. The face you've got on under the one Walt gave you is even worse."

"Claire," I began, "I'm just about broke. No," I added, "I *am* broke. Any day might be my last day driving 117. Between the economy and the fact that I mostly deliver to people who don't have much money to begin with. I'm sorry to have to tell you— you should know, that's all. It means no more fancy restaurants. For a while at least."

She folded her hands in her lap and made a show of pursing her lips. "Okay," she said. "It's tough news. It changes everything, Ben. When I first saw you flopping on the ground under my kitchen window, I said to myself, 'Claire, there's the man for you. Probably has a secure, well-paying government job.'"

"You don't care?"

"Of course, I care," she said. "But you care more. I know you do. That's more important. I'm not even surprised you're going broke. Everything is either twenty thousand dollars or free. Walt says you don't run a business—you run a charity."

"I know what Walt thinks," I said. "For a long time I did okay."

"It isn't just a job, though, is it?"

"No," I said. "I guess it isn't."

"It's part of who you are. It's something you love. Maybe there's a way. I'd never want you to give up something you love."

"Did someone ask you to give up something you love?" I asked.

"Kind of. Dennis created a situation where I had to, or thought I did." She hesitated and pulled up the one sock that had almost come off her foot. "Yes," she said, as if she had just that minute decided. "He did. He had passion for his music, for the cello. I quit college to work so he didn't have to. Not that he ever tried. He just let me do it. Maybe he didn't come out and ask me to give up the cello, but it amounted to the same thing. He should have stopped me. Told me not to do it. We could have worked it out. There's a lesson in that, Ben. If someone you love asks you to give up something you love, don't do it."

It sounded like good advice: advice that I would take, except going out of business wasn't a choice for me. I didn't really want to talk about Dennis. That wasn't a choice either.

"He must still love you," I said. "He's going through a lot of time and expense to find you and get you back." I wanted to ask her what she was going to do. Instead I just let my words hang in the air between us and hoped she answered the question I couldn't bring myself to ask.

She answered quickly. It wasn't something she needed to think about. "It doesn't matter if Dennis loves me. He doesn't, though. What he loves is that cello. He isn't searching for me. No one is really searching for me."

Recalling my last attempt to mention the cello, I knew I was on dangerous ground. "The cello?"

It was no longer dangerous. I was relieved. She simply nodded. "Our divorce is almost final. I shouldn't have taken it. The cello was our only community property that meant anything to him. Turned out there was more community involved than I knew about."

"Another woman?"

"Yes," she said, without sadness. "I don't care. I don't even care about the cello, really. Not *that* cello. Not anymore. I'm going to call him and tell him to come and get it. Just him, though. I won't give it to her or her family." She obviously knew the other woman's name and wouldn't use it. Claire needed to call the woman "her." Even if Claire no longer loved her husband, using the other woman's name would bestow a dignity and power she couldn't bear.

Claire brightened. "I wonder if what you need is a good bookkeeper?"

"Are you interested in the job?"

"I'm pretty sure I've already submitted my application."

"Then it's yours."

"Slow down, mister. I'll have to think about it. I've been out of the job market for a while. I'm kind of enjoying the interviews. I have concerns."

"About what?" I asked.

"Lots of things. Job security for one."

I told her I understood. "What else?"

Claire lifted herself up and straddled me. We faced each other. "Then of course there is the compensation package."

I groaned.

She might have been small but she was no feather, and I was a busted perch. She pushed me backward onto the porch floor and leaned over me. Her breasts skimmed my chest. Her long black hair fell around my shoulders. She began to move her hips. "Sir, I'm ready for my next interview."

"You'd have great job security, ma'am," I said. "But, frankly, I'm a little concerned about the compensation package."

Claire kissed me and gathered her hair behind her back. "That's what negotiations are all about. I'm sure if you try you can come up with something that meets my requirements."

It took awhile. Sure enough, I managed another interview.

27

On the way back to the diner I stopped at Bernice's grave. Several pieces of red flagstone had been set in the ground as a stairway up to an area that had been cut back into the hillside, almost a grotto. There were fresh flowers next to the marker. *Bernice Chun-Ja Butterfield Beloved Wife 1936–1972–1987.* The way Walt had done the dates didn't even wrinkle my brow. In a way, I would have been surprised if he hadn't memorialized the year of the rape, the year she really died to herself and to Walt, and the year Desert Home ended.

Claire had been in the bathtub when I left. I'd carried and heated the water for her. I needed to take a shower, several of them, and put on clean clothes. There was no sense doing the first until I had the clean clothes. She shouted from the bathroom that she was going to call Dennis from the pay phone at the diner sometime later in the day.

The walk back up the trail to the diner was slow and could barely have been described as walking. If Claire hadn't been such an effective painkiller it could have rightfully been called a death march. I stepped between the mounds of earth, and the white adobe diner shimmered under the noonday sun.

The booth we had sat in during dinner lined up directly with the entrance to Desert Home. I wondered if that was what Bernice had been staring at over her untouched coffee all those years.

Maybe she saw the future there, of Claire and me, and it gave her some peace. As I stood on the trail staring across 117 at the diner, I could almost see Bernice Butterfield staring back at me through the window.

The Victor was right where I had left it against the Quonset. As usual, Walt knew I was on the property before I did. He stepped out of the doorway of the Quonset with only a few telltale signs of our fight. A butterfly bandage held his torn lip in place. There was nothing in his movements that hinted at anything but a good night's sleep. It was disheartening. I looked and felt like hell and I was pretty sure I'd won. Walt didn't toss me a hello, not that I expected one. He didn't take a swing at me either, which I found a welcome and reassuring sign.

He pointed to the Victor. "Clean it up the way it was when you took it. Then bring it in."

I sighed loudly.

I got the hose and turned the water on. Walt opened the door just long enough to put out a bucket of soapy water and soft rags. It might have been entertaining to watch as I tried to wash and polish the Victor, the kneeling, the tight work with my fingers to get off all the dirt and blow out the sand from around the engine. It would have been like watching a surgeon try to operate with an Erector Set for hands.

Walt came out just once and inspected. He grunted and pointed to some spots I had missed. Without a word he returned inside. When I was finally done, or prayed that I was done to Walt's satisfaction, I held the hose over my head just to feel the cool water on a battered face that had now been burned by the afternoon sun.

I knocked on the door of the Quonset. Walt barked at me to come in, which I did, pushing the Victor. He was sitting at his

workbench, hunched over some small part that he was either as-
sembling or disassembling. A bare lightbulb hung a few feet above
his head. The rest of his workshop was in shadow. Without looking
up, he said, "Put it back in line. I'll finish cleaning it later."

He didn't even inspect my work. He just wanted to tell me I
hadn't done a good enough job, meaning the job he could do, that
he always did, *the* Walt Butterfield your-baby-could-eat-off-my-
exhaust-pipe standard. I jockeyed the Victor back into its place
and took a few more minutes to shine up the chrome and catch a
water drip or two.

I stood next to him at his workbench. "Thank you," I said. I
gave him a minute or two to say something back to me. Of course,
he didn't. I had been drinking water from the hose and had to
relieve myself. I asked Walt if the back door to the diner was open
so I could use the bathroom.

He paused in his work and looked me over, almost smiling.
"No need," he said, and tipped his head toward the rear of the
Quonset. He returned his attention to whatever he was fiddling
with on the bench. "Use the one back there. But be careful of my
objet d'art."

I told myself that Walt and I were making progress. He'd never
let me use the workshop toilet before. I hadn't even known there
was one.

I carefully made my way to the rear of the workshop, twisting
and turning through the maze of crates. It was no use asking Walt
to turn on a light or two, just to be courteous. Two stacks of large
boxes sat so close to the door that I had to turn sideways to get it
open. The restroom seemed like an afterthought, narrow and put
up out of rough plywood. The flimsy spring-loaded door snapped
shut behind me while I batted at the air trying to find the pull
string for the light. Little restrooms like that rarely had a switch.

The stench of urine was overpowering in the closed room. It wasn't like Walt to have a room, even a restroom, that wasn't clean and smelling fresh. I found the light cord and pulled it. It didn't catch the first time and I had to pull it again. When it came on it wasn't much of a light, no more than forty watts.

I wondered what Walt meant when he told me to be careful of his objet d'art. To my knowledge Walt didn't collect art, unless you considered his motorcycle collection art. Most men probably would. There were never even any stills from the movie days on the walls of the diner like might be expected. Just inside the door on my left, tacked to the wall, was a photograph. I reached up and directed the bare bulb at the photo so I could get a better look.

I recognized the two men. I guessed who the woman was. It wasn't much of a guess. All three were laughing. One of the men was a young Walt. The other was Lee Marvin. The three of them were standing on a boat dock somewhere tropical, the blue ocean in the distance, serene and eternal. Bernice was between the two men next to a fish, a sailfish or marlin, hanging from a block and tackle. The fish dwarfed all three of them, but none more than Bernice. The men were turned toward her. She was bent over with her laughter, her happy face to the camera, and what could have been tears on her brown cheeks. If only from this photograph, I would have known Claire was her daughter.

I moved the light closer. Small print at the bottom of the photograph identified it as *Property of MGM*. It noted the photographer and the date—1962. The caption read: *Co-star Lee Marvin and friends on the set of* Donovan's Reef. *Island of Kauai, Hawaii. Directed and produced by John Ford.*

Maybe the photograph wasn't art, though I understood why Walt had kept it all these years. What I couldn't understand was why he kept it tacked to a wall near a toilet in a small, windowless restroom that stank of urine and mold way in the back of his workshop. It was the only picture of Bernice I had ever seen, with or without Walt. I figured Walt had reasons that made sense to him even if they wouldn't make sense to anyone else.

I let go of the bulb. It swung gently back and forth. I looked down at the sparkling white toilet bowl and floor. Then I glanced at the wall in front of me.

It took a few seconds to focus my eyes through the shifting shadows made by the swinging of the bare bulb. The face of the corpse was contorted in its dark, shrunken skin. Its hair flowed long and stringy out from under a cap that read, *Da Nang AFB 1969*. The clothes, a fatigue jacket and jeans, still clung to the shriveled body that had been nailed with long spikes through its shoulder blades into the plywood behind it. The legs were draped on either side of the commode as if it were riding the toilet. The urine smell was not coming from the toilet. It came from the corpse.

I fell more than backed out of the restroom, gasping for air, crashing through the narrow door and into the crates of motorcycle parts. Pieces of metal burst from the crates and rolled in all directions across the workshop floor. I stumbled toward the front of the Quonset, dodging Walt's chevron of cycles, my eyes on the thin lines of sunlight spilling from around the edges of the door. I didn't open the door; I kicked at it with my boots using all the strength I had. The door shattered and flew off its hinges. I rushed through, my hands clutching for fresh air and the sliver of open ground between the diner and the Quonset.

I was still gasping for air when I returned to the workshop a minute later. Walt hadn't moved. He sat on a stool hunched over his project. He didn't look at me. "I thought you might like to meet your potential father-in-law. One of them, anyway."

I stood behind him quivering. "Goddamn it, Walt!" I shouted. When he didn't respond I stepped into the pool of light over his bench and slapped off the crap in front of him onto the floor. "You crazy fucker!"

Walt's eyes narrowed as his project scattered across the concrete floor. "Watch your mouth, Ben. There's more where last night came from." Calmly, he got up from his stool and retrieved his project and returned it to his workbench. He sat down on the stool and began to work again. "This is an Amal carburetor. They're rare and nasty little things to rebuild."

I tried to gather myself. "Walt, you're crazy."

He must have succeeded in doing something to the carburetor. "There we go," he said to himself. Turning the part over and over in his fingers, he said, "You think so?"

"Yes," I said, whispering between my teeth, "I do." I thought about the corpse for a minute. "Did you kill him?"

"No, Ben, I didn't. I didn't save him either. He was the one who ran off into the desert. I couldn't go after him. I had to get Bernice and Bobby to the hospital. It took some time out there. I'm not in the saving business. That's the preacher's job. And apparently yours."

I said out loud what came to mind. "The fourth man."

"No," Walt said. "The first man. He was pulling up his jeans when I came through the back door." Walt paused and looked up at the bulb above his head. "The next one had already started on Bernice. The other two were waiting for their turns. One of them couldn't even wait. He was masturbating while he watched.

"You know, Ben," he said, "Lee and I were just kids in Korea. We thought we'd seen it all. The real horror of war is always waiting for you at home. It's waiting, I tell you. We were so damned happy when we got back. We'd made it. We survived. But it's always waiting. Waiting. You let down your guard. And there it is. You can't ever let up. Give up."

I wasn't sure what Walt was talking about. I was pretty sure I didn't want to know. A few days after the rape, he'd come back to the diner to clean up and change clothes. Just to relax, he went for a ride. Several miles down 117 toward Rockmuse he saw a figure crawling just north of the highway. "I knew it was him before I ever saw his face. He damn sure knew who I was. What he didn't know was how much I'd seen."

Here it was, the story that had never been told. I waited for Walt to tell me what had really happened. Why it had happened. But he didn't know why. "Soon as he saw me he started wailing from his knees, pulling at me. His tongue was swollen from thirst. I could make out his words well enough. He begged me to understand he had nothing to do with what happened to Bernice. Said he'd tried to stop the others. I stood out there in the desert for an hour or better. Just let him waste what little time he had left. The only new bit of information I learned was that the man had been hitchhiking. The other three had picked him up outside Rifle, Colorado."

"Do you remember his name?"

Walt gave me a grim smile. "Ben, why in the hell would I care what his name was?"

"He might have had people somewhere," I said.

Walt swiveled around on his stool until he faced the rear of the workshop and the restroom. He spoke toward the room with its corpse. "If he did, they're better off without him. If Jesus himself had done what that man did, I'd have his bony ass riding bareback on my privy."

I couldn't help smiling a little. Walt hadn't said anything particularly funny. He was serious as a judge, which was strictly what he was. "I believe you," I said.

"I brought the body back here. I'd just built that little water closet. Seemed like a fitting final resting place."

Part of me agreed. I joined Walt looking back toward the small room. Neither one of us had anything more to say for a few minutes.

"You love Bernice, don't you?" He didn't say it or mean it exactly as a question, simply a confirmation.

I didn't correct him. I knew that he'd meant to say Claire, though in his mind he thought of them almost as one person. Maybe I should have taken a moment before I spoke. A moment or an hour wouldn't have changed what I had to say. "Yes, Walt," I said. "I believe I do."

"When you two get married, I'll deed you Desert Home as a wedding present. Every square inch of it. Not that it's worth much to the world. You've never had a home, have you, Ben?"

I told him I hadn't.

"You'll have one then. You both will. She could do worse than a truck driver. From what she's told me, she already has. Just keep fresh flowers on our graves."

"Graves?"

"I want to be buried next to Bernice, if you don't mind. There's room for Claire, and you, too, if you want. Bernice would like that."

"Are you putting God on notice, Walt?"

He thought about that for a moment. "I think I am."

"I think you've got a few good years left," I said.

Walt ignored me. "I'd like the diner to go . . ." It seemed to me as if he were trying to recall a name. It wasn't a name. ". . . back to the desert," he said. "Just let it go. You know how things fall apart out here. Leave it be. Nature will take care of it sooner than you'd think."

Walt winked at me. "I feel like a nap. I didn't sleep well last night."

"Walt?" I didn't know how to ask him the question. I knew I shouldn't ask it at all. "Why'd you keep the corpse?"

Walt got off the stool and walked to the empty doorway. He raised his face to the bright desert sky. "Ben," he said, "I can't give you a good reason. I guess I just like to take a piss on him once in a while, knowing he's in hell. He's in hell with nothing but flames and that photo of the three of us for a view. God help me, sometimes it makes me feel better. You can bury him if you want to." He took a few more steps toward the back door of the diner and stopped. With his back to me, he asked, "You still think I'm crazy?"

I told him I did.

"Maybe so," he said, with as much surrender in his voice as I'd ever heard. "I damn well earned it."

"I'll replace your door," I said.

"Yes," he said, "you will." He went inside the diner for his nap.

28

I borrowed some of Walt's tools and set about trying to repair the door I had kicked down. It was mostly in pieces. The following week I would have to buy a new one, and probably a new frame. Cobbling pieces together to have something to hang on the hinges would have to serve. The door to the restroom had to be in about the same condition. I wasn't ready to go back there. When I did, maybe in a few days or a week, I'd remove the first man and bury him somewhere in the desert. It wouldn't be proper, or even legal, not that there was a chance he would object. Even less chance I would be held accountable by the law if the instant funeral was ever discovered. He had served his purpose and overstayed his welcome.

True, Walt was crazy. Just because he was crazy didn't mean I couldn't agree with the sense he made. It did make sense to me, crazy sense. I tried not to think about whether that meant we were both crazy. It did get me to consider heaven and hell while I worked on the door.

Sometimes I believed in hell; sometimes I didn't. There hadn't ever been a time I believed in heaven, though for Walt and Bernice, I was willing to make an exception. Thankfully, it wasn't up to me when it came to Walt. Whatever he had done, or not done, he'd paid handsomely in this life for his choices. I doubted he would have considered them choices at all. If for no other reason than pure loyalty to Walt and the way I felt about Claire, this was one of those times I believed in hell, or wanted to. Not for him, but for the men who raped Bernice.

I also felt a certain strange gratitude to the man. After all, if not for him, or maybe the others, neither Walt nor I would have Claire. Walt knew that I would bury him sooner or later. That was what he wanted. He couldn't just come out and ask me. Claire was right. Walt was changing. My preference would have been for him to change a little more quickly, at least prior to our dinner the night before.

When it came to heaven or hell for myself, God could put me right back on 117. He'd get no argument from me, although I might respectfully request that he pick up the fuel costs and see that my customers paid me, on time, if possible. It's not heaven or hell, just a straight stretch down the middle of the two. Maybe a little of both. Just 117.

Claire came around the corner of the diner. "What's all the pounding?" She looked at the shattered door then back at me. "Is Walt okay?"

"He's taking a nap."

She gasped. "He's unconscious!"

I went to her and kissed her cheek. "No," I said, "he's really taking a nap." I glanced over my shoulder to the window of Walt's apartment. It was open, and the drawn curtains moved slightly.

"A nap? I've never known him to take a nap."

"Well," I said, "he's taking one now. He threw me a bone. Said he didn't sleep well last night." We heard a short cough from inside his room. "Trust me, Claire, he's in fine shape. I promise."

She seemed satisfied that no harm had come to Walt.

"I just made the call to Dennis. He's on his way. I gave him directions." My face twisted when she said his name. She raised her voice a bit and directed it toward the open window. "I told him to come alone and not to stop at the diner. Not for coffee. Not for directions. Not for anything." We both waited for another cough and got one. "Should I ask about the door?"

"No," I said. "Someday you can ask Walt if you want to." There was no cough this time.

Claire followed me into the workshop while I replaced Walt's tools. "Dear Ben," she said, "you have to get home and take a shower. A long, hot one. Stop and pick up some lye soap and a box of steel wool. I don't want to tell you what you smell like."

"You don't have to," I said.

"Since Walt is taking a nap, would you take this?" She pulled the revolver from a small leather bag that was slung over her shoulder. I recognized it as the one she had pointed at me with such skill. "The second day I was here Walt insisted on giving me the gun and lessons on how to use it. He said there were some vicious animals out here. I needed it for protection. But I haven't seen much in the way of animals. The only time I ever brought it out was when you came back."

"I remember," I said.

Walt hadn't been thinking of snakes and coyotes when he gave Claire the gun. He had been thinking of the kind of animals that drive up in a Chevrolet Biscayne one desert evening. Claire probably knew that was what he had been thinking.

"I could tell you knew how to use it," I said. "I'm not glad you pointed it at me. I am glad Walt gave it to you. You should consider keeping it."

She held the revolver out to me. "I think you should take it. I don't like to admit it, but I've got a temper. I don't want anything to happen."

I told her I understood and took the gun.

"I just want to give Dennis the cello and tell him he's a poor excuse for a man."

"Thought you'd have said that by now."

"Many times."

"You think maybe he's forgotten?"

I watched the smile do its slow travel across Claire's face. "I know you don't want me to see him, Ben. But I want to. Then it's over."

Would it ever be over? I wondered. "If you want it over," I said, "it will be over. If it doesn't turn out that way, I'll understand."

"You wouldn't fight to win me?"

"Sure I would," I said, "if you wanted to be won. Of course, there are some women who can't be won; they just like men fighting over them. I'd like to think you're not one of those women, Claire. I'd like it if there wasn't anything to win, just giving."

"Good," she said. "That's the way I feel, too. When I first found out about Dennis I was prepared to fight for him. After a while I realized all either one of us meant to him was that damn cello. I might have fought for him if for one minute I thought it was just a matter of showing him how much I loved him. Then I realized just what you said, you can't ever win what isn't freely given. I realized I didn't love him anymore. I hadn't loved him for a long time. If I still loved him ... if I loved him, this morning would have never happened. I hope you know that."

"I'd hoped that was true," I said. "I wouldn't want you if it wasn't."

"Remember when I asked you about your rules?"

I nodded.

"I wasn't just thinking about your rules. I was thinking about mine, too. Until I give Dennis the cello back I'm still married to him. Now please, please, go home and take a shower." She blew me a kiss. "I want to kiss you, but the way you look and smell makes me want to gag."

"You sure you want me to come back tonight?" I asked. "I mean, if Dennis is on his way? I don't think you want me to be there when you talk to him. I shouldn't be there." I thought of her temper. I thought of my own. "Or maybe you think I should be—in case something happens."

"No, I don't want you there. He said he couldn't get here until at least tomorrow night. I understand your concern, though. Walt will be nearby. I'm sure of it."

So was I.

"If you're not at the house by seven, I'll take one of Walt's motorcycles and come looking for you. I'll make dinner. And mister, you better have cleaned up. Do you understand?"

"Yes, ma'am," I said.

"Now go!"

Claire escorted me to my truck and watched me climb into the cab. It took a couple of attempts to successfully manage the climbing. She started to come over to assist me, and I waved her away. "Don't," I said. "I have my pride."

"Where was your pride last night?"

She walked alongside the cab as I maneuvered out onto the white gravel apron. When she reached the front of the diner, she stopped. From there she blew me a kiss and waved good-bye to me as I pulled out on 117. It was a small gesture, perhaps even unimportant, except no woman had ever done it before. My eyes stayed on my side mirrors until she had disappeared, and then for a while longer.

29

I made it into Price late in the afternoon. On Sundays the gates to the transfer were locked at two. I wouldn't be able to park my truck in the yard or get my pickup. It was just as well. The fewer times I had to get in and out of a truck or a pickup the better. The Price police and my neighbors didn't like me parking my truck and trailer on the city street in front of my duplex. I might get a parking ticket. I didn't care.

A pregnant teenager sat on my front steps. This one was larger and heavier than Ginny. It occurred to me my duplex was sending out a homing beacon to pregnant teenagers. She didn't look lost. She seemed to know exactly where she was and for whom she was waiting. She watched me as I parked my truck and trailer and greeted me with a shy smile that revealed the effects of a hard life on soft teeth. I made my way up the walk. A pile of cigarette butts lay at her feet.

She got right to the point. "You're Ben Jones, right?" Her name was Miranda and she was a friend of Ginny's. "Have you seen Ginny?" she asked.

"Not for a couple of days," I said. "Is she missing?"

Miranda nodded gravely. "She told me you two were kinda friends and where you lived. I asked around until I found the right house."

Miranda took a close look at my face. "You don't look so good. Are you okay?"

"No," I said. "I had a tough night."

"You look like you've had a tough life," she replied.

I could have said the same about her.

I wasn't too concerned about Ginny and admitted that yes, Ginny and I were "kinda friends." Miranda wiggled her eyebrows up and down. I felt compelled to tell her that Ginny and I didn't have that kind of friendship. "I used to date her mother a long time ago," I said, hoping that was all I needed to say. It wasn't.

"Why would that make any difference?" she asked.

"Believe me," I said, feeling some anger, "it makes a big difference. She's seventeen and I've known her since she was a little girl."

"Okay, okay," she said. "I don't care. My old man is around your age."

"I'm happy for both of you." I didn't much care for the "old man" slang. "I'm sure she's fine," I said. "Did you call her other friends? Work?"

"Ginny doesn't have many friends. Since she got pregnant the guys haven't been much interested. The girls we hung out with are still in high school and they don't want much to do with her." I suddenly felt sorry for Ginny, sorrier than I had, though no less proud. "I've been letting her stay with me," she continued, "but my boyfriend doesn't like it. He says having one bun warmer around is enough. He threatened to go back to his wife if I didn't tell Ginny to hit the road. She still sleeps at my place a couple times a week. During the day when he's at work."

"What about work?"

"That's really what has me worried. I stopped by Walmart to say wassup, and the assistant manager said she didn't show up for her shift. She's so fired. And that job is all she has in the freakin' world."

Now I was seriously concerned. I sat down next to Miranda. She sniffed the air. The smell didn't seem to bother her much. "I haven't seen her in a few days," I said. "Can you think of anywhere else she might be?"

"She has this thing about going out in the desert by herself. I don't know where. Different places. She car camps. But she's about to pop. If the baby comes when she's out somewheres all alone . . ."

That was one bad possibility. Another was that she had come across her own variety of animals in a Chevrolet Biscayne. "What happens when you call her on her cell phone?"

Miranda started to cry. "It's been disconnected."

"What about the college? She mentioned she was taking a class. Maybe her professor knows where she is?"

"I don't know nothin' about that." Her big body began heaving with the sobs. "She's so smart. She's not like me. She had straight As in high school before she got knocked up by that bastard."

The mention of the bastard made me think about Nadine. "Maybe she and her mother patched it up?"

Miranda shook her head. "I called. Her mom hung up on me." Another sad possibility crossed her mind. "*You* didn't do anything to hurt her, did you?"

"Never," I said, and patted her shoulder. "I like Ginny. In fact, I admire the hell out of her. She's a great kid." I corrected myself. "She's a great woman." There was a rising guilt in me about not letting her stay at my place. It was warm and safe. What would it have mattered? If—when—she showed up, I would make the offer. "Let me give you my phone number," I said. "When she shows up or you hear from her, let me know."

Once inside I remembered I didn't have a phone anymore. I wrote down the number of the transfer station and went back outside. I told Miranda that it was a work number and to leave me a message. "Next week I'll stop by the college and see if I can locate her professor. Maybe he knows something."

Miranda made a couple of unsuccessful attempts at lifting herself off my steps. I offered her a hand. When she was on her feet, she asked me if I would take her number so I could text her if I heard from Ginny. I hadn't sent a text in my life. Even if I had a cell phone I wouldn't know how.

I took her number.

Miranda scribbled it on a matchbook she took from her purse. She took out a fresh cigarette from a pack.

"I'll call you," I said. "You know you shouldn't smoke when you're pregnant."

"I hear that a lot. But my boyfriend says it's not true. Doctors put that out there so they can make an extra dollar off us pregnant girls."

There wasn't anything to say. That boyfriend of hers was all the wrong stuff. She offered me a cigarette. "I don't smoke," I said.

She laughed. "You pregnant?" She lit her cigarette and waddled off down the street. "Text me!"

The shower water bounced off my body and ran brown and red for five minutes. After it ran clear I filled the tub and began scrubbing, carefully cleaning around the wounds so they wouldn't open up. That was the limit of my hot water for a while. Some of the wounds wept red and tinted the bathwater a vivid pink that reminded me of the evening at Desert Home and the mesa light pouring onto Claire as she played her silent cello. I closed my eyes and soaked and listened to the faucet drip.

I might just return the tractor-trailer to the leasing company. It might go better for me if I gave it to them rather than having it repossessed. There was no sense in postponing the inevitable. If Ginny hadn't shown up by then, I would go to the college and try to find her professor. I realized I'd let go of any ideas I had about saying good-bye to 117. In time folks would know I wasn't going to come around anymore and life would go on out there and in Rockmuse just as it always had, only without me.

It was better not to say farewell, better for them and better for me. Like what Walt wanted to happen to his diner, just let it go. Let the desert take it all back. Everything was on loan anyway. Maybe that was part of what Walt was trying to say in his workshop. Bernice had only been on loan to him and he let his guard down, and she was gone, repossessed in the blink of an eye. It took him forty years. Now he was letting go, giving her back to the desert.

The best part of 117 was Claire and Walt. I wondered when the time came for Claire to let go of the cello, of Dennis, if she wouldn't try to hold on the way Walt had done. It was possible, no matter what she said, that Claire would return to her husband and that the loan of her was already over, or soon would be. What the desert wants, in the end, it takes.

I showered again with lukewarm water and gently patted myself dry, leaving spots and streaks of fresh blood on the towel. The mirror helped me inventory the damage. My whole right side where Walt had kicked me was bruised blue. My face was swollen, especially the jaw where Walt had elbowed me. The only way I could get my left eye fully open was to use my fingers. I could see through it, except what looked back at me from the mirror was a red marble. The worst casualty was my ear. It was thick with blood and appeared to need my hair to keep it from falling off. It should have had stitches. I used almost a full tube of antibiotic and downed three Advil. The good news was the toes on my left foot didn't seem to be broken. They were blackened and stiff as nails. It hurt like hell when I wiggled them, but wiggle them I could.

I limped into the bedroom and gathered up my clothes. They went straight into a plastic bag to be thrown away. My skin and hair had picked up some of the stench from the urine-soaked corpse. I tied the plastic bag and washed my hands. I sat naked on my bed. Never in my life had I felt so tired and battered. Only the thought of seeing Claire at Desert Home kept me from collapsing backward on the bed and not moving for a week.

30

Claire thought her husband would arrive at Desert Home sometime on Monday. With no way to get my pickup out of the transfer
yard and my trailer still loaded, it made sense to just spend the
day making the last of my deliveries. Being on 117 and busy might
help me keep my mind off knowing that Claire and her husband
were together, maybe in a way I couldn't stand to think about. I
took on diesel at the truck stop and made it to the diner by six
thirty. Walt didn't show himself and I didn't bother to knock.

Instead of walking straight to Claire's house, I veered off the
lane and up along the ridge that divided 117 from Desert Home.
Both Claire and Walt seemed to have this ability to sense the
presence of people without seeing them. I hugged the ridgeline,
staying out of sight of the house.

A quarter of a mile away I hunkered down among some desert
flowers and waited to see if Claire would come out. It was a silly
test. I didn't think of myself as a silly man. Waiting to see if she
appeared, even as sore and tired as I was, increased my anticipation of seeing her. I wanted her to feel my presence. From a distance, I wanted to see her small body and dark hair, as I had seen
her so many times before. I needed to see her waiting for me.

The longer I waited the more uncomfortable I became. My
muscles began to spasm and cramp. Soon I was experiencing a
different kind of discomfort. I began to wonder if her husband

was already there or if something had happened that prevented her from appearing. The list of the something-wrongs occupied me for another minute or two. Seven o'clock came and went and still she didn't show. The last thing that occurred to me was that I might be wrong about her ability to sense people. She was simply inside, waiting.

I found Claire outside sitting on the porch with her eyes closed, letting the last light of the setting sun dance on her eyelids. I stood quietly and watched her, the smells of the dinner she had prepared making my stomach growl. Still, she didn't move and made no effort to recognize my presence so near to her. Her hair was free and wild on her shoulders, her hands folded peacefully in her lap.

"Claire!" I shouted, and ran up on the porch and grabbed both of her arms in my hands and lifted her out of the chair.

She opened her eyes and laughed. "I win! How long were you going to hide up there on that ridge?"

My knees buckled. I dropped to the porch. I pressed my face into the pleats of her long western skirt. I couldn't speak. For one brief moment I knew what it would be like to lose her. She knew what I was feeling and put her hands to my head without saying anything.

She knelt in front of me and kissed my cheeks, first one and then the other. "So much for games," she whispered.

We ate on the porch, mostly without speaking, listening to the sounds of evening. The plates we balanced on our laps were tin and heavy, from another century. She had found them in the cupboard along with a few mason jars, two of which we used for water.

Claire spoke again of her mother, of the unrealized plans Bernice had for Desert Home. I listened as she spoke, sometimes re-

ferring to herself and her mother as if they were interchangeable.
The effect was unsettling. Desert Home was her mother. I wrote
off my outburst to fatigue, though the feeling of loss still lingered
on inside me. When I glanced at Claire she, too, seemed to be
feeling as if we were somehow trespassing on history. What we
saw and felt was already strangely past. We touched each other
often during the meal, casually, for the reassurance of the physical reality of each other and ourselves.

"Do you suppose Walt would sell it to me?" Claire asked.

"You'd have to ask him," I said, wanting to tell her that Walt
would give it to us. And if there wasn't an us, he would probably
give it to her. "It's hard to figure Walt," I said. "My guess is that
he already has given it to you. It's your inheritance from them
both. You said you love it here. You've been happier here than
anywhere in your life." I heard myself speaking in the past. I set
my half-full plate down on the porch. "I'm so tired, Claire."

She did the same with her plate and lay with her head in my
lap. She pushed off her boots with her toes. "Me, too," she said.
"I've been thinking I don't really need to see Dennis again. I'm
not sure I even want to anymore. You and I could go away for a
day or two. I'd just leave the cello in the house. I wouldn't even
need to leave a note. You were right. Anything I could say to him
I've already said a hundred times. All he wants is his cello."

"Could you do that?" I asked.

"I know you're afraid, Ben. Don't be. You're as much a part of
my happiness here as Desert Home." She raised her lips to mine.
"Do you want me to skip seeing Dennis?"

My answer was yes, but I knew if she didn't I might always
wonder what might have happened if she had. She might wonder.

"No," I said, "I don't want you to see him again. What I want
doesn't matter. This is between the two of you. Even if you don't

want to see him again, you need to put that cello in his hands. You took it to hurt him in the only way you could. You'll know if you no longer love him when you give him the cello. When he takes it he'll know you don't love him. I *am* afraid, Claire. If you don't see him but give him the cello, I'll be afraid forever."

We left the plates on the porch. She led me through the empty house to the bedroom. The cello and bow leaned against a bare wall. A mattress made up with white sheets and a blue blanket rested on the floor in the center of the room. Beside the mattress was a small night lamp.

She unbuttoned my shirt. "We'll decide in the morning."

"You'll decide."

She touched my forehead. "You've got a fever."

I lay down on the bed and watched as she undressed. When she was naked, she carefully folded our clothes and set them against the other wall. Each movement, no matter how small, meant something to me, as if she were dancing and the dance told a story I could feel but not understand. I was falling asleep with my eyes open. I heard her switch off the lamp.

She brought her body close to mine. "No more interviews tonight," she whispered.

"I could interview all night," I said.

"You will, mister. Tomorrow night. And the night after. And the night after that."

Later I awoke, knowing her warm body was no longer next to mine. I got to my feet and stood in the doorway of the bedroom. She was sitting on the green metal chair in the living room just as I had seen her that first evening. She was playing the cello in the weak light of the waning moon, her bow arm moving slowly. The notes were full and strong and filled the house and passed around and through me, each time leaving a part of themselves behind. Then her cool fingers were on my arms leading me back to bed. She smelled of desert air and fresh rain. I glanced over my shoulder into the living room, and both the green chair and the cello were gone. The starlight reflected off the hardwood floor where they had been.

"I can still hear you playing," I said.

She stroked my forehead with her fingers. "Oh, Ben," she said, "I am still playing. I am always playing." She placed her head on my shoulder and her left hand across my chest. I listened as her breathing slowed and she returned to sleep. I kissed her hair, inhaling all of her that I could hold, and held my breath as I fell asleep.

31

We awoke at dawn. The soft sunlight angled through the bedroom window as if it didn't want to bother us. She was wearing a man's white T-shirt. I didn't recognize the T-shirt, but I recognized the faded oil stain on the left shoulder. The shirt was a gift to her from Walt. It was a thin, threadbare cotton, and it fit her like a silk envelope.

I tried to lift Claire's T-shirt over her head. She resisted. "You can't be serious."

I assured her I was very serious. "Like a carpenter with two broken legs at the bottom of a beautiful staircase. Maybe I can't climb the stairs, ma'am, but at least let me admire the workmanship."

She removed the T-shirt. I let my eyelids close as a way of keeping the image of her inside me. She snuggled next to me. I apologized for being so much trouble during the night. We stayed awake and quiet for a long time.

Claire broke the silence. "My advice to you is not to win any more fights with Walt."

I told her I planned on taking her advice. "If it hurts this much to win," I said, "I don't want to know what it's like to lose." I added, "I hope Walt has said all he has to say on the subject."

"You had me pretty worried last night." Her voice trembled as she spoke. "You were delirious some of the time. You suddenly got up and stood in the doorway looking into the empty living room. I didn't know what to do. You must have stood there for fifteen minutes. I tried several times to get you back to bed. You wouldn't go. I think you were seeing me play the cello. You had this expression on your face like you were listening to something."

"I was," I said. "I remember. I can still see you there. I can still hear you. Though if you asked me, I wouldn't be able to describe what I heard."

She had her mind on something else. I waited to hear what it was.

"You're right," she said. "I have to put the cello in Dennis's hands. If I don't, I can't stay here with you and Walt—with my mother—in Desert Home."

We lay together for a long time as the room gradually filled with sunlight, and I thought about the cello and her husband on his way. She didn't tell me what she was thinking. She didn't need to. The cello against the wall might have well been Dennis. I wondered why I didn't hate it, all their years together standing there.

We spent the early morning lounging in bed and on the porch without much conversation as we both thought about the coming day. Midmorning Claire and I walked silently hand in hand back along the sandy lane toward the diner, pausing briefly at her mother's grave. She let go of my hand when we reached the end of the lane and put her arms around my waist. The diner shimmered in the heat on the other side of the highway.

"Soon," she said, "Dennis will have his cello and I'll be here in Desert Home with you and Walt."

I kissed her and walked across 117 to the diner. The front door was open. I turned to look back at Claire. She was gone.

Walt sat at the counter facing the front door with a cup of coffee in his hands. "How's she holding up?"

"Do me a favor, Walt?"

"What?"

"Punch me again. I'd like to be unconscious today."

"Funny," he said, "I was thinking of asking the same favor of you. Except I need to be on guard duty when he shows up. That and I'm not sure you could get the job done."

I let that comment go, partly because I agreed with it. "You think there's going to be trouble?" I asked.

"Maybe," he answered. "I don't know him, but I know Claire some. I hope not." He swiveled the stool around to face the counter. "I noticed she returned the gun I gave her. Probably a good idea."

I agreed with him. "I need to stay busy today," I said. "I still have freight in my truck so I'll be out on 117 all day."

Walt offered to cook me breakfast. I declined, and he acted as if he didn't believe me. "You haven't eaten, have you?" I said I hadn't but I wasn't hungry. "Sure you are. Your body's healing. Bacon and eggs. Toast and butter." He slipped off the stool and headed for the kitchen. "That will fix you up. I'll have you on the road in twenty minutes."

I took a seat at the counter and mumbled, "Whatever you say, Dad."

Walt showed his head in the stainless steel pass-through. He glared at me. "What did you say?"

"Nothing," I said. "Not a damn thing."

In less than five minutes he put down a plate of eggs, bacon, and toast. I was hungry. He took the stool to my right and watched me eat, suppressing a grin. Five minutes after that there wasn't a crumb on the plate. Gulping the last out of a mug of coffee, I stood up.

Walt reached up and put his big left paw on my shoulder and

firmly pushed me back down on the stool. "Sit down," he said. "We need to talk."

When someone says *we need to talk*, what he or she usually means is *you will listen*. Any conversation that takes place will be accidental. I was listening.

Walt cleared his throat. "Just so you know," he said, "after this husband thing is over, there are going to be some changes."

I asked him what kind of changes.

"Changes," he barked. "One in particular." He made sure he had his eyes on mine and I was prepared for the significance of whatever he had to say. "No more nights in Desert Home until you two are proper."

I was glad I had already eaten breakfast. It gave me the necessary strength to hold my face together. After a suitable pause, I said, "Yes, sir."

My answer might have been a little too much for him. He doubted my sincerity. He shouldn't have. I was absolutely sincere. If that was the way Walt felt, Claire could spend nights with me in Price.

"Are you mocking me, Ben?"

"No, sir," I said. "I hope you'll make this speech of yours to Claire, if you haven't already."

"I don't need to make it to Claire. I'm telling you. If I see your ragged ass down there late at night or early in the morning, you'll think the other night was your senior prom. You understand?"

I gave Walt another "Yes, sir." Just to make certain, I said, "By 'proper' you mean married, right?"

"You know damn well that's what I mean. That's her mother's house. I still own it. No hanky-panky. The people who raised her are gone."

I had guessed as much.

"She doesn't have anyone except that musician ex-husband." He said "musician" as if it didn't have a thing to do with music.

As far as I was concerned, the phrase *hanky-panky* was more interesting. It amused me some. I bounced it around in my head for a few seconds. It was as good a term as any and better than most.

"You don't think you're getting too far ahead, do you? What happens if I ask Claire to marry me and she turns me down? Or are you planning on asking her for me? Maybe on account of the hanky-panky you figure on just telling her she has to marry me?"

The idea that Claire might have a different plan was not a possibility Walt had considered. He had no intention of considering it now. "I'm just giving you fair warning," he said, and clamped his jaw shut. The conversation was over. He picked up my plate from the counter and took the mug from my hand. "Now get to work."

To my way of thinking, for what it was worth, I figured I now had received Walt's blessing. Twice. He had everything all set in his head, and he was confident everything was now set in mine. If Claire decided, for whatever reason, that marriage to me wasn't what she wanted, I would be to blame. That would be the end of my friendship with Walt forever. It was a risk I was willing to take. He would have it no other way.

The truth was, neither would I—the marriage part, not the hanky-panky. Claire would want time, and I wanted her to have it, as much as she needed with or without the hanky-panky, though preferably with. If at any point she said no, or even if she left with Dennis and never returned, a part of her would always remain with me, proper in my heart in the only way it could be. In that I had no choice.

I aimed the truck toward Rockmuse. I repeated "hanky-panky" out loud to myself a couple of times and bet that Walt and Bernice had hanked and panked up a storm, probably before they were married. Maybe not, but I wouldn't have bet on that. Men were often far different in their roles as fathers than they were as suitors, the memories of which kept them, out of necessity, both vigilant and violent, and even tender in moments, to their daughters. I wondered if I might have that chance someday. I hoped so.

32

I finally made the first of my farewell deliveries around noon. I had decided to drive east most of the way to Rockmuse for my first delivery and work my way west up 117 back toward Price. Either way involved backtracking. Doing it the way I had chosen simply meant I would do the long drive at the beginning, which suited me fine.

The two hours it took to get to my first delivery allowed me time to get my mind straight about accepting whatever happened with Claire. In Walt's version, which was the only version possible for Walt, everything went just the way it was supposed to go. Claire would hand off the cello to the husband. The husband would say thank you, more or less, and leave. Anything more, and Walt would be there to see that it wouldn't be much more. End of story.

My versions allowed for every possibility I could imagine, including the husband leaving with Claire and the cello, Claire refusing to hand over the cello, Claire returning with the cello to New York. Maybe it was being orphaned and alone all my life, but I always steeled myself for the worst outcome I could envision. That way I could shrug and be almost happy with anything that fell short of the worst. It was a peculiar life skill and one I had gotten damn good at.

I'd done my worst-case-scenario preparation. There would be no surprise, no matter how it went.

My first stop was the University of Utah dig site three miles south of 117 in the center of a one-mile-square depression. I had been told the area once held the last large body of fresh water as the great inland sea disappeared. It was a depository of sorts, a prehistoric landfill, where creatures, and later people, had gathered and lived and eventually settled to the bottom like so much solid waste in a treatment pond.

University faculties and students from all over the West converged there over the summers. I had delivered all their supplies for years. Now, with budget cuts, they used more student interns to bring in supplies and equipment. A lot less supplies and equipment were brought into the dig site because fewer faculty and students could afford to come to work at the site.

As access roads go, the dirt road to the site had been kept in good shape. The county had seen to it that the surface was regularly scraped and the ruts leveled out.

This year was different. The slashes were long and deep. The drive was slow and tedious. When I began to descend into the depression I saw why. The site—usually full of activity, tents, workers, cars, and pickups—was empty, except for a small travel trailer and a beat-up old Nissan SUV. I could see the shape of a man sitting on a camp stool beneath a makeshift awning that flapped lazily in a light breeze.

I parked near the trailer, climbed down out of the cab, and waved to him. He waved back without lifting himself off the stool. As I approached, he said, "Didn't you get the memo? The apocalypse has come and gone."

Up close he was older, his face sharply lined like the ruts in the road that led into the site. "Where is everybody?" I said. "I've got a load of Schedule 40 galvanized pipe."

"Take it back," he said amicably. "The university hired me

a week ago to be the caretaker for the summer. Make sure no one gets away with any illegal bones. Big budget cuts." As if he wanted me to get the idea of the size of the budget cuts, he made a slow sweeping motion that took in a three-hundred-sixty-degree view of the site and the desert in all directions.

"I can't take it back," I said. "There's nowhere to take it. It's been paid for."

"Well," he said with a sad smile, "that's the government for you. Buying shit they can't afford that will never be used." He pointed to a stack of wooden pallets and crates a hundred yards away. "Put the pipe over there."

I spent the better part of an hour unloading the pipe. It was hot and unforgiving work beneath the hard noon sunlight. Sweat poured down my face and chest as I worked. I enjoyed the physical exertion. My muscles began to loosen as I got into a rhythm of lifting the lengths of pipe and tossing them into neat piles. When I was done I sat on the liftgate for a well-deserved rest.

The old man appeared at my elbow with a canteen of water. "The name's Jasper."

I told him my name and took a long pull on the canteen. "You're out here all summer alone?"

"Yep," he said. "And my pay is commensurate with what I do. Which is absolutely nothing. Government work," he said by way of explanation, and spat dark brown tobacco juice onto the dust. "For entertainment I watch the sun rise and the sun set. Between the two I *wait* for the sun to rise and the sun to set." He spat again and winked. "It's not honest work, but it's work. The first real steady job I've had in two years. I'm not complaining."

I started to tell him that I drove 117, and if he needed anything to let me know and I'd deliver it. Force of habit. I caught myself and said nothing when I remembered I wouldn't be driving 117. "My guess is," I said, "you kind of enjoy your work out here, such as it is."

He smiled. "I do at that," he said. "At night I've been climbing up to that ridge over there and watching the stars. Television for the desert rat. Couple nights ago I took in the sights of a desert fire. Didn't last long, though. Beautiful while it lasted, like fireworks."

Desert fires are rare and don't last long. There simply isn't enough to burn. Unlike a forest fire, desert fires are left alone. Usually a fire is the result of a lightning strike or, once in a while, a careless camper. Campers might have been the cause of the fire Jasper saw. There hadn't been lightning for over a week.

"Where did you see the fire?" I asked.

He pointed north, in the direction of 117. "Out there. Like I said, it didn't last long. One big flare-up. It blinked for a while. Why?"

"No reason," I said. "Just curious." I faced north and pointed. "You stood on that ridge up there?"

Jasper rubbed his face with both hands as if to wake up. He squinted upward and nodded. Dreamily, he said, "Once in a while you can catch a shooting star. The night sky kind of reaches around you up there like a starry bubble."

I asked him to sign for the pipe. He scribbled his initials and I gave him his copy. I told him to be safe. Almost as an afterthought, I asked him if he had lived a long time in Utah. His answer surprised me.

"No," he said. "Born and raised in Washington State. Lost my job to the digital revolution and my pension to Wall Street. My wife died. I've just been moving from place to place. I like it here, though. You?"

"All my life," I said. "And probably what comes after."

We left it at that. On my way out I slowed near the ridge he had indicated and followed the line of sight due north. There was nothing out there that I knew of, and not an area where you'd expect hikers or campers to go. In fact, there had only been one person out there two nights ago—Josh.

The next few deliveries went quickly. I wondered about the fire Jasper had seen. Maybe it was just a campfire. Josh would have been cold while he waited for daylight. What concerned me was that for Jasper to see it, it would have had to be one hell of a big campfire and there wasn't much there for Josh to burn. Jasper's choice of the word *flare-up* made me think of *flare*. Perhaps Josh was attempting a signal fire with the hope of being rescued. Maybe he had been rescued. Jasper only saw it the one night.

Layers of soft wide clouds were building to the west in front of a late-afternoon sun as I headed my empty trailer back toward home, which for a moment I envisioned not as my duplex in Price, but Desert Home and Claire. My place in Price had never been my home, only where I slept. After two nights with Claire, it seemed as though it wasn't even that anymore. Dennis might be in Desert Home with Claire, or have been there and gone. Or they were both gone. I wanted to know which it was. At the same time I didn't want to know. The compromise presented itself as I approached the turnoff to the Lacey brothers' place. My intention was to occupy myself for a few minutes by checking in on Duncan.

A red handkerchief twisted in the wind from where it had been anchored to a pile of rocks. Though seldom used, many of my customers put out a brightly colored rag of some description to request me to stop for a pickup, or to place an order.

33

Fergus was sitting on one of the plastic crates beside the cable spool table. On the table, partly hanging off the edge, was an oblong package tightly wrapped in black plastic and sealed with silver duct tape. Fergus looked like he was expecting me. There was no way he could have known when I would show up. He didn't wave or stand. I parked in their turnaround. He sat with his hands folded in his lap and watched me as I climbed down out of the cab.

There was no use hurrying. It was maybe twenty-five steps to the table. By the twelfth step I knew what lay stretched over the table in front of Fergus. I took the crate across from him and sat down. Neither one of us said anything for a few minutes. We just sat there with the crude body bag between us like a centerpiece at a sad dinner party. Fergus didn't look at me or the bag that held his brother. He stared south toward 117.

"When?" I asked.

Fergus gently rested his hand on the black plastic. "Yesterday." I waited for him to continue. He began to stroke the plastic. "He was feeling better."

Fergus had been sleeping. When he awoke he saw Duncan stringing barbed wire from their old Jeep along a hillside behind their boxcars. The roll of wire was in the back of the Jeep. The end was nailed to a fence post. Duncan stood between the two.

"He was just standing there, looking back toward me with this silly grin on his face. He sort of waved. I saw the Jeep begin to creep down the hill. He probably didn't bother to set the emergency brake. He didn't even try to get free. Maybe Duncan didn't notice the barbwire tangled around him until it was too late. I didn't even make it out the door before the barbwire cinched him around the waist like a tourniquet. Damn near cut him in two. He was still alive when I got to him. Not a damn thing I could do, Ben." He paused. "I keep telling myself it wasn't a bad way to go. We had a few minutes for our good-byes."

"It's got to be tough to lose a brother," I said.

Fergus stopped stroking the plastic and gave it a pat. "Even harder to lose your only son."

"Your son?"

"We wanted it that way. You and the few others we've had contact with over the past forty years assumed we were just a couple of crazy brothers living out here. It got easier to sell as we got older. I was only eighteen when he was born. His mother was seventeen. We figured being brothers kept us a little safer."

"Safe from what?"

Fergus needed to think about my question. I let him think. He made his decision. "From the law, Ben. FBI mostly. Our name isn't Lacey. It's Tinker. I'm Joe. My son's name was Teddy. Ted. We're originally from Baltimore. Showed up out here in the middle of the night. Before that, the closest we ever came to this much sand was the Atlantic shore."

It didn't seem all that important to know why they were wanted men. The bullet scars I'd seen on Duncan's chest made sense. "What do you want me to do?" I asked.

"Don't you want to know why we've been hiding out from the law all these years?"

I told him I didn't care. I did care, though only a little.

He wanted to tell me anyway.

"Teddy and a friend robbed a bank. Only trouble he was ever in. Thought they'd do it just the once. He was only twenty years old. It's not like he had a brain in his poor little head at that age. His friend shot the guard. Killed him. The guard shot his friend. Toby, his name was. He died where he fell. They'd known each other since they were in kindergarten. A teller emptied his revolver into Teddy. He was half dead when I broke him out of the hospital. We drove for three days. The whole time I was expecting him to die. If he'd lived or died, better with me than in prison or by lethal injection."

"What about his mother?"

"She gave her blessing. Knew we'd never see each other again. And we didn't." Fergus, or Joe, smiled up into the sky. "As prisons go, this was a good one. Still a prison."

"I saw the putting green," I said. "Just like the Wall Streeters and bankers."

"Yep," he agreed. "We even supplied our own barbed wire."

I didn't think there was much left to be said. "Give me a hand. We can put him in the refrigerator unit. I'll take him into the funeral parlor in Price." Fergus made no move to help me. "Or do you want me to help you bury him here?"

He sighed. He took his eyes away from Duncan's body. "There's something else you should know." I let him take a moment to find the courage to tell me what I already suspected. "I'm wanted, too. When I took my son I didn't have much money. It ran out fast. Outside Muncie, Indiana, I robbed a gas station. Then a bank in Trinidad, Colorado."

"Anyone hurt or killed?"

He shrugged. "Maybe," he said. "Probably. I was out of my

mind. I'd been driving for two days. I didn't really know how to use a gun. It just seemed to go off by itself. Teddy was lying in the backseat bleeding and unconscious."

"You want my sympathy?" I asked.

"Your understanding, maybe."

"Sure," I said. "What exactly do you want me to do?"

"Take him into Price or Salt Lake. Somewhere he'll get a decent funeral. That's it." He thought a moment more and added, "The boy was so lonely out here. I guess I don't want him to spend eternity the same way."

There was nothing in his tone to suggest that was all he had to say. I just waited on him to get it all out. When he didn't, I grew impatient and finished for him. "You want to be left out of it?"

He nodded, and I added, "You think funeral homes have night deposit slots for bodies?"

"I got lucky with the bank in Trinidad," he said. "If you want to call it luck. Two hundred thousand and change. I could make it worth your while."

"You couldn't possibly make it worth my while," I said, with no room in my tone for misunderstanding. The thought of starting a life with Claire that way, with stolen money, wasn't something I could have lived with.

"I've never taken money for doing something illegal," I said. In fact, I had never really done anything illegal, for gain or not. At least not something I'd had a chance to think about. "Your money is stolen," I said. "Even if it weren't, taking payment might take the fun out of what for me could be considered a crime spree—if I get caught."

"You'll do it, then?"

"I'm not sure what I'll do. No promises. I'll take the body. If I turn you in, either because I want to or I don't have any other choice, you have to go without trouble. You understand? That's the best I can offer."

He took my offer. We slipped Duncan in over the butter brickle ice cream. "There is one thing you can do for me," I said. "You have any idea where those boxcars came from?"

Fergus said he did. "That's where the railroad left them. We covered up the tracks. This used to be a siding."

"You built your house on the tracks?"

"Sounds stupid, doesn't it?" It wasn't exactly a question.

I opened the little inspection cubby on the exterior of the trailer and took a peek in at Duncan in his black plastic sleeping bag. "No," I said, "not at all. Especially when you compare it to everything else you and your son did." I closed the inspection door.

"Didn't have a choice," he said.

I avoided looking at him. "Sure you did."

34

I had no idea what I was going to do with Duncan's body, or with the unwanted knowledge of what he and his father had done. For a little while I had succeeded in forgetting about Claire and her husband. It was almost a vacation.

At the turnout for Desert Home, I saw Walt on my left near the top of the hill leading to the archway. He waved me in.

Before I could get out of the cab he jumped up on the running board. "He's been down there about an hour. Took his rented SUV down the road across from the diner. On top of everything else, he's an idiot."

He reached to steady himself on a mirror post. I could see the butt of a handgun beneath his short leather jacket. "You think you're going to need that?" I asked.

Walt gave my question more thought than I expected. "I hope not," he said.

"Don't shoot anyone accidentally," I said.

He jumped down and glared up at me. "I don't shoot people accidentally," he said. "I shoot them on purpose."

We walked up the hill toward the arch. "An hour's a long time," I said.

Walt's answer was to the point. "They've been married a long time. You probably shouldn't be here."

"Probably not," I said. "But it doesn't take an hour to hand over the cello."

Walt put his hand on my shoulder. "Don't go down there."

I wasn't going to, and told him so. It wasn't true—part of me was already starting down the other side.

"She knows you're here, right?"

"She knows," he said. "She doesn't need to see me."

"Maybe she is your daughter." It was something that had been playing in the back of my mind for quite a while. I meant it as a kind of joke. As soon as I said it I was filled with regret. Such a comment wouldn't sit well with Walt. When he didn't say anything, I looked over at him. He was staring stone-faced down at the house.

The two of us knelt on the sandy ground just out of sight below the rim of the hill. One of us was praying that there was nothing going on inside the house but talk. Walt could have been hoping for the same thing. I liked to think so. Both of us just wanted to see Dennis come out of the house with the cello and leave, alone.

"Why don't you go down there," I suggested. "Just to make sure everything is okay?"

Walt glanced over at me with a mixture of understanding and pity on his face. It might have been a mixture of contempt and pity. It was an expression I'd never seen before, not on Walt Butterfield's face. "She's with her husband, Ben," he said quietly. "Unless there's a sign of trouble brewing, neither one of us belongs there. You can't change whatever is happening behind those doors. It would be wrong to try." He rocked back on his heels and stood up. "It's time for you to go."

He walked me back to my truck. "Maybe she'll stay this time. Maybe not."

"I thought this was her first visit," I said.

"She showed up on my doorstep one morning about a year ago, right after she and her husband separated. I knew right off who she was. I let her cool her heels, hoping she'd go away. Stubborn girl. She stood outside the door to the diner or sat roasting in her car off and on for most of the day. She knew I was there. And she knew I knew. She wore me down. Late in the afternoon I let her in. She walked straight to Bernice's booth and sat down, like she'd been doing it all her life. She had her choice of any seat in the diner.

"All she wanted was for me to tell her about her mother. She knew about everything else. I made us a little something to eat. Before she left she asked for a keepsake, anything that was her mother's. I gave her those boots she wears. Had them made up special for Bernice just before ..." He stopped. "And a little gold locket Bernice wore, with our wedding photograph inside. Then she asked for something to remember me by. Kind of surprised me."

I asked him what he gave her.

"A quilt my mother made for me when I was a kid. She looked it over and put it in a bag. She thanked me and left. Never expected to see her again. Didn't want to see her again. Claire looks so much like her mother. It was like losing Bernice again. A few months later I wrote to her and told her it would be okay with me if she wanted to phone me or visit again. I gave her the number to the phone booth and said that if I was around I would hear it ring. Two weeks ago it rang. She was calling from New York. She wanted me to come and pick her up at the airport in Denver. I picked her up. She sent some of her belongings ahead. Used her mother's Korean name instead of her own. Said she had her reasons. I thought maybe it had to do with her husband."

Walt looked back over his shoulder toward the archway, as if Claire was standing beneath it.

"Why are you telling me this?" I asked him.

"Thought you should know since you and Claire are together now."

"I hope so," I said.

"There's something else," he said, "just between the two of us. Bernice and I had been trying to have children for years. Then those men violated her." He scuffed at the dirt with his boots. I could tell for a moment he was in the diner again that evening. "She was still in the hospital when we found out she was pregnant. I couldn't stand the idea. I wanted the doctors to flush the damn thing and send it straight to hell. No matter how I felt, Bernice wanted to keep it. She begged me, but I wasn't having any of it. We argued. She said she would leave me if I harmed the baby. It wasn't just the baby. Those animals broke her all up inside. Carrying the baby and childbirth might kill her. I agreed to let her have the baby, though I didn't visit her until after it was born. It wasn't the rape and beating that took away her speech. It was having the baby. A stroke. By the time she recovered, the baby was gone, adopted. Healthy damn kid. I still had Bernice. She hated me as much as I hated those men. Until Claire showed up, and I saw her, I hadn't realized what I'd done to Bernice. What I'd done to myself."

"A second chance?" I ventured.

Walt nodded.

"I hope you take it," I said.

"Just thought you should know," he said.

Walt walked back up the hill. What he really wanted me to know was that he had as much at stake as I did in whatever was going on inside the house, maybe more. Walt had made Bernice give up the baby. He had kept the corpse. Now he was trading back.

The sun was beginning to set. The wind was gusting, full of sand as it crossed 117. It made the sunlight dirty, like a bandage stretched over the sky. If I didn't keep my speed down, the sand would take the paint off my truck and trailer right down to the metal.

The flashing blue and red light bars of the two police units faded in and out of sight behind the windblown sand. They were parked side by side along the shoulder in front of the diner. When the officers saw me coming they got out of their vehicles and motioned me to pull over into the diner's parking lot. One car was a Utah Highway Patrol cruiser; the other was a Carbon County Sheriff's unit.

There was little doubt in my mind they had been waiting for me. I had no idea why, especially the need for two of them.

35

I pulled off 117 onto the gravel and inched the nose of my truck forward until it was within a few yards of the two men. They looked a little nervous while they stood their ground. I recognized the highway patrolman. His name was Andy. We'd met on several occasions, none of them seriously official. He was a nice Mormon guy a few years younger than me with short blond hair and an easy way about him.

The three of us stared at one another through the windshield. They wore sunglasses. Not because of the sun—because of the blowing sand. There was nothing easy about the way they stood. In case there was any misunderstanding, they had put on their hats and pulled the brims down low and tight on their heads. It was cop sign language for "I'm on duty."

I climbed out of the cab and said hello to Andy. I extended my hand. The wind and sand snatched up my greeting and sent it twisting over the roof of the diner. Andy didn't take my hand. The sheriff's deputy took a step backward and rested a thumb on his sidearm. The gun was still in its holster. Its cover was unfastened.

Andy glanced at the deputy. "We have orders to take you in to the highway patrol headquarters in Price."

"Take me in?"

"Escort you in."

"It takes two of you to escort me?"

"Deputy Tanner is here to ride along with you."

"Am I under arrest, Andy?"

"Trooper Smith," he said.

"Am I under arrest, Trooper Smith?"

"Not unless you refuse."

"Can I ask what this is about?"

The deputy spoke up. He had a thick neck and a broad chest. He puffed it out in case I might not have noticed. "You could. It wouldn't do you any good." His right hand on the butt of his gun, he reached around his back and produced a pair of handcuffs with his left. He rattled the cuffs between us. "What's your pleasure?"

It was clear to me Andy didn't care much more for his partner than I did. "No problem," I said. "I'd rather Andy ride with me. You're too tough. I might get hysterical and drive off the road. My insurance would go up."

The three of us spent a long minute listening to the wind roar between us. Though I didn't like the deputy, that wasn't why I wanted Trooper Smith to ride along with me. The bad weather meant it was going to be at least an hour's drive into Price. Maybe in that time Trooper Smith might turn back into Andy and tell me what the hell was going on.

Trooper Smith broke the standoff by simply walking to my truck. He stepped up on the running board and removed his hat. A gust of wind caught a small clump of wispy blond hair and stood it straight up. In the soiled red light he reminded me of the cartoon character Woody Woodpecker. For no reason I could fathom, I thought of Duncan Lacey's corpse in the refrigerator riding herd on the remaining cases of butter brickle ice cream. Without bothering to nod at Deputy Tanner, I followed Andy.

The deputy stood his useless ground while I maneuvered my rig onto 117. He still held the handcuffs, trying not to look like the last guest at a bad party. The wind took his hat. Our last glimpse of Deputy Tanner was as he chased his hat across the diner's parking lot. Nothing commands less respect than a barrel-chested cop chasing his hat, especially if he's holding handcuffs in one hand.

The wind rocked the cab from side to side. Neither one of us spoke. Nasty crosswinds howled loudly through the body fairing. We couldn't have heard each other speak if we had tried. The empty trailer was a metal sail. It caught the wind broadside, occasionally sending us snaking sideways onto the soft shoulder.

Andy took off his sunglasses and his hat.

Sooner or later there would be rain. The cauldron of wind and sand would stir up some moisture and the result would be even more messy and treacherous. Walt would stay on the ridge above the model home for as long as it took, no matter what the conditions. All night if necessary. This wasn't a possibility I wanted to consider. I cursed at the weather, forgetting about the sensitive ears of my Mormon passenger.

Once we had turned north toward Price at the junction with U.S. 191, the wind slapped harmlessly at the trailer from behind. The sun sank deeper into its brown bed.

Andy stared straight ahead toward Price. "You're an okay guy, Ben."

"But?"

"But I think you've really stepped in it this time."

"Stepped in it?" I repeated. "Is that an old Mormon saying? Or a legal assessment of my situation?" When he didn't say anything, I said, "I get it. This is serious. I'm telling you, for the record, I haven't committed a crime. I'm innocent."

My comment lit up a smile on Trooper Smith's face. "I doubt that."

"Are you going to tell me what this is about?"

"I don't know, Ben. That's the truth." Andy checked the side mirror. Deputy Tanner was riding our tail with every flashing light he had. Talking to the mirror, Andy said, "What I know is that all the big phones started ringing this morning. There were even bigger phones making the calls."

"How big?"

"Big. Attorney general. Special investigations captain." He whistled softly. "Governor."

I tapped the brakes. Deputy Tanner swerved onto the shoulder to avoid becoming a flashing blue and red suppository. "That explains the presence of Deputy Tanner," I said. "I guess the governor calling makes me an advancement opportunity."

"You staying out of trouble?"

When I said I was, he remarked that the condition of my face suggested otherwise.

"Walt Butterfield," I said, as if that should explain everything.

It did. Andy shook his head. "Last year he punched a tourist who refused to leave without getting a piece of pie." Trying to sound as if he were inquiring about nothing more important than the time of day, Andy asked, "Anything unusual happening on 117?"

It had been an interesting couple of weeks. I had discovered an abandoned housing development, gotten laid, and was in love. In the process I'd had the shit kicked out of me by an old man who, although he might be my best friend in the world, kept the corpse of his dead wife's rapist in his bathroom. Almost as an afterthought, there were both halves of a fugitive bank robber in my refrigerator unit.

"Unusual? You mean in general or for 117?"

"I mean like millions of dollars unusual."

I glanced over at Andy and felt my knuckles go white around the wheel. "No," I answered. "That would be unusual. UFOs. The occasional killing. Last year I heard about a talking dog, which, by the way, was true. The dog only spoke French. No one paid much attention. That's the usual. If everyone—man, woman, child, and talking dog—sold everything they had and then borrowed everything they could, among them they couldn't raise a million dollars. Except maybe Walt. Millions of dollars? Now, that would be unusual. The entire town of Rockmuse wouldn't bring more than a couple of dollars. That's if you could find a buyer."

"Millions are involved," he said. "That's all I know. And you, Ben. You're involved somehow. I'm just following orders. Doing any more is a couple of notches above my pay grade. Whether you know it or not, you stepped in something that smells. Being innocent probably won't help. If you were a Mormon it might not help."

Andy's remark about not being a Mormon struck a serious chord. I was no one, doing a nothing job a hundred miles up the asshole of nowhere. I wasn't a Mormon. I tried, more or less successfully, to convince myself that whatever the trouble was, it had nothing to do with Claire. Runaway wives didn't usually merit this kind of attention from the law. If they did, the local law wouldn't have time for the fun stuff like homicides and drugs. The idea that Claire and her husband might somehow be the source of my immediate woe wouldn't quite go away.

"I've been thinking of converting," I said.

Andy didn't respond, not that he needed to.

I'd heard that the Mormon church had been converting dead Jews for years, going that extra mile to save souls. Of course, I wasn't as worried about my soul as I was my skin. But saving the souls of long-dead Jews? This was exactly the kind of pioneering spirit you had to admire, if it didn't piss you off too much. It didn't sit all that well with the Jews. Recently they had struck a deal with the Mormons to knock it the hell off. No word from the souls on how they felt either way.

By comparison, run-of-the-mill evangelical Christians were a bunch of slackers. They confined their proselytizing to the living. All the same, I had a vision of church elders running around Jewish graves with nets, scooping souls out of the air like Hebrew butterflies that were destined to be dried and mounted with pins under glass on an LDS ancestry register. The thought made me laugh.

Andy took notice of the laugh. "Glad to see you still have a sense of humor. You're going to need it."

That was true. I hoped I had enough to go the distance. I'd be riding this problem out as I usually did, without a safety net. Like every other house-renting, paycheck-to-paycheck, heel-dragging working American, it wouldn't matter if I stepped in it by accident or was pushed, or simply whiffed it as I walked by. With the powers in play, guilt or innocence had nothing to do with anything.

Andy understood this reality as clearly as I did. The stink, real or imagined, had attached itself to me, and there was nothing I could do about it. I was a falling man. At this stage all I was really curious about was how the concrete was going to feel against my head. It was almost exciting.

Andy instructed me to drive my rig into the gated impound lot next to the squat brick one-story building that served as the local headquarters for the Utah Highway Patrol.

The parking lot in front of the entrance was full of cars. Most of them were Price City police and sheriff cruisers. It was a frightening display of jurisdictional camaraderie, like carrion eaters making elbow room for each other at a tiny buffet.

I set the brake, turned my engine off, and looked around the cab as if leaving home for good. At least the leasing company holding the paper wouldn't have to bother Bob to unlock the gates at the transfer station. Andy put on his hat and sunglasses.

I held out my wrists. "You want to accessorize me, Andy? I don't mind. Someone needs to look good. It might as well be you."

Andy peered out over the rims of his sunglasses. "No," he said. "I don't need to look good. I am good. I'm a Mormon." He forced a smile and slapped me on the shoulder. "Good luck, Ben."

I took a deep breath. "I'm going under, Andy. Bankrupt. I'm drowning in red ink. Today was my last run. If I'd stumbled across millions of dollars I'd know it. And I'd be a million miles away from here."

Andy shook his head. "Not a chance."

"What makes you so sure?"

"Everyone knows you've been struggling. Run off with millions of dollars?" The idea made him laugh. "You wouldn't take five dollars. You can't even bring yourself to collect what's owed you by the people who need you. You're a decent, honest man, Ben. Flawed, like all of us, but honest."

"Is that your professional opinion?"

"Better," he said. "That's my Mormon opinion. Not that it makes any difference."

"Can I ask you a favor?"

He nodded.

"Tell Walt where I'm at?"

Andy nodded again. "Anyone else?"

I thought of Ginny. "No," I said.

My door opened. Deputy Tanner jingled the handcuffs up at me. In a voice as quiet as iron and yet courteously measured, Trooper Smith leaned around me and said, "Get out of here, Tanner."

The deputy walked away like a spurned suitor. Andy said, "I'm not supposed to tell you, but this is just questioning, Ben. It might not turn out as bad as you think. Just don't be an asshole."

"Me? What happened to honest, decent?"

Andy sighed. "You are. But you are not exactly unknown to law enforcement around here. From time to time you have been an honest, decent, and stupid asshole. Don't make this worse. You have to trust."

Without much enthusiasm, I said, "I guess I'll trust the system then."

"Not the system, Ben. God."

"Okay," I said, knowing I had no choice. But I couldn't help remembering that advice hadn't worked out so well for Jesus.

36

Andy followed me through the side entrance down a narrow corridor lined with red brick and cops without pastries. They seemed
to be licking their fingers all the same.

I went through the metal detector, followed by the wand, and
then the pat-down followed by the wand again. They weren't taking any chances with a desperado like me. The fact that I didn't
set off any buzzers seemed to disappoint the crowd. Near as I
could tell, there were deputies from two counties, a handful of
Price officers, and a couple of Utah troopers, one still dressed in
jeans and a white T-shirt, as if he had been yanked off his sofa at
home. His badge was pinned to his shirt.

Andy opened a metal door stenciled with a black 1. It struck
me as a bit odd. I knew for certain there wasn't a 2 or a 3. He
pointed to a metal chair, one of two, at one end of a metal table,
one of one.

"Take a seat, Mr. Jones." I was Mr. Jones again, and Andy was
Trooper Smith.

There wasn't a one-way mirror. Law enforcement had gone
high tech. The black marble lenses of two cameras rested discreetly at opposite corners near the low ceiling of the tiny room.
I sat down. Experience had taught me that no matter how big a
hurry cops were to bring you in, once you got there you were in
for a wait. It was an opportunity to ferment your misdeeds and let

the little bubbles of fear rise to the surface. The hope was you'd pop like a champagne cork at the first question.

I rested my forearms on the cold table, folded my hands, closed my eyes, and climbed the hill above Desert Home. I saw Claire on her porch. She was waving good-bye to a man I had never met and, if my luck held, never would. He got into the compact SUV I'd seen earlier and prepared to leave with the only thing he cared about—the cello. It was as satisfying a daydream as I have ever had. I was startled when I heard his car door slam shut behind me—it was the door to the interrogation room. I kept my eyes closed.

The legs of the metal chair across from me screeched against the floor. Something large and soft landed on the table, probably a file. I smelled Right Guard deodorant and sweet tobacco. A man sat down and made himself comfortable. He stared quietly at my closed eyes. Another man stood behind me near the door.

After a while the man grew impatient watching my eyelids. "Do you play a musical instrument, Mr. Jones?"

Without opening my eyes, I said, "I'd have to say no. Though I confess I've played my own flute."

The man at the door stifled a hitch of laughter. A look passed between the two men. I felt it graze the side of my head. It was that kind of look.

The man at the door said, "Give this man your attention, Ben."

The man wasn't Andy. It was a familiar voice I couldn't place. He knew me well enough to call me by my first name, and he wasn't bothered by the informality. I let my eyelids drift slowly up to reveal the man in front of me one slice at a time. He wore a brown tweed jacket that was too small for him, a white shirt, and a red knit tie that strangled a thick neck. His thinning gray hair and the round rimless glasses he wore were out of place on such a large body. Even his mustache and goatee seemed too small for him. He looked like a retired NFL lineman who had awakened one day to find himself an overweight high school math teacher. He offered me his hand. "My name is Ralph Welper. My friends call me Doc."

We'd never met, but I knew who he was from Ginny's description. I ignored his hand. "Let's give it a few minutes," I said. "Maybe I'll come up with a name that better suits you."

I glanced over my shoulder to the man at the door. It had been a long time since I had last seen him. "Hello, Coach," I said, almost happy to see him. "Under the circumstances, should I call you Captain?"

"I always preferred Coach," he answered. "You don't have to address me at all. Just direct your responses to Mr. Welper. I'm only here as a kind of chaperone."

"For him or me?" I asked.

In addition to being in the Utah Highway Patrol, Dunphy had been my high school baseball coach. Usually teachers doubled as coaches. He was the exception. He had been an all-American in college, pitching for Brigham Young, followed by a year in the minors.

While I spent twenty years driving 117, Coach Dunphy had been transferred all over Utah as he moved up the ranks. I'd heard he'd made captain. At over six feet, he was still every bit of the lanky kid who at one time had the eleventh fastest pitch in the American League. He was casually leaning with his back against the closed door. His gun-blue uniform fit like a tailored suit. He didn't answer my question, not that I expected that he would.

Dunphy instructed me to take the man's hand.

I complied. Briefly.

Welper said, "I wasn't aware that you two were acquainted."

He was genial enough, but obviously bothered by the connection. "As pleased as I am to be the cause of your little reunion, I'd like to get down to business."

"That's fine," I said. "Can I ask you a question first?"

He nodded, eager to have the conversation under way.

"Is there a young kid, a teenage girl, or maybe a boy, in your neighborhood? Someone you're friendly with?" He was obviously surprised at my question. He shrugged. "Sure, a couple of them, I guess. Why do you ask?"

"I was just wondering if you were screwing one of them? How would you feel about me asking one of them if you were?"

Captain Dunphy barked my name in rebuke. Mr. Welper held up his hand to reassure the captain. He removed his round glasses and set them on the file folder between us. He knew I was referring to his conversation with Ginny. "I wouldn't like it one damn bit," he said. "But if doing so was part of your job, I'd understand it."

I turned toward the captain. "Why don't we ask Captain Dunphy what part of your job calls for talking to a pregnant teenage girl the way you did?" Welper didn't like the way our conversation was going. The captain shifted his weight against the door and said nothing. My guess was Dunphy didn't know of Welper's conversation with Ginny. He might not have cared even if he had known. I liked to think he might.

Welper apologized, except there wasn't any apology in it. He opened the file and skimmed the contents of the top page. When he was done he made a point of letting me know he was doing an inventory of bruises and scabs on my face. "It seems you have a taste for violence, Mr. Jones. Several years ago you shot and almost killed a man."

"I shot him with his own gun. He was trying to rob me."

"Understandable. Did you think you missed him with the first three shots?"

I didn't answer.

"And the drunk and disorderlies here?"

"That was a long time ago," I answered. "In my own defense I admit I was drunk. I wasn't all that disorderly. It's a fine distinction cops don't always appreciate."

"What about the man you beat so badly he took his meals through a straw for six months? Was he trying to rob you?"

"No," I said. "I objected to his sense of humor. Like I said, I was younger then. I'd probably object differently these days. Maybe not. The point is, those charges never came to much. Simple assault. Time served. Ten days if I remember right."

"I'm curious," he said. "Seems like an extreme reaction to what it says here was just a joke."

"Depends on the joke," I said.

Captain Dunphy pushed himself away from the door and walked quickly to the table. He leaned on his hands between us. "I'll tell it just like Ben heard it. Then you decide, Mr. Welper. Then I'll expect you to move on.

"One night in a bar a forty-year-old roughneck learns that Ben here is an orphan, maybe half Indian and half Jewish. He says he heard a joke that reminded him of Ben. A boy goes home to his mother and father. His mother is Jewish and his father is African American, though that isn't the word he used. The boy says he has a problem. He wants to buy a neighbor kid's bicycle. The parents ask him what the problem is. The boy says since he's half Jew and half black he can't decide whether to Jew the kid down or just steal the motherfucker. The roughneck says to Ben, 'Since you're an Indian, what would you do, chief? Jew him down or just get drunk and forget about it?'"

Welper stared at me. I imagined a window behind him.

"What's the matter, Mr. Welper?" Dunphy asked. "You're not laughing. Neither did the judge, who, by the way, was Jewish. The charges were reduced. The judge made Ben promise to control his temper and his drinking. To my knowledge he's made good on both."

Welper pushed himself away from the table. "Mr. Jones's face tells a different story," he said. "I need a word alone with you, Captain," he said.

When Welper had left the room, I said to Dunphy, "Walt Butterfield."

The captain nodded. "I know. Trooper Smith told me." Keeping his voice low, he said, "I'm going out in the hall to have a word with Mr. Welper. When we come back in you both better have a change of attitude. I don't like him or the way he operates. To answer your question, I'd say I'm here as much for you as him. If I were you, I wouldn't count too much on the past. Mr. Welper doesn't know God, but he has friends who do. Together they got the old man out of bed for this one."

I thought about Andy's advice. I had to trust someone. Captain Dunphy wasn't God, but for someone in my position he was close enough. I wouldn't argue the point. "Why am I here?"

"That's a good question. Welper has a good answer. Or thinks he does. If he doesn't tell you, I sure as hell will. I don't give a shit. I'm forty-one days away from retirement. They can all kiss my Jack Mormon ass. I just hope you haven't done anything stupid, Ben." He left the room.

A few minutes later they returned. Welper slid a glossy eight-by-ten photograph toward me. "You know that man?"

"Yes," I said. It was a photo of Josh Arrons. He was in a workshop of some kind. Several parts of cellos and violins were suspended from the wall behind him. I thought of Claire waiting for me and forced myself to perk up for Welper's benefit. I hadn't been the valedictorian of my high school class, but I tried to put the same tone of exuberant innocence into my answer. "He's a reality television producer."

"That's what he told you. I'm an insurance investigator. The truth is, he is working with me. Or was. My company insures the most valuable cello in the world. That cello is missing."

"Damn," I said, ignoring the news that Josh wasn't who he said he was. "What's the most valuable cello in the world worth?"

"You already know that, Mr. Jones. In the neighborhood of twenty million dollars."

"What makes you think I know anything about a twenty-million-dollar cello?"

He shot me a self-satisfied smirk. He couldn't wait to tell me how smart he was. "Not long after the cello disappeared—stolen, really—my company put up a website. Innocuous appearing. It was a long shot. You spent two minutes and thirty-six seconds on the Internet reading about that cello. Our IT people were tracing your computer through its IP address. There were a few other hits on the site. None for longer than a minute. But you, Mr. Jones, you rang all the bells. The woman who stole the cello took a flight from New York to Denver. She didn't rent a car or take public transportation. Someone picked her up at the airport. The surveillance cameras at the airport lost her. Colorado borders Utah."

"The cameras lost a woman with a cello in the airport? You'd think a woman with a cello would have been easy to track."

"She didn't have the cello with her. And she didn't check it. I wish she had. Suppose you tell me why a high-school-educated truck driver, and occasional self-taught flute player, was on his employer's computer researching rare cellos at five in the morning? A computer he uses maybe twice a year to check billing and weather? And why he lied when his boss asked him about it?"

"I lied because I didn't want to tell him I was reading up on cellos. If I have to explain that to you, you're an idiot. You really think I might have something to do with your missing cello?"

"Maybe. Maybe not," he answered. "You might have possibly wandered across it. Have you?"

"I might have," I said. "There's all kinds of shit lying around in the desert."

Welper glanced over to the captain, who told me to answer the question.

"Sure," I said, "I saw *a* cello. I don't know if it's the one you're searching for. The one I saw was missing its price tag."

I did know. I knew Claire had to be the woman in the airport. I assumed Walt had been the one who picked her up in Denver. What I didn't know was that the cello was worth twenty million dollars. Or if Walt knew she had the cello. Or even if he cared one way or the other. What I did know was that it didn't make any difference to me. It did explain a little about why the husband's priorities got derailed. I did know why she didn't have the cello with her at the airport, not that it mattered much now. Some of the odd freight Walt had received must have been the cello. I couldn't help smiling even as I realized Claire hadn't been completely honest with me.

Welper leaned across the table. "You're smiling, Mr. Jones. That tells me you're thinking when you should be talking. You don't seem all that shocked to learn that the cello you saw is worth twenty million dollars."

"Twenty million doesn't mean anything to me."

"Why's that? Are you a rich man, Mr. Jones?"

"You know I'm not. It's the other way around. The cash register in my head won't ring up twenty million. It's unreal. I can't even imagine an amount like that. It has no more meaning to me than moon rocks. Now, if you'd said fifty grand, that would have shocked me. Twenty million for a piece of old wood?"

Welper cringed. "Where did you see this old piece of wood?

"Out in the desert."

"Exactly where out in the desert?"

"A woman had it."

Welper pulled another photograph from the file. "Is this the woman?"

Of course, it was. "That's her," I said, hoping he might forget that I'd been vague in my answer to his question about where I'd seen the cello. "What's her name?"

"Claire Tichnor. Exactly where and when did you see Mrs. Tichnor?"

"Out on 117. Her car was broken down," I lied. "My memory would be a lot clearer if you'd just come to me when you first suspected I had information."

I shrugged and tried to look like a helpless high-school-educated truck driver. It was a role I was born to play. "I didn't care about the damn cello. I just thought if I ever saw her again I might impress her by knowing something about cellos. That's why I was on the Internet at five in the morning. Jesus, what do I know about cellos?"

"That's what you thought, was it? Take a few minutes on the web and increase your odds of getting laid?" Welper laughed. "Maybe with one of your local barflies. You'd need a million years to have a chance with a woman like that."

I wanted to tell him how quickly a million years goes by in the desert. I kept my mouth shut.

"But that's what your little girlfriend thought, too—there had to be a woman."

There it was. My little girlfriend. Mentioning Ginny that way straightened my spine just as Welper expected it would. "Yeah," I said, "my *friend*. Why else would I go to Walmart in the middle of the night looking for cello music?"

"When did you see Mrs. Tichnor?"

I answered as if he were asking about the first and only time I'd seen her. "I'm not sure. The day before I got on the computer. Whenever that was. You'd know better than I would."

"Where are Mrs. Tichnor and the cello now?"

I shrugged. "I couldn't tell you. It's a big damn desert."

"You're holding back, Mr. Jones. That's not a smart move. There's more at stake than just a rare cello. A lot more."

"I think we've already established I'm not very smart. The question now is, how stupid am I? What could be more stupid than someone like me lying to someone like you about a twenty-million-dollar cello?"

"I can think of two. Kidnapping. Maybe murder."

37

I shouted, "I don't know anything about a kidnapping or murder!"

Captain Dunphy didn't waste any time getting to the table. "Neither do I," he said. "That's the first I've heard of it." He demanded a chair and a notepad from one of the cameras. In the few seconds it took for the items to arrive, he towered over Welper, grim and silent.

"Up till now we've been having technical difficulties with the tape." He spoke to the camera. "I've been assured that it's now functioning properly."

I understood. Until a minute ago Welper's connections had kept my interrogation off the record. That had changed in a big way. The expression on Welper's face told me he was aware of the change, and he wasn't happy.

I settled down. "I think maybe somebody ought to read me my rights," I said. I was reasonably certain Claire couldn't have had anything to do with a kidnapping or murder. The same for Walt. Of course there was the little matter of the corpse he'd kept in his bathroom. I began to wonder about Claire. About both of them. Maybe I was just the stupid truck driver everyone thought I was.

Dunphy said, "You're not under arrest. Yet. You are here voluntarily." He waited, daring me to disagree. When I didn't, he said, "But you're correct, Mr. Jones. And I'll start with Mr. Welper here. You have the right to remain—"

Welper blustered. "You're joking."

Dunphy continued until he was finished. "Do you understand these rights as I have explained them to you?"

Welper nodded.

"Say yes or no. Clearly."

Welper said, "Yes." He waived his right to have an attorney present.

Dunphy did the same for me, and he said to both of us, "From here on out, I will be asking the questions. I'll start with you, Mr. Welper. A moment ago you suggested you had knowledge of a kidnapping and murder."

Welper got busy trying to backpedal. "It's a possibility. I have no direct knowledge of either." It wasn't working.

"Let's start with everything of which you do have direct knowledge."

"We don't have time . . ."

Dunphy cut him off. "If you'd started out the right way, you wouldn't feel so pressed for time. Trust me, Mr. Welper, we *do* have the time."

Welper whispered, "Are you sure you want to do this?"

It sounded like a warning to me. It must have sounded the same way to Dunphy. He responded that he was absolutely sure. He expressed his certainty in a voice that could have been recorded from the parking lot.

Welper was still trying to act as if nothing had changed. Somewhere in his head he was still convinced he was running the show. "I don't want the truck driver here."

Dunphy seemed to be thinking Welper had a good point. I pushed my chair clear of the table. I was okay with leaving, if only as far as the hallway. "Mr. Jones," the captain said, "stays put. Remember, he's here at your invitation. Just one of the many courtesies I was asked to extend. Those courtesies have expired, Mr. Welper."

I was content to be a spectator for the better part of an hour. I wasn't particularly interested in Claire's life before she arrived at Desert Home. I closed my eyes and did my best to send a message to Welper and Dunphy that I wasn't interested. Several times I tried to imagine myself under the archway above Desert Home. I wanted the sun on my face and to see Claire on the porch, alone, looking up at me. I couldn't manage it. I was listening to every word and getting an education I didn't want about cellos and Claire's past.

The captain stopped Welper from time to time to scribble and ask follow-up questions, stating and restating what had been said, moving backward but never forward. Or so it seemed. He knew his job and exactly how to do it. Claire had pretty much told me the truth, which was a relief. For his part, Welper had been telling the truth as well, what little he had been willing to share before Dunphy took over. I only got a few surprises. None of them had anything to do with kidnapping and murder.

When Claire was a senior in college she used all of the inheritance from her adoptive parents to buy an option, a first right of refusal, on a very rare cello, the same cello described on the website. Five hundred thousand dollars. At the time, it was owned by one of her college professors. He needed the money and didn't want to sell the cello while he was alive. It had been in his family for generations. He was fond of Claire. The opportunity to buy the cello in the future was an expression of his admiration for her talent. He had considered Claire his most gifted student. Welper added, with a sick wink, that maybe what the professor, who was in his fifties, really admired was an altogether different set of gifts.

Dunphy made a point of ignoring the comment.

Upon the death of the professor, whenever that might be, Claire would have the right to match any bid when his estate put the cello up for auction. If Claire happened to predecease him, the option money, which was otherwise nonrefundable or unassignable to a third party, would be returned to her estate from the proceeds of the sale. The professor was a cagey old fellow. The cello could not be purchased by Claire and resold. At least not for twenty-five years. How Claire might raise the eventual sale price, which she must have been aware could be in the millions, was not known. At twenty-one, she probably hadn't thought that far ahead.

Three years ago the professor died, and the cello went to auction. Claire had been married for a long time. She had given up playing the cello to support her husband. Not long before the cello was to be auctioned, her husband acquired a girlfriend. Not just any girlfriend, a beautiful young Chinese national from Hong Kong who was a rising star as a violinist. She also had a doting and very wealthy father who had embraced capitalism long before China made it officially possible. Welper thought the appearance of a wealthy girlfriend months before the auction was more than a coincidence. Who had engineered the coincidence, the husband or the girlfriend, was difficult to know.

A chance to purchase this particular cello would have brought out the opportunism in a lot of people—investors and collectors, as well as musicians. The relationship benefited everyone but Claire. Daddy, who came up with the millions to exercise the option, benefited most. Claire was told only that a group of foreign investors had loaned them the money, in exchange for which the husband retained exclusive but restricted use of the cello for his lifetime. The investors retained the right to "showcase" the cello internationally for at least one month a year, with or without the husband. Claire signed off on the deal.

As soon as the ink was dry on the sale, the husband filed for divorce. It was, in Welper's words, a rocky divorce. It only got rockier when the judge ruled that while the "first right of refusal" was Claire's alone, she would receive no monetary compensation for the husband's use of the cello. In effect, the husband was awarded sole custody of their major asset, which was not an asset at all, just a simple right to access—a form of straw purchase that met, though just barely, the terms of the professor's option. The husband's attorney argued that possession of the cello was essential to Mr. Tichnor's livelihood as a professional musician.

Welper took a deep breath. "Maybe the worst part for the former Mrs. Tichnor wasn't losing the cello. She quickly learned not just of the girlfriend, but of the father's financial involvement. In effect, Mrs. Tichnor lost the cello, her husband, and her five hundred thousand, with the former husband as the beneficiary. The final insult came when the judge ordered Mrs. Tichnor to pay the husband spousal support for five years."

Dunphy asked, "That's when the wife stole the cello?"

"Yes and no," Welper answered. "She played nice for a couple of months. Even made the first few spousal support payments. Then she attempted to kill the ex-husband. Poison. Or that was the initial assumption. I don't think she planned to kill him. It was part of a plan to steal the cello. She met him at a midtown bar in the afternoon. He later said she just wanted to say good-bye and good luck. No hard feelings and so on, as if there were a chance in hell. Anyway, he agreed. An hour later he was rushed to the hospital. She even went with him, the concerned and still-loving ex-wife. Also part of the plan, I think. It wasn't until two days later that the doctors told him he had been poisoned. Tough to prove. No charges were filed. Not yet.

"The same evening as Mr. Tichnor lay in the hospital, Mrs.

Tichnor showed up where the Chinese princess was playing a charity benefit for the Manhattan Friends of Chamber Music. Dressed in an evening gown, she casually made her way through the social upper crust of New York. After chatting with various people and sipping champagne, she approached the other woman, who had just taken her place for the evening's featured event. No one was paying much attention. She said a few words to the princess, which no one heard and the princess said she couldn't remember. She grabbed the violin from the woman's hands—a violin worth a quarter of a million, which thankfully my company didn't insure—and swung it like a baseball bat. She hit the princess hard enough to knock her out of her chair. In the turmoil that followed she calmly walked out and disappeared."

It took every ounce of concentration to keep my eyes closed. Dunphy said, "You getting all this, Mr. Jones?"

I didn't respond. I was getting all of it, even the parts I could barely stand to hear. Claire had a temper. The temper troubled me. Welper was right, Claire's temper was of the worst variety—cool and methodical. Returning the gun to Walt had been a damn good idea. There had to be another reason why she knocked the princess out of the park, especially in front of so many witnesses, not that she needed another reason. Either way, Claire's temper was a good reason for Welper to fear for the safety of the cello.

According to Welper, Claire had taken the keys to the husband's practice studio in a secure building. Probably on the way to the hospital. People at the building had been used to seeing her.

"The next day, while the husband was in the hospital and the princess was recovering from largely superficial head wounds, no one knew the cello was missing. She had given herself a head start. Mrs. Tichnor disappeared. She had been smart enough to use her employer's account to buy a plane ticket to Denver. Four hours before departure. In her own name. She was also smart enough to make it round-trip. Ever since 9/11, one-way tickets have been scrutinized. One-way tickets are the first to get attention."

Dunphy asked, "Why did Mrs. Tichnor come to Utah?"

Welper answered that he had no idea. The husband said she had made the trip at least once before. Mr. Tichnor didn't know why. At the time they were going through the divorce and were not on speaking terms.

"How did she get the cello out here?"

"We don't know that either. We weren't even certain she had the cello with her here." Welper glanced at me. "An accomplice maybe. She's a loner. No family or close friends. It's not like she could just put a twenty-million-dollar cello in an envelope and mail it to herself. We checked all the high-value transport companies. Until Mr. Jones here, we thought she might have even destroyed it. Its size makes it bulky. I don't think her plan was to demand payment for its return. It doesn't really matter. She's here now. Or was. And she has the cello."

Dunphy asked to see the police report. Welper fumbled with his glasses and took his time responding. When he did, the answer surprised me. It also surprised Dunphy.

"What do you mean a report was never filed? How can a twenty-million-dollar cello get stolen and a police report not get filed?"

"The consensus was we had a better chance at recovery if we kept the police out of it. This was not a professional theft. It was the result of a domestic dispute. If it was just about money the cello would have been safer in the hands of a pissed-off ex-wife." He shrugged. "Anyway, I agreed. That's also the way the princess and her father wanted it. So did Mr. Tichnor."

Dunphy raised his voice. "And yet, Mr. Welper, here we are. Just mushrooms. Kept in the dark and fed shit."

Welper didn't have a response. The expression on Dunphy's face told him that no response was best.

"Just so I'm clear, no reports on the theft or poisoning? Or the assault?"

Welper nodded.

"So you and your company just thought you'd show up out here in Utah and do whatever you damn well pleased. Is that about it?"

Welper said he had notified the Price police, who had been cooperating.

"They should have known better," Dunphy said. "They might not have been so cooperative if you had been more forthcoming with the details."

"Mr. Jones acted suspiciously, so we assumed he was involved. I still think he is. I think the cello is still in Utah, along with Mrs. Tichnor."

"What constitutes suspicious behavior in your world?"

"Same as in your world, Captain. When someone doesn't act the way he might rationally be expected to behave."

Dunphy ordered me to open my eyes.

Welper had produced a photograph of my distressed motorist, Carrie. "You recognize her?"

I asked if I could get my wallet out. I tossed the photo Howard Purvis had taken across the table next to the captain.

"She flagged me down on 191," I said. "She wasn't dressed like a working girl. Just the opposite. She was very friendly. I declined her friendliness. Another truck driver had seen her. He happened to see her downtown the next day and took this photo just in case. We thought maybe she was setting me up for a hijack."

Captain Dunphy said, "You hired a prostitute to get close to

Mr. Jones? And when that didn't work you assumed he was acting suspiciously?"

For the first time Welper got his blood up. "Ms. Delacroix is not a prostitute. She's a trained field investigator. Mr. Jones claimed he had a wife and kids at home. He was very convincing. Ms. Delacroix said she almost believed him. Yes, I'd call that suspicious behavior. Why would a single red-blooded American male walk away from an attractive opportunity if he wasn't hiding something? Especially a truck driver?"

"He just told you. What Mr. Jones isn't saying is something you wouldn't understand anyway. Right now the only person who looks bad here is you, Mr. Welper. Now tell me about the television producer."

"When Mr. Jones wasn't interested in Ms. Delacroix, we had to come up with another plan on short notice. Once again he acted suspiciously. We asked for and received the cooperation of the freight company." Welper added, "It took some convincing, but Jones went for it."

I said, "Yeah, I'm stupid and gullible. On the other hand, I have a couple grand and you have nothing. I'm curious—was Bob Fulwiler in on that?"

Welper smiled. "No. We set that up through corporate. He was easier than you. It was almost sad how enthusiastic he was. Not like you. We couldn't understand why a truck driver wouldn't jump at a chance to be a reality television star. Again, unless he had something to hide. And you certainly acted like you had something to hide. Josh practically had to beg you to let him ride along with you. Even then you kept him in your truck most of the time."

Dunphy was running on an empty patience tank with Welper. He was fighting his disgust and fatigue by taking longer pauses between questions, carefully choosing his words. "I know exactly why Ben here didn't want to be on television. It's pretty much the same reason any decent human being with an ounce of self-respect and a normal desire for privacy would have. There are some people who don't yearn to be celebrities by flying their laundry for a camera. The reason you think it's suspicious doesn't have anything to do with being an insurance investigator. It has everything to do with who you are."

Dunphy's disgust was tinged toward anger. "You roll into Utah and set up shop. You have a prostitute—excuse me, field investigator—take a run at Mr. Jones. When he declines, that makes him seem suspicious. You follow that by dangling some asinine reality show. When he doesn't want to open up his life for the entertainment of millions of viewers, he's even more suspicious."

The captain abruptly stood. "You're free to go, Ben." Then to Welper, "And I'd like to tell you what you're free to do. Instead I'll just tell you you're free to go as well. As long as it's out of Utah. And take your field agents with you. When and if a stolen property report is filed, give us a call. Long distance."

38

I wasn't waiting to be asked again. I was up and moving with no intention of slowing down for any parting pleasantries.

Dennis was on his way back to New York with the cello. At least I hoped he was. I was eager to see if Claire had stayed behind. With the divorce and the girlfriend, the odds that she would be waiting for me seemed better than ever. Besides Claire's temper, the biggest surprise was that she had led me to believe the divorce wasn't final. The only reason she might lead me to think otherwise was to keep me at a distance. Maybe she knew in her heart that even though the divorce was done, she and Dennis weren't. They would always have unfinished business. The cello was just the box where they kept it.

Welper didn't move from his chair. "I can't leave without Mr. Arrons."

"Can't or won't?" Dunphy grabbed my arm. "Not so quick, Ben."

Welper's voice was soft, almost resigned. "I can't. I won't. My son-in-law is missing. I'm afraid he's gotten in over his head."

"What's your son-in-law got to do with this?"

"My son-in-law is Josh Arrons." Welper was suddenly uncomfortable. "He's not exactly a trained investigator."

Dunphy sighed. "What *exactly* is he?"

"A cello maker. A luthier. I invited him along because I thought

he might be useful in identifying the del Gesù cello. He was supposed to stay put in Price at the Holiday Inn and wait until we
called him. When Ms. Delacroix failed, we had to put something
else together in a hurry. He was available. I thought it would be
safe enough. If he'd done just what he was supposed to it would
have been. Unfortunately, he took matters into his own hands."

Dunphy was unmoved. "Missing is not the same as kidnapping or homicide. File a missing-person report. Or maybe you'd
prefer to keep the police out of it. As usual."

"I'll do whatever I need to do. Please. I'm afraid he's been the
victim of some kind of foul play. Forcefully detained. Badly hurt.
Even murdered."

"I think you're overreacting. Why would he take off on his own?"

Welper sent a grim nod in my direction. "If Mr. Jones hadn't
turned Ms. Delacroix down, Mr. Arrons wouldn't have been involved. She'd never failed before. She certainly never failed with
someone like Jones. Packed up her wounded pride and left town
in a huff. So we improvised with the reality show story. I was in
Logan running down another lead when Josh got the idea to follow
Mr. Jones. By the time I got back, Josh had rented a Jeep in Moab.
He left me a note at the hotel. Probably because he didn't want me
to stop him. The note said he was going to follow Mr. Jones."

"What day was that?"

"He rented the Jeep on Friday. The note was written early
Saturday morning. No word from him since the note."

Dunphy said, "Ben?"

"He was in one of those fire-engine-red Moab rental Jeeps," I
said. "Hard to miss. But I don't know where he is now. I kind of
liked the guy. Those Jeeps usually have homing beacons in them.
Check the rental company."

"Did that first thing this morning," Welper said. "He rented the Jeep for a week. The beacon must have malfunctioned. They aren't getting a signal. Maybe it's been disconnected."

Dunphy was out of patience. "File your report. It hasn't even been seventy-two hours. If he hasn't shown up in another day or two, I'll authorize the search. That's the best I can do."

Welper wasn't about to leave it alone. He was begging. "Can't you start the search tonight? I'll pick up the bill. Every penny. Overtime. Whatever it takes. Whatever your opinion of me, just put it aside. Money is no object."

Dunphy said, "Mr. Welper, of the few certainties I've come across in life, one of them is that when a person says money is no object, the opposite is most likely true. Money is the only object—or will be."

"If you can get the ball rolling, I'll write a check right now."

Dunphy was still on top of his game. "You seem to be in a big hurry. It makes me think there's something you haven't told me. I'm giving you one chance. What is it?"

This was not a time to hold back. Welper didn't, though he took his time getting started. "I was confident Jones would have some answers. I still think he knows more than he's saying. It doesn't seem like I'm going to get any more. Now I'm worried."

"About what? Be specific," Dunphy asked.

"The father of the Chinese princess is a businessman. You know what I mean?"

"You mean he's a criminal?"

"Yes," Welper said. "Powerful, slick, and untouchable. From what I hear, methodical and ruthless. He's not the kind to file a police report. He's the kind to take back what's his in his own way. Whatever and whoever it takes. We had a gentleman's agreement that he'd stay out of it for two weeks. Those two weeks are up. For all I know he's got his people on the ground here in Utah.

With his resources he probably knows as much as I do. Including about Mr. Jones here. Probably more."

"Why would a cello maker risk getting crosswise with Chinese thugs? And alone at that?" Dunphy knew the answer. He wanted Welper to say it.

"I didn't tell him about the Chinese thugs. There was no need. He was supposed to stay out of the way. Maybe he would have taken off anyway. I think maybe he wanted to impress me and come home a hero to my daughter. It was stupid."

"Not as stupid as you've been. If he's found trouble, it will all be on your head." Dunphy said he'd return in a few minutes, and left the room.

"Does Mrs. Tichnor know about the father's line of work?" I asked.

There was a lot going on behind Welper's eyes. "Not at first. Probably now. She's smart. Everything she's done has been carefully planned. Why do you care?"

"I just do," I said. "I care about your son-in-law, too. Probably more than you do. I think what you're really afraid of is how your daughter will react if harm has come to her husband."

My concern about Ginny had been growing. Maybe Welper and his crew hadn't been the only ones watching me. I wasn't too concerned about Claire. At least her safety. She had Walt and the secret of Desert Home. But Ginny couldn't say the same. Even if the Chinese weren't responsible for Ginny's disappearance, Welper might be, one way or the other. He seemed like the kind of man who might do anything if he convinced himself it was part of his job, even leveraging Ginny to get to me. If he thought I was holding out, or if I'd done something to his son-in-law, he might have taken Ginny as a bargaining chip. She was pregnant. She had no one. She was the only personal link to me that he knew about.

Which meant that the father's camp could have made the connection as well.

"If it's any consolation," I said, "I don't think there are any Chinese poking around 117. There aren't many people out there. A car full of Chinese would stick out like a sore thumb."

Welper screwed up his face so I would know he thought I was an idiot. "Don't you think they would know that? With all the wars going on, the world is filled with highly trained mercenaries. It's a growth industry. I strongly doubt he'd use Asians for exactly that reason. Men in Han's position have their own private armies on retainer."

"It doesn't matter," I said patiently. "If you'd only lived out there for ten years, you'd still be considered a stranger. The same goes for the town of Rockmuse. They can spot outsiders from a mile away. No matter what color they are. If there are people poking around and asking questions, I'd say there is a better chance they'd be the ones to disappear."

"That would be the case with Josh as well, wouldn't it?" he asked.

I didn't want to admit it. I had to agree that it would.

Welper dropped his chin. He leaned across the table and lowered his voice. "Now let me tell you what I think. I think you know a whole lot more than you've said. I'm a little off balance because of Josh, but I'm damn good at what I do. You've got your former coach running interference for you. Enjoy it, because it won't last long. I've got cards I haven't played yet. If you're between me and Mrs. Tichnor and that cello, you are between the proverbial rock and a hard place. I guarantee you this: you will get crushed. If you've had any part in bringing harm to my son-in-law, any part at all, I will come after you. If you have information, now is the time. The last time. Don't hesitate. Don't hold back. Do you understand?"

I thought about what he'd said. "I might be able to help with Josh. Not because of you or the cello, or anything else but Josh."

"Let's hear it."

"Let me finish," I said. "You said your piece. Here's mine. My little friend, as you call her, has been missing for a couple of days. Maybe she's one of those unplayed cards you just mentioned. You know anything about that?"

"Not a thing," he said. "I only talked to her that one time." He sounded convincing. He should have stopped right there. He didn't. "Kids like that go missing all the time. Drugs. Alcohol. One bad choice after another. Most show up eventually. Some don't. And when they don't, it's not a big loss to society. In fact, sad though it might be, it's a blessing. Kids like that are a drain on everyone else. My guess is that she'll show up. Now tell me what you know about Josh."

It had been quite some time since I'd gone after someone in a blind rage. It took every ounce of self-control I had to keep from going after Welper. I took a few shallow breaths. "Let me tell you about my little friend," I said. "She's bright as hell. Sure, she's made some mistakes. Who hasn't? But she's seventeen, homeless, alone, pregnant. She works the night shift. She's going to college."

Welper cocked his head to one side. He enjoyed my speech and the anger behind it. To his way of thinking he was gaining the upper hand. "Well," he said. "I guess I had your little friend all wrong. Make sure I get an invitation when she graduates from Stanford."

We sat for a minute without speaking. I relaxed a bit and worked up a smile for him. "I'll do that," I said. "But let me tell you what's going to happen if she gets hurt because of you. And by hurt, I mean anything from simple inconvenience to death, hers or the baby's." I let him wait. "Nothing. Not a damn thing."

Welper laughed. "Nothing? You need to brush up on how to make a threat."

"No threat. Nothing," I said calmly. "Because I'm nothing. I'm just a high-school-educated truck driver. I'm probably not even that anymore. I'm in debt. My rig is about to be repossessed. I have no family. I'm not even a Mormon. I'm broke. If it weren't for the money Josh paid me, I wouldn't have enough money to eat. You can do any shitty thing you want to Ginny and me, or anyone else that gets in your way. You can say it's not you, it's the job. You have power. I understand power. I understand it the only way someone without power can understand."

"What's your point?"

"No point." I shrugged. "I'm invisible. I have nothing to lose. I think your cello will show up. I think Josh will show up. I think you'll go home and go on being successful and powerful. You'll get even more powerful friends to call when you need a favor. You'll forget you ever met me. This whole cello deal will be a story that won't even entertain your grandchildren. Then some night you'll be in your bed. Not asleep, just drifting maybe, that time when small, unimportant things go through your head. Maybe during one of those times I will be an answer to one of your life's trivia questions, the truck driver in Utah. Just for a second or two. Maybe in those seconds you'll think of Ginny, too. You'll think for those couple of seconds that people like us who don't count and have no power just might be the most powerful and dangerous people in the world. The thought will go as quickly as it came. You will sleep like the dead."

"Now *that* sounds like a threat."

"Strange it sounds that way to you. All I remember saying is that nothing will happen. Nothing at all. Sometime in the future."

When Dunphy came back in, Welper and I were sitting quietly. He paused at the door and took in the silence and the two of us. "Looks like I missed something important."

"Nothing at all," I said.

Welper was busy trying to stare me down.

Dunphy said, "We'll start looking for your son-in-law tomorrow."

Welper thanked the captain. "Mr. Jones was just telling me he thought he could be of assistance in locating my son-in-law."

"Is that true?"

"I can show search and rescue the general area where I last saw him. It might not help, but it's a place to start."

"Can you make a map?"

I told him it would be better if I could just show them. The captain said he understood. "Be here tomorrow by ten."

Welper stood. "One more thing," he said, "I'd like to take a look inside Mr. Jones's truck and trailer."

"You'll need a warrant for that. Unless Mr. Jones has no objection."

I did object. For a moment I didn't know why. "No," I said.

My answer didn't sit well with Dunphy. "That's your right, Mr. Jones. Mr. Welper here will make a few calls, and a judge will sign a warrant. It will take some time. Meanwhile, your truck and trailer will stay in our impound lot. The warrant will take even less time if I think we need one. I'm beginning to think it would be a good idea."

There was only a small chance they wouldn't find Duncan's remains wrapped up with the ice cream. If they did find it, all I had to do was tell the truth. Not so good for Fergus. Under the circumstances, I had no choice. I might have had to tell the truth anyway. I hadn't had much time to consider what I was going to do with the body that wouldn't lead to Fergus going to jail, which was where he belonged.

"Go ahead. I don't have anything to hide," I said. Probably what everyone who has something to hide says.

The corridor was empty. The three of us walked out into the dimly lit impound lot. The wind had died down. The damp air was charged with electricity. I felt the hairs on the back of my neck move as if insects were crawling under my skin. A bolt of lightning flashed to the south under rolling fists of dense clouds. A few seconds later came the thunder. I lifted the sliding door, exposing the empty trailer. Several bursts of lightning splintered the dark horizon. Dunphy paid no attention. He aimed his flashlight into the trailer. Welper and I looked out toward the lightning. Maybe he was thinking of Josh. I was imagining Claire again, and Walt. It was going to be one hell of a night out on 117.

Dunphy hoisted himself up into the trailer. "I don't see anything. It looks empty to me."

Welper struggled to get a meaty leg high enough for a foothold up into the trailer. "Give me a hand."

I thought about giving him a hand with my foot. Dunphy flashed the beam in Welper's face. "Stay where you are."

Welper insisted he was coming up. Dunphy repeated his order. Welper got a foothold and stood waist-high against the open door searching for a way to pull himself the rest of the way up. Dunphy nudged him back down to the ground with the toe of a boot.

Welper hit the ground and dropped to one knee. "I'm coming up," he insisted. He was the dumbest smart guy I'd ever met. "Don't make me go over your head, Captain."

I couldn't believe my ears, but Dunphy did. "You've already been over my head," he said. "I'll be damned if I'll have you up my ass." Welper put his fingers on the edge of the trailer floor right where Dunphy's boot heel could find them. He swore as he jumped backward and stayed where he was.

The two of us watched as Dunphy's flashlight beam bounced around the walls and floor of the trailer. It seemed as if he might stop and not go any further. I began to think that would be the end of it. The beam found the chrome handle that opened the small door to the refrigerator unit at the far end of the trailer. He opened the door and squeezed himself through. He was inside for a few minutes. I thought I heard him moving around in the cramped compartment. He came out carrying something.

"What's that?" Welper asked.

Dunphy tossed a half-gallon carton of butter brickle ice cream up and down in his left hand. "Butter brickle ice cream. My wife loves this stuff. Can I buy this from you, Ben?"

I told him he could have it.

"No gifts," he said. "It might be construed as a bribe."

"Ten dollars," I said, and put out my palm.

"Bullshit," he replied. "I'll give you five."

He hopped down from the trailer and handed the ice cream to Welper while he extracted five dollars from his wallet. Welper stared at the ice cream and continued to hold the carton while Dunphy went through the cubbyholes and glove box in my cab. He was thorough. He checked under the seats and above the visors. "We're done here."

"Can I go now?" I asked.

He told me to wait a minute and turned his attention to Welper. "Mr. Welper, be here tomorrow morning at nine to fill out a missing-person report on Mr. Arrons. If you're not here or you don't fill out a report, wherever he is, that's where he'll stay until you do."

Welper walked away, still holding the carton of ice cream. After a few steps, he turned and threw the carton at Dunphy. It missed and bounced harmlessly off a tire.

It was an amusing little tantrum. "Isn't that an attempted assault on a police officer?" I said.

"Technically," Dunphy said. "But what self-respecting lawman could write that up without laughing?"

I climbed into the cab and told Captain Dunphy I would be back at ten as promised.

"You and I need to talk about Duncan Lacey." He let what he'd said sink in. "But not tonight."

"You saw him?"

"Both halves."

It was a wash as to what shocked me more, the news that he knew who was in the makeshift body bag or his decision not to mention it. Dunphy hadn't used Duncan's real name. It was possible he didn't know of his past.

"Why didn't you say anything?" I asked.

Dunphy started to leave, then changed his mind and came back. "Not tonight. It looks like an accident to me. He's not going anywhere, is he?"

I shook my head in reply.

"Good. I'm a one-shitstorm-at-a-time guy." He reached into his lapel pocket and handed me his card. "Just in case you think of something you've forgotten to tell me." He raised his eyebrows. "Or you could save me the phone call and tell me now." He waited for me to talk. When I didn't, he bent over and picked up the carton of ice cream. "This stuff is an aphrodisiac to Mormon women. Especially my wife."

His footsteps on the gravel echoed across the quiet impound lot.

39

The gates of the transfer station were locked. My pickup was inside. I cursed the company for refusing to give me the code. A long-haul rig pulled up behind me. The driver figured out I didn't have the code and opened the gate. I followed him in and parked in my usual spot. I debated about what to do with the keys to my truck—take them with me or leave them in the ignition for the leasing company. They might not come tomorrow, but they could come any time.

It only took a few minutes to grab my personal belongings from the cab and stuff them into a plastic bag. I put the keys over the visor and left the door unlocked. No sense making their job harder. Duncan's frozen body would be my parting gift. I'd ask Captain Dunphy what he wanted me to do when I saw him next. I climbed into my pickup and watched in my rearview mirror as my red brake lights reflected against the galvanized gate closing behind me. I turned onto the frontage road and headed for home, which wouldn't be home for much longer.

The porch light of my duplex was on. I looked up and down the street to see if I could tell which parked car belonged to Welper or the Chinese contingent. I made a fist with my right hand and opened the door with my left. The light from the porch sliced across my dark living room until it came to rest on a pair of pink Converse All-Stars dangling from the footrest of my recliner. I took a deep breath and swallowed hard. On cue, Ginny unleashed a loud sleeping snort. Her breathing returned to normal. So did mine.

Once again she was asleep with her dress hiked up and her hands cradling her round belly. I knelt next to the chair in the dark and fought the impulse to touch her hair. I rested my head on the arm of the chair.

I woke with her warm hand on my face. Still half asleep, she said, "Jesus, Ben, does your face feel as bad as it looks?"

"About the same," I answered. "Where have you been, kid? Your friend Miranda dropped by. She was worried about you."

"How about you?"

"Didn't give it a second thought. Where were you?"

She reached down and picked up something off the floor on the other side of the chair. "Saving your ass, old man. Turn on a light, you perv."

She was holding what looked like my blanket, carefully folded and shrink-wrapped in clear plastic. I asked her if it was my blanket. "You didn't have it dry-cleaned, did you?"

"No. You don't dry-clean eighty-five thousand dollars."

On a wild hunch Ginny had driven to Salt Lake City after watching an episode of *Antiques Roadshow*. She took the blanket with her. "It's what they call a 'pre-contact' Indian blanket. They're really rare. Jesus, I never thought there was so much to know about blankets. Yours was made in the Southwest before the indigenous people had contact with white men. The first person I showed it to—I thought she was going to faint. She started crying."

"Was she sure?"

"She wanted to run some tests and show it to some other experts. I refused to let it out of my sight. I swear, Ben, you'd think they were having a community orgasm. She put me up in a hotel. A nice one. With room service." She added, "And a minibar!"

"Wow," I said.

"She asked about you. I told her what I knew. Hope you don't mind. I would have phoned—if you had a phone. Eighty-five thousand is what she'll pay. She said she wanted to be fair. There's a chance it would bring more at auction. If you don't sell it to her, or decide not to sell it at all, then she'd like to be reimbursed for the hotel and the testing and maybe a little extra. Pretty cool, huh? But you'll have to pay taxes when and if you sell it."

"Yeah, kid," I said, "pretty cool. Even after taxes."

"Now for some bad news. I did a profit-and-loss statement, factored in your accounts receivable. A whole bunch of neat stuff. It's all on an Excel spreadsheet on my computer. Basically, if you keep driving 117 without making some serious changes, your blanket money will be gone in a year and you'll be right back to square one. On the upside, I think I'll get an A in my class."

"I'm proud of you," I said. "You already have an A from me."

"I thought you'd be happier," she said.

"I am happy," I said, wondering if what she had told me could actually be true. "I'm tired, Ginny. Most of all I'm happy you're okay."

"You mind if I sleep here tonight?"

What could I say to the pregnant teenager who seemed to have come to my rescue? I wanted to tell Claire. I wanted Claire to meet Ginny. I wanted us all to have dinner at the house in Desert Home, even Walt. I wanted to buy Claire her own cello. I wanted Ginny to have enough money to get herself and the baby properly settled. I wanted to sleep. I wanted everything to be exactly as it was, because it had become better.

"Go to sleep," I said. "If you go into labor, do it quietly."

Ginny yawned and smiled. "Asshole." She closed her eyes and stuck out her weaponized tongue at me. "Ben, would you do me and yourself a favor? Take a damn shower. You stink. Pregnant women are really sensitive to smells. But you'd stink to me even if I weren't."

"Right now, Mom," I said.

"That's a lot of money, Ben. You could start over, if you wanted."

"Maybe," I answered. "Except when people like me start over they usually just start over doing the same damn thing."

She was asleep again.

Everything had changed and still stayed the same. At the top of the list was Claire. All the rest was gravy. I pulled an old green army blanket off my bed and covered Ginny, vaguely wondering if I could be covering her with thousands of dollars. On my way to shower my eyes fell on my old percolator—five thousand; the antique La-Z-Boy recliner—two thousand; plywood chest of drawers—a thousand. I was just another millionaire laughing under the hot water.

I couldn't sleep. The clock on my bedside glowed minutes past midnight. Did my mother know what she had wrapped around me? Was it the only gift she had to give me? Did she even care? Was it even hers to give? More thunder coughed in the distance. All at once rain began to fall. It beat the roof and sides of my duplex and splashed down the gutters into the alleyway. Dennis was on his way. Walt was in his bed. Claire was clutching a pillow and thinking of me. Lightning cracked nearby. My window shade threw off a bright yellow like firelight.

My thoughts came to a halt with Josh and refused to move on. It wasn't until that second that it occurred to me I might have killed Josh by leading him out into the desert and abandoning him there. The caretaker at the dig site had seen a fire. A signal fire? 117 was due south from where I'd left him. Maybe not even ten miles. A mentally impaired Cub Scout could have found his way to 117 from there. Sunset west. Sunrise east. But he wasn't even a Cub Scout. He wasn't a reality television producer or even an insurance investigator. Josh was simply a luthier trying to impress a father-in-law who wasn't worth the effort.

The prospect of Josh running afoul of a cadre of cello mercenaries seemed a better end than what I could imagine in the desert. He quickly became the thorn in my new paradise. I had no choice. How soon I acted might make all the difference, if he was out there at all, and if I could find him in the darkness. If serious harm had come to Josh in the desert, it would tarnish all my good fortune.

I dressed and drove straight back to highway patrol headquarters and called Captain Dunphy. It was after one in the morning. The dispatcher was the only person there. Dunphy listened and advised me to wait until morning. He knew I would ignore his advice. "I'd hoped when you called you'd have more to say. Tell the dispatcher to radio Trooper Smith and have him meet you at Walt's diner. You need to have someone with you."

"Why?"

"If you find him, you'll need a credible witness as to his condition and the circumstances, especially if he's dead. If he is dead, I don't want one grain of sand out of place. And then there's the probability you might run into unfriendlies. You want to do that alone?"

I didn't, not even with Andy, or Walt. "You worried about me, Coach?"

"On 117? Not much. But don't disregard my instructions about partnering up with Trooper Smith. He knows that area pretty well. Not like you, though. And he needs the overtime."

He hung up.

40

Not another soul was on U.S. 191 coming to or going from Price. The dispatcher told me Trooper Smith would meet me at the diner as soon as he could get there. I pulled up in front of the diner. The sky had completely cleared, leaving behind the scattered reflections of stars in the puddles of water on 117. I parked in front, between the antique glass gas pumps and the front door. I thought Walt might come out. I wasn't surprised when he didn't. I couldn't be sure exactly what time it was—my guess was around two. It had been a long day for the old fart, and he needed his sleep.

I rolled down the window of the pickup and listened to the desert pop and crack from the disappearing weight of the night's rain. There was a sweetness to the air that begged me to breathe it in and hold it as long as I could—cool, and laden with moisture and the scent of desert flowers. It was a smell that had always reminded me of the mother I never knew, or maybe just of childhood. I wanted to go to Claire's, if only to stand outside on her porch while she slept. I got out of my pickup and stared back up 117 toward its junction with 191. No headlights.

What could be the grim business of searching for Josh reminded me that I had needed a motorcycle to lose him. A motorcycle might be helpful in finding him.

The hastily mended door to Walt's shop was easy to open. I did it quietly without turning on a light. Taking the Victor without his permission would come with some sort of penalty—later. If I ended up finding Josh sooner and alive, whatever the penalty, it would be worth it.

I pushed the Victor around the corner of the diner as Trooper Smith was getting out of a white highway patrol 4×4 pickup. He'd left the engine running and the lights on. There was a nod of approval, and between us we easily lifted the Victor into the bed of his pickup.

Inside the truck, Andy asked, "Does Butterfield know you're taking one of his children?"

"No," I said, "but I've borrowed it before."

"Is that the story behind your face?"

"Actually," I said, "it is. Different child."

Andy put the pickup in gear. "He ever let you borrow the Vincent?"

I didn't answer. I realized the Vincent hadn't been in the workshop. There was only one reason it wouldn't be with its siblings: Walt wasn't back. I didn't want to think about what could be keeping him. I began to slip from my perch on top of the world.

"Where to?"

"I wish I could tell you," I said. "We'll have to feel our way around in the dark for a while." I told him to keep driving 117 east toward Rockmuse.

The starlight helped, though not as much as daylight would have. Several times I had Andy slow and take side roads that led nowhere. Once, if not for the four-wheel drive, we would have been stuck in the mud.

I hardly recognized the right road even when we found it. The ruts had widened and deepened to the point that they were impassable even with four-wheel drive. Many were the size of miniature canyons, still brimming with black water. Andy expertly avoided them by detouring out into the desert and paralleling the road. It was slow going. The Victor bounced hard against the fender wells in the bed of the pickup. It occurred to me I might have to use my blanket money to buy Walt a new Victor—if he let me live.

After a particularly ugly jolt, the nose of the pickup took a steep dive forward and the front bumper buried itself into a wash still half full of runoff. We had to get out and dig to free the tires. We were both caked with mud when we got back inside the cab.

"He followed you out here?"

I didn't answer.

A few minutes later we were moving again and rejoined the road. Andy finished his thought, as I knew he would. "You led him out here on purpose, didn't you?"

I didn't answer that question either. Somehow we made it to the burned-out ranch. Andy killed the engine. We sat for a few minutes in the darkness, listening to the pickup's engine cool.

"Consider this," Andy said. "If that man is badly hurt or dead, you're going to have to live with what you've done. You pointed this desert at him like a gun. Why wouldn't you just get out of your truck and tell him to get lost all by himself? You'd phrase it differently. I'm sure of that."

"Coulda-woulda-shoulda," I said. "The captain tell you about the cello and maybe some bad men?"

"Every law enforcement agency in the area has an eye out."

"Maybe Josh ran afoul of them? You think of that? Maybe there's another explanation that doesn't have anything to do with me."

"Maybe," he said. "You just keeping telling yourself what you need to hear, Ben. You might get lucky. For the record, you're a better man than the one who did this."

I didn't feel like a better man. I was thinking of Walt and

the missing Vincent. And Claire. The money, even Ginny's return, couldn't elevate my mood.

The Victor refused to start. Its exhaust sputtered a rich gasoline haze in the turnaround. We put it back in the bed of the pickup. Andy and I started walking east about a hundred feet apart. Each of us had a pack with flares and a medical kit. There was a search grid in my head. About a half mile out I still smelled the burned gas and oil of the Victor. After maybe another quarter of a mile the odor had taken on a bitterness that I knew was not from the motorcycle: it was the acrid stench of burning rubber. There was one other odor that was like that. Burning flesh. What I smelled could have been a little of both.

Andy was the first to come upon the charred wreckage of the Jeep. It had hit one of the domes of rocks that sprouted up at random, and then rolled a short distance down an embankment and landed on its passenger side, where it had caught fire. The ragtop had been burned away along with the dashboard. Andy shone his flashlight into what was left of the driver's seat. It was empty.

"That might be good news," he said.

We moved in expanding circles away from the crash site. Josh had made it several hundred feet from the Jeep. We followed articles of burned clothing. He had crawled to high ground and was crumpled beneath a scrub pine wearing only his underwear and socks.

He was unconscious and on the living side of death. Probably not by much. Andy and I worked quickly to cover him with thermal blankets and check him for obvious injuries. His pulse was weak. The broken leg was obvious. A thick stream of blood had pooled at the base of his skull. It was still three hours or more until dawn. Andy set splints around Josh's neck, back, and leg. All of the splints had to be improvised from scrub pine. I lit flares

and watched Andy take off in the direction of the highway patrol
pickup to see if he could radio dispatch to send help. If not, he
would have to drive to the diner to use the phone.

Josh moaned. I knelt beside him, patting his lips and face
with water from the canteen I carried.

He opened his eyes and tried to speak. After I got a little water
down his throat, he tried again and began to cough. I thought
he'd lost consciousness again when he said with a hoarse whisper,
"I knew you'd come back."

"Sure," I said. "The world can't afford to lose even one luthier." I said *luthier*, but I was thinking *father and husband*.

"You know?"

"I had the displeasure of meeting your father-in-law." I asked
Josh not to talk and reassured him he was going to be fine. With
any luck he was reassured. I wasn't. Beneath the dirt on his face
he was badly burned, and not from the sun. There were also burns
on his chest, arms, and legs. Internal bleeding and head trauma
were both possibilities.

He took a few more sips of water. "This is water, isn't it?"

"What else would it be?"

"The sweat off your balls." His weak laugh turned into a
cough that spewed blood down his chin.

The headlights of the highway patrol pickup swept the dark
sky above our heads. Andy parked at the edge of the embankment and made his way carefully over the uneven ground toward
us. The look on his face told me he hadn't had any luck raising
the dispatcher.

"It might take too much time to drive to the diner to call Life
Flight," he said. "We'll have to risk taking him with us."

We dumped the Victor over the side of the pickup and replaced it with Josh, who had lost consciousness again. During the

long, slow ride back to the diner I stayed in the bed with Josh. I was there to keep his body stabilized and as comfortable as possible. It was all I could do to keep us both from bouncing out of the truck.

Just before dawn the Life Flight helicopter landed in the middle of 117 in front of the diner. Andy had been forced to use the pay phone. 117 had lived up to its reputation for spitefulness when it came to modern communications. Andy and I watched its flashing lights approach in the clear predawn sky. Shortly after it landed, Captain Dunphy arrived in a cruiser. He had his blue and white light bar going but had dispensed with the siren. Welper was with him.

Welper hovered over Josh as the paramedics transferred him from the pickup to a gurney. Josh was semiconscious. That didn't stop Welper from swearing at him, calling him a stupid son of a bitch. I was standing nearby. Welper suddenly turned and rushed me, swinging wildly. He was easily blocked. I slapped him hard and he staggered backward. Dunphy put himself between us. Welper had already lost his taste to continue, at least with his fists. His mouth was still at it.

"I told you what would happen if any harm came to my son-in-law."

Dunphy told him to shut up.

"You know where to find me," I said.

Welper turned on Dunphy. "You, too," he said. "You won't be able to protect him. This wouldn't have happened if you'd done your job in the interrogation room."

Dunphy dismissed Welper as easily as I had the wild swings.

One of the medics shouted over the rhythmic beating of the chopper blades. He waved me to come over. I leaned inside the open door. He pulled the oxygen away from Josh's face. With my ear next to his lips, I could barely hear what Josh said. The medic replaced the mask. I shouted for Welper. Once he was inside, the chopper took off. The three of us watched it speed across the horizon as the first yellow rays of daybreak rose behind us.

Dunphy was the first to break the new silence. "What was that all about?"

"Josh wanted to tell me something," I said. The captain waited for me to say more. I obliged him. "Nothing much. Sort of a thank-you, I guess."

Andy shook his head. "I hope he makes it." Andy and the captain both had the same thought and looked at the diner. Andy said, "With all this racket in his front yard I can't believe Butterfield hasn't come out."

Dunphy said, "Let's get out of here before he does."

We all got in our vehicles. The captain and Trooper Smith churned up the gravel and were gone. I sat in my pickup waiting for the heater to give me some warm air and prayed, or whatever nonbelievers do, that Josh would survive. I did like him. I looked out my window into the empty sky and smiled. Josh's parting, but I hoped not final, words to me were, "At least I'm not swinging from a cargo net."

I wanted nothing more than to see Walt walk out of the diner. I knew he wouldn't. He wasn't there. In case I was wrong and he had returned, I went to the Quonset to see if the Vincent was there. It wasn't.

Though it made no sense, I searched the workshop, halfheartedly checking such unlikely places for a motorcycle as beneath his workbench, among the crates of motorcycle parts, even in the tiny restroom where the corpse over the commode grinned at me as if it knew where the Vincent and Walt were. We stared each other down for a long minute. The corpse won.

41

I stood outside the restroom and glanced at some of the boxes I had delivered a few weeks earlier, plus another one that had been delivered by DHL more recently. They had been set apart and stacked in the rear of the Quonset. There had been more.

The names on the return addresses caught my attention. All were Chun-Ja. I knew who Chun-Ja was now. The cartons had to be how Claire had managed to get the cello out of New York to Utah, except none of them were big enough to hold a cello. Welper was right. She couldn't have just put something that size in an envelope and mailed it to herself. It wasn't as if she could buy carrier insurance to cover a twenty-million-dollar cello. It didn't really matter. The cello was on its way back to New York. Whatever was in the remaining cartons wasn't any of my business.

The trail across the road from the diner was a muddy, slippery mess from the rains. So was I. Partway down I stopped and watched the sun begin to rise over Claire's house. I wanted it to still be Claire's house. Patience might be the better part of virtue; I no longer cared about either. From where I stood I couldn't see the front of the house where Dennis's compact SUV had been parked. I made my way down the slippery trail past Bernice's grave and stayed high on the hillside until I got a good view of the house.

The SUV was gone. There was no sign of Walt or Claire. One

or both would know I was nearby. I waited for a couple minutes and approached the house. The green metal chair sat on the front porch.

The front door was open wide to the sunrise. Inside was quiet and cool. My mind raced trying to come up with logical and trivial explanations for Claire's absence, and Walt's. Perhaps they were on the Vincent together. I saw one of Claire's turquoise cowboy boots. It lay off to the side of the bare living room floor not far from where I'd first seen Claire teasing her silent music out of the red light.

Something crunched under my boots—a few large splinters of dark wood. I picked them up and rolled them between my fingers. I held the boot in my other hand. I returned to the kitchen, hearing my own footsteps echo behind me as if someone were following. I was alone.

I stood at the kitchen window where Claire had first seen me. The happiness didn't last. My eyes lifted toward the southern horizon, where the new sun sliced through strands of deep shadows hugging the brown desert floor, probably mud from the night's hard rain.

It was just a blink, a shimmering glint of metal that disappeared as quickly as it appeared. I placed the boot and the splinters on the counter, walked outside, and stood beneath the kitchen window with my back to the wall. When I saw the metal again I began running toward it, stopping to resight and adjust my route before running again. It appeared so close. Each time I stopped it seemed to get farther away. The sun was rising quickly. I ran faster, knowing the changing angle of the light could extinguish the reflection at any moment.

I came to an abrupt stop at the edge of the reservoir. I tried to catch my breath and bent over. When I looked up it was gone.

I closed and opened my eyes and imagined the location where the reflection had last appeared, between two rocky peaks, to the left of an alluvial fan, to the right of some scrub brush. I jogged faster, my lungs burning, my eyes focused on what I couldn't see.

A quarter of a mile up a muddy wash, the gouge in the desert deepened until the walls were above my head. It was possible I could have passed by and never seen the small strip of chrome caught between rocks above my head. It looked like a strip of car window molding.

Farther up, the wash forked. Always staying to my right, following the downslope of the watershed, the wash divided itself into a labyrinth of cavernous scars. I sloshed through the shallow water. The high sun beat down on the desert floor several feet above me.

The SUV stood improbably balanced on its grille, the hood half buried in the mud and its ass end pointed to the sky like it had been dropped from a great height. It was disguised as a large mound of wet dirt and debris. From ten feet away it would have been impossible to identify. From the rim it would have been impossible to even see. The driver's-side window was open. A lifeless hand dangled from its edge. I reached down and felt for a pulse. There was no one around to introduce me to what had been Claire's husband.

The inside of the SUV was filled to its headliner with oozing mud and rocks. His neck was enclosed in muck, along with most of his face. There were finger-shaped gouges in the thick mud near his chest. Someone had tried to dig him out. I continued down the wash for several hundred feet shouting Claire's name. That was when I saw Walt, encased in mud. His body was embedded upright in the side of the arroyo wall. He faced forward as if he were emerging from a door beneath the desert.

I dropped to my knees. His eyes opened, their sockets white and expressionless holes. Moments passed as I carved him out with my hands. I jerked him free from his tomb. We tumbled together into the shallow water. Fine silt bubbled from between his lips. Walt coughed. His mouth erupted with the stink of bloody water and mud. His lips moved to form my name.

I looked up and down the arroyo. Claire had to be nearby. I could almost feel her. Walt groaned and coughed up more darkness. The flash flood must have been like being caught in a churning wall of water, rocks, and mud. It had to have been Walt who tried to save Dennis, digging wildly with his fingers even as the second wave of water rushed toward him. If Claire was nearby, she probably hadn't survived, but I couldn't be sure. I left Walt and slogged up the muddy arroyo searching for her. I didn't want to stop, but Walt was still alive, and if I got him out he might stay that way. I returned to Walt.

He was old but as densely packed with muscle as a young man. I hoisted him over my shoulder and stumbled back the way I had come. As we passed the SUV I heard a faint voice cry for help. It sounded like Claire. In that moment any voice I heard would have sounded like Claire's. Between my failing strength and my hurry to locate Claire, I could have been more delicate in shedding Walt's weight. He grunted when he hit the ground. I shouted her name as I scrambled across the wash to the SUV.

It wasn't Claire. It was Dennis. "Where is she?" I demanded.

His unfocused eyes rolled. "Help me. Please."

I slapped him and asked again. I got the same answer. I put my lips so close to his face I got sand in my mouth. "Tell me where she is or I will let you die."

He either didn't know or was too injured to understand my question. Or he didn't want to answer. Behind me Walt vomited again and rolled onto his side. I couldn't try to save them both. My guess was that Dennis wasn't going to make it no matter what I did.

No sooner had I begun to lift Walt to my shoulders than Dennis spoke again, clearly and with purpose. I lowered Walt, this time with more care. I stood at the window. "I'll make you more comfortable if you tell me where Claire is. That's the best I can do."

He replied with two words. "The cello."

"What about it?"

"Save the cello," he said.

Disgusted, I said, "Save it yourself."

His next words surprised me. "Are you Ben?"

"Yes," I said. There was only one person who could have told him about me.

I wanted his final words to say something, anything about Claire. That wasn't what I got. He was dying and confused. What little he said was more than I could stand to hear. His last words were to her: "You shouldn't have done it, Claire."

He choked, and his last breath escaped from him.

Getting Walt to the rim of the wash was a struggle. When I finally succeeded, I saw the Vincent a hundred yards away, flat on its side near the edge of the meandering arroyo. I used my belt to strap Walt in front of me and fought a constant battle to shift gears and balance his dead weight as we made the long, rough journey back.

In his room I lowered him onto his bed. I noticed long furrows through the dried dirt on his face. Tears. After a couple of attempts to speak, he said, "I fell asleep."

To Walt Butterfield those few words had to have been the most painful he had ever uttered. They were a revelation and admission that he was, as I long suspected and he feared, human after all. It didn't matter that he was an old man, or that he had spent hours in the sun and wind, and more hours in darkness with the wind and blinding rain as he looked down on the house and Claire. In the case of Bernice it was bad timing. Still unacceptable, but not this. He had simply fallen asleep as any tired human being might have done hours earlier. He had failed. In Walt's world there was no greater failure than a man's inability to protect those he loved. There were no excuses, no pardons. I had no doubt in my mind that he loved Claire, even if she wasn't his daughter.

I asked Walt if he wanted me to take him to the hospital or call an ambulance. He shook his head. He knew his decision might result in his death. It was a decision I was bound to honor. I didn't agree, though I understood. Death might be what he wanted, even what he had longed for since that evening at the diner so many years ago.

42

The sun was already low in the sky when I headed back to the SUV in my pickup. I didn't hold out much hope of finding Claire, alive or dead, but I had to try. My only other reason for returning was to mark its location for the highway patrol and search and rescue. If I didn't get there before dark it might be weeks before search teams found the site. My exhaustion was complete. I begged God for a miracle, even though two miracles had already been granted. Claire might still be alive.

Only a couple hours of direct sunlight remained by the time I arrived. I used an hour of it searching for Claire before I finally gave up. I tied red grease rags to nearby scrubs that clung to the top of the arroyo and finished just as I heard the first rumble of thunder and saw clouds building to the east. From where I stood above the SUV, I thought I saw the tuning pegs of the cello jutting up above the mud-filled rear cargo area of the vehicle. Dennis had told me to save the cello. I wondered if I should. Along with the desert night the new threat of rain meant the possibility the SUV would be swept away again. It might be lost forever or completely destroy the cello.

I took the tire iron from my pickup and labored to pry open the exposed back hatch door of the SUV. There was too much inside pressure from the mud. In a fit of foolishness, I braced my back against the embankment and used my legs to push the vehicle upright onto its tires. Dennis's head slumped through the open window.

In a rush against time, I swung the tire iron as hard as I could against the rear cargo window. The broken window released the pressure with an explosion of mud, and the tailgate popped open. The mud flowed out and exposed the back of the cello. I carefully dug the cello loose from the rocks and mud. The cello should have been freed enough to be pulled out. Something held it in place. I tried lifting it straight up. It came loose from the mud with a sucking sound. The something that had been holding it down was a turquoise boot. The boot was still lodged in the hole it had made. Claire, in a rage, must have driven its pointed toe into the delicate face of the cello. Beneath the cello was Claire.

I stared at her face in the dark oozing interior of the SUV. The cello had shielded her enough that most of her upper body was clear of dirt and water. A needle of sunlight moved across her eyes. She blinked and took a full, painful breath.

"Ben," she whispered.

I pushed the cello out of the way. Her breath was irregular. She exhaled air in shallow gasps. The cello had kept her alive but I feared the tremendous weight of mud and rock had crushed her chest and heart. I dug furiously with my fingers to free her, and as gently as possible lifted her out of the cargo compartment and carried her into the cool shadow of the arroyo. It took all my strength and balance to run up the slippery embankment with Claire cradled in my arms. We reached the top just as the first new trickles of water began to fill the arroyo in advance of another flash flood.

I slid her light body across the front seat of my pickup. I still held the turquoise boot in one hand. I let it drop to the floorboard. Claire reached for my face. "Take me home," she said.

Thunder and lightning chased us as I sped across the desert, dodging rocks and gashes cut by the rains. Her body slumped against mine. I wrapped my right arm around her to lessen the blows to her body. The pickup shook and rattled as I raced toward Desert Home and 117.

The setting sun pushed through a thin layer of pink clouds to the west as the desert in front of us began to sink into shades of yellow. The rain clouds disappeared and the eastern sky opened. Claire's body relaxed against mine. Rounding the edge of the reservoir, I pulled her closer and kissed her black hair.

I slowed down then and drove slowly until we stopped in front of the porch.

"We're home," I said, gazing out through the dusk at the dark porch. "You know," I said, "the first thing I notice about a house, any house, is its windows. Then its porch—whether it has one and what direction it faces. I am partial to east. Any desert dweller will tell you, the true beauty of a desert sunset can only be appreciated by looking in the opposite direction."

My eyes settled for a moment on the single green metal chair. "It's nice if there is a comfortable chair on the porch. The last thing that might catch my eye is the roof. I don't like a roof that's too pitched. If I want a hat I'll buy a hat. A sharp-pitched roof has always put me off for some reason. How about you?"

I buried Claire next to her mother.

43

It was a rare, cool afternoon in August, ten weeks to the day since Claire died. I sat on the porch of the house in Desert Home. In my hand I held a small, unopened package posted to Walt from New York, from Chun-Ja. I also held a letter I had read several times. It was from a law firm and had been sent to Chun-Ja in care of Walter Butterfield. Both had been sent by U.S. mail, where they waited patiently at the post office for Walt.

I'd picked up the two custom headstones I had ordered weeks earlier and spent the morning installing them over the graves. My plan was to bury the package and envelope beneath Claire's headstone. When the time came I changed my mind.

I expected Preach to appear beneath the archway. On my way into Price the previous evening I had spotted him at the junction of U.S. 191 making camp for the night. I asked him if he'd drop by and perform a little religious service for me. He said he would. I drew him a map.

The discovery and sale of my blanket was big news in Price and, to a lesser extent, Utah and nationally. For a town the size of Price with only one small newspaper, the word of big money spreads faster than the Word of God, which has pretty much always been the case everywhere. It was big money, more than anyone expected, especially Ginny and me.

I'd sold it to a museum in Taos for $153,000. It wasn't the

highest offer, but it was an Indian-run museum. The curator, an old Pueblo man, told me up front I'd have to carry a loan for about $50,000 until they could raise the rest of the money. He said he'd draw up the paperwork. I told him we could just shake on it. I'd trust him. He nodded his gratitude.

Maybe it was less an issue of trust than the fact that the blanket was, in a way, going home. That and maybe taking something on faith eased my guilt about selling my mother's only gift. Except, given the circumstances, she might have thought giving me up was a gift of sorts.

For a brief time the news of the blanket and my story brought idiots out of the woodwork. I received several letters from men and women claiming to be either my father or mother. One of them may well have been telling the truth. I never answered any of them.

Hollywood called after I got my phone turned back on. A man identifying himself as a reality show producer said he wanted to do a show following me as I tracked down my parents. "The Native American angle will really sell it," he said. That was a while ago. His ears were probably still ringing from my well-considered two-word response.

I used a chunk of the money to buy the headstones, one for Claire and one for Duncan Lacey, even though I knew Duncan wasn't his real name. Neither was the name on Claire's headstone.

Captain Dunphy had been tipped off by an anonymous caller about the two Laceys with hints they might have a criminal past. By the time highway patrol got out to the Lacey place, what with Josh in the hospital and the cello madness, Fergus had killed himself. They found him hanging from a steel crossbeam in his boxcar home. Shortly after that the full story of the Laceys came out—their true identities and what they had done. It wasn't even serious news by then. The newspaper printed the story in a single column next to a big advertisement for fresh cherries and beef brisket. Afterward no one cared what I did with Duncan. I'd more or less promised to give him a decent burial. I intended to do just that. He had company. Good company.

Claire was another story. No one knew what had happened to her or the cello. That suited me just fine. I had notified the highway patrol of where I had seen the SUV. After two days of rains and flash floods, it took them a couple of weeks to finally relocate it. The animals and weather, combined with the constant friction against rock, had removed most of Dennis from the driver's seat. The body might just as well have gone through a hundred wash cycles with a load of gravel.

The cello, or what was left of it, was still in the back, broken and caked in mud. Ralph Welper was a happy man, though only for a week. The cello in the back of the SUV turned out not to be the del Gesù cello. It was a good copy that Claire had commissioned in the two months she was playing nice with Dennis.

John waved to me from the archway. I waved back and watched him walk down the hill toward me, his back slightly hunched as if he were still pulling his cross. He hadn't asked me what kind of religious service it would be. He just solemnly replied that he would be there. If he'd known it was a funeral service he might have asked the name of the departed. Maybe not. He knew Duncan's body had been released to me. He knew nothing about Claire, and the name on the headstone wouldn't change that.

I placed the letter and the package on the porch. We shook hands, and I led him behind the house up the trail to the little grotto. "Here they are," I said. "Could you say a few words?"

The big man took his time reading the headstones. He started on the far right and worked his way left. First he read the worn words from Bernice's stone. He sounded out the Korean slowly. "Chun-Ja." Next came "Yun-Ja, Beloved Daughter." I was prepared to tell him that Chun-Ja was Korean for Spring Girl and Yun-Ja meant Flower Girl. He didn't ask. Claire would have liked the name I gave her.

He smiled when he saw Duncan Lacey's stone. "Beloved son," he read. "Yes, he was," he added. "Thanks for doing this, Ben." He looked back and forth between Duncan and Yun-Ja. "No dates of birth or death?"

I changed the subject rather than answer his question. "I assume you were just trying to get Duncan some medical attention when you made the call to the highway patrol."

He answered without taking his eyes off Duncan's headstone. "It doesn't matter, but how did you know?"

"I guessed," I said. "That day on the highway when I stopped to find you with Duncan, you said he'd been coming to church. Later I figured he might have told you about his past. After the episode on the highway, you probably wrestled with your conscience and decided on what you had to do."

"You going to tell me about Yun-Ja?"

"Someday," I said. "Not now. She has family where she is. I hope that's enough."

The reverend began. I thought he might end with the usual ashes to ashes. He had made a different choice of scripture.

"The sea gave up the dead that were in it, and Death and Hades gave up the dead that were in them, and all were judged according to their works. Lord, I commend these souls to your keeping. Amen."

We walked back down the trail and sat on the stairs in the

shade of the porch. I asked John if he cared for a smoke. He said he would. We began the usual imaginary rolling and lighting ritual.

He inhaled first. "This is Walt's place, isn't it?"

I answered that it was, though Walt had sort of put it in my care while he was convalescing.

"I heard he took a bad spill on his motorcycle a couple months ago. How's he doing?"

Until the week before I would have been unable to answer John's question in the positive. Walt had long ago mended from a broken collarbone, a dislocated elbow, and probably a concussion, as well as a laundry list of lesser breaks, all of which I ached to claim credit for as having occurred during our fight. He took his sweet time going into the hospital. He waited almost a week. I didn't coach him about what to say.

He'd managed to get himself there on the Vincent. It was all his idea to say he'd fallen off his motorcycle, which must have hurt more for him to say than any part of the truth of that night above Desert Home.

Walt and I had an unspoken gentleman's agreement. Neither of us had said one word about any of it, not to anyone and certainly not to each other. He'd kept more to himself than usual, if that was possible.

The weekend before, as I was working on the house, I heard the growl of the Vincent coming down the trail behind the house. He idled for a few seconds at the graves before continuing. I was busy cleaning the windows. He stopped just long enough to tell me that I was doing a lousy job and that some of the siding had come loose on the north side. He politely, for Walt, suggested I take care of it immediately and try not to fuck it up. Then he roared off into the desert. I knew the house had come to me.

John passed me the cigarette. "Nice place. You should live here," he said.

I answered that I might someday. I picked up the small package and turned it over and over in my hands. The truth was, I already lived there. I just slept somewhere else. The blanket money paid for Ginny and her new baby girl to move into the recently vacated duplex adjoining mine. Sometimes I heard the baby crying at night. I complained, but I liked hearing her through the wall. It was comforting and helped me sleep.

"You get a package?"

"Walt did," I said.

I explained that I had been in Rockmuse and picked up Walt's mail. Something he hadn't bothered to do for months. The postmaster gave it to me because he heard about Walt's accident.

"Don't suppose he needed it very badly. Wonder what it is?"

"I know what it is," I said. "Strings." I pulled out the letter. "Same thing in this."

The preacher wisely left it at that.

Claire had sent the cello strings by U.S. mail without knowing that Walt, like most of 117's residents, avoided the post office. There were two other pieces of mail. One was the business license renewal for the diner. The other was the letter from a law firm in New York. Both the package and the letter were addressed to Chun-Ja in care of Walt Butterfield. I opened them without shame.

The letter confirmed a phone conversation and gave Claire a summary of a DNA test. All the hair samples submitted for analysis were from a male subject who was statistically a match for her biological father. Strands that I guessed she got when she innocently requested a keepsake from Walt. She must have suspected, or at least hoped, Bernice had been pregnant when she was raped. There was a chance that Bernice herself might have known. Maybe not. Maybe the trauma robbed her of that knowledge.

It didn't seem at all strange to me that Claire wouldn't have told Walt she had proof she was his daughter. She wanted him to claim her as his own without any more proof than his own gut. Given enough time, he might have done just that. Only afterward would she have shown him the letter. Maybe never. I liked to think that by the time they began dancing in the diner Walt had already begun to sense she was his biological daughter.

I kept the letter and package with the strings and didn't give them to Walt. All I gave him was the business license renewal for the diner. Learning after Claire's death that she was his daughter would only have killed what little was left of him. I didn't want that. Though we didn't speak of her, she had once been ours, was still ours. Each of us held the knowledge of our relationship with her. There was no one else.

John and I passed the cigarette back and forth in silence for a few minutes.

"When are you coming to church again?" he asked.

"Next time I need a new wrench," I answered.

"I'm thinking of getting an altar. And maybe a new heater. One that works in the winter."

"Sounds fine," I said.

"Last month the church got an anonymous gift of three thousand dollars."

"Good for you," I said.

"Good for the Lord's work," he replied.

John put the cigarette out in the sand. "Gotta go," he said. He gave me a sunburned wink and added, "I left my cross double-parked." He stood up and took a few steps and turned. "If you don't mind me saying so, Ben, I think you're spending too much time alone."

"No, I don't mind," I said. "You think spending more time with people will change that?"

He didn't have anything else to say. I watched him walk up the hill and disappear on the other side of the arch.

Once, during one of our roadside smokes, the reverend had said that most people associate the desert with what is missing—water and people. "They never think of the one thing the desert has more of—light," he said. "So much light."

All the light in the world won't help a blind man see what's right under his feet. Not Ralph Welper anyway, or those like him. Two weeks earlier he had marched down the road from the archway. I was tidying up the graves and watched him make his way to the house. He must have seen my rig in the turnout.

The oaf stood right on Claire's grave when he told me he was still convinced I knew more than I'd said. I just let him talk. Welper vowed he would find the real del Gesù cello if it was the last thing he did. I thought it would be fitting if it did turn out to be the last thing he did. "And that damn woman, too," he added.

I asked him if he had any new leads. He said Claire had been spotted in Rome. It took all my energy not to smile. Apparently Claire had joined Elvis on his eternal tour.

"Is that all you came to say?" I asked.

He handed me a box. "I promised Josh I would deliver these in person along with his thanks. They had to do some skin grafts. He's going to be fine. But don't expect any thanks from me."

I asked him why he was still around Utah and not in Rome. Turned out he was doing his best to stiff the State of Utah for the search-and-rescue costs as he had promised. Dunphy had been smart enough to get him to agree to it in writing. When Welper reneged, as Dunphy suspected he would, Welper's powerful connections had deserted him. The state had filed suit to collect.

"It's a matter of principle," Welper said.

I agreed that was exactly what it was.

The package Welper had given me contained the CD that Ginny had made, and several more, all cello. A note from Josh repeated his thanks and mentioned that he and his wife planned to return to Utah for a vacation.

"I'm curious," I said. "Why couldn't Mrs. Tichnor's husband spot a fake cello?"

"Because it was a good copy," Welper said. "Not expensive but perfect in details that only someone who had been intimate with that particular cello would know. The scrollwork especially. The face and back were distinctive, as if made by two different luthiers, which was true. Experts say the father made the back and the son made the front. He had no reason to think the cello wasn't authentic. Anyway," he added, "in that pair she was the brains. And for all I know, the real talent."

Welper had not just been standing on Claire, but the del Gesù cello I'd buried with her. It was still in the special crates she'd shipped it in, and still in pieces set in perfectly molded foam packing. All she had done was take it apart, just like the copy she had made. Tough, close work, though I learned it was done all the time by luthiers who repaired cellos. It just never occurred to anyone she would or could do it with the del Gesù. Each piece of the two cellos had been sent separately through different carriers.

I saw the crates again in Walt's workshop when I went in to dispose of the corpse in his restroom. All I was looking for was something to remember her by. I had unknowingly delivered parts of the del Gesù cello myself. Walt must have known she was coming and helped her arrange to ship things ahead. Using the Korean name of her mother as the shipper was the tip-off that the crates were intended for Claire.

She'd made a small mistake by using the U.S. mail to send the strings. She didn't know Walt rarely checked his mail in Rockmuse.

I never believed Claire had planned to keep the real cello, or harm or destroy it. I had my doubts that moment in the back of the SUV, when I saw her boot stuck where she had kicked in the front of the cello. What I didn't know then was that it had all been a show for Dennis, to make him think she had destroyed what he treasured most. The biggest flaw in Claire's plan had to do with Dennis. She made the fatal error of thinking that because she had loved him, she knew him. She was so certain he wasn't the violent type. Every type is a violent type. Given the right circumstances, Gandhi himself might have attacked someone with a meat cleaver.

When she kicked in the cello, Dennis must have flown into a rage and strangled her. She didn't have a chance to get the truth out. The strong fingers of a cellist must have made short work of Claire's delicate neck. Unaware that she was still alive, or maybe not caring either way, he threw her into the SUV with the pieces of the fake cello and took off across the desert. Who knows why he didn't go back the way he came. Maybe Walt woke up just then and chased him into the desert. Even if Walt hadn't fallen asleep, it all happened so quickly there was nothing Walt could have done. I'd like to tell him that someday, not that he'd listen.

The chances were small I would ever listen to the CDs Josh sent. I would probably always prefer the music Claire heard and I could only imagine. It was something we shared. I didn't want to give that up for something as unreliable as reality.

These days I sometimes catch Bernice out of the corner of my eye. She is sitting in her window booth and staring out into the desert. Like everyone else who knew the story, I always thought it was the vacant and aimless stare of a broken mind. Now I believed she was simply watching the changing desert light move across her dream of Desert Home and a life, a hope, for a child she would never know. It was a life half lived in that distance.

I locked up the house and climbed the hill to the arch. Every time I reached the halfway mark I heard Claire's voice calling after me. I always stopped and looked back. This time would be different. I prepared myself and was determined not to turn around. I did, though. I looked down at the porch and the one green chair, and out over Desert Home, then east toward the sunset reflecting off the mesa.

The first month I drove 117 I decided to go to the end of the road—just to say I'd done it. The pavement terminated with an abrupt edge as clean and final as if the asphalt were a piece of blackboard lopped off by a pair of industrial shears. There was no barricade or warning of any kind. The end of my world.

It was the kind of long, average day that an ordinary miracle might slap the boredom off your face.

The sun descended behind me. I got out and leaned against the front bumper and finished a bit of sandwich left over from lunch. The truck idled quietly behind me. I tilted my head and stared up the granite wall. In the blink of an eye I was awash in an unearthly glow. It could have been a minute or ten thousand years. I forgot my name. A gust of wind swirled the light and dust into a rose-colored column that reached steadily upward until it punched a cotton-candy hole through a wide patch of baby blue sky.

Over a hundred miles back to the junction with 191, and I

didn't recall any of it. When I undressed for bed that night my boots spilled pink light.

Someday the arch of Desert Home will rust and disappear, along with the house and the streets and the reservoir shimmering in the distance. But the ghosts will be real. Real people once lived there, if only for a handful of sunlit days. I might come to think of them as family someday.

The preacher knew what he was talking about. The desert is home to light.

ACKNOWLEDGMENTS

It has long been my opinion that the writing of a novel is not unlike a marriage, subject to all the ups and downs, unbridled passion, frustration, boredom, literary infidelity, trial separations and, sometimes, red-faced anger and, on occasion, even divorce. I offer my gratitude to the following people who served as confidants, supporters, and counselors, whose assistance took the form of being literary Gandhis, Nazi cheerleaders, and quizzical Zen monks.

Ann Rittenberg, William Kittredge, C. J. Box, Roland Merullo, Karen Kargel, Laure-Anne Bosselaar, Scott Gibson, Susan Schwartzman, Tom Barrows, Patti Morris, and Martin White.

Though his name also appears on the dedication page, hardly a day goes by that I don't feel fortunate for the hours of encouragement and invaluable questions and thoughts I received from Sterling Watson. He seemed to know what I was going for even before I did, and then never let me forget it.

Thanks to Sam Manganaro and his staff at Vincent Works in Dolores, Colorado, for their help in researching vintage Vincent motorcycles.

Thanks to all the wonderful writers and friends associated with The Solstice MFA program at Pine Manor College in Boston, Massachusetts, among them: Meg Kearney, Tanya Whiton, Sandra Scofield, Steven Huff, William Hastings, Venise Berry, Robert Lopez, Kerry Beckford, Susan Lemere, Mike Miner, Teresa Sutton, Melissa Ford Luken, Cindy Zelman, Jaime Manrique, Carol Owens Campbell, David Yoo, Rick Carr, Alison McLennan, Joe Gannon, Gabriel Cleveland, Jacqueline Brown, and Dzvinia Orlowsky.

My enduring gratitude goes out to Jack Estes, publisher of Caravel Books, who said yes after so many said no.

My deepest bows to my agent, David Hale Smith, and to all the amazing and supportive people at the Crown Publishing Group, especially my editor, Nate Roberson, who have embraced me, and my work, with such abiding faith and made this beautiful and revised new edition possible.